THE ENGLISH
LIEUTENANT'S LADY

AN OREGON TERRITORY ROMANCE

EVELYN M. HILL

CHAPTER 1

Tongue Point, Oregon Territory
October 1845

Geoff heard the *click* of a rifle being cocked in the bushes behind him, and then a woman's voice, deadly calm. "Stand up—slowly, now—and keep your hands where I can see 'em."

He obeyed without question. Several years of service in Her Majesty's Army had taught him not to argue with people pointing weapons at him. Not at the moment, at least. Once he got his hands on the pistol at his belt, this would be a different conversation.

Her voice came again. "Turn around. Let's have a look at you."

Slowly, hands raised, he followed her orders. The sunlight fell through a gap in the trees overhead, almost blinding him. He blinked. As his eyes adjusted to the light, a young, dark-haired woman stepped onto the path. She was a tiny thing, the top of her head almost level with his shoulder. But the eyes that studied him were as steady as the rifle in her hands. The one that she was pointing straight at him.

He cleared his throat. "Good afternoon, madam." Civility never hurt at a time like this.

"Are you calling me a madam?" She tilted her head as though trying to determine if the word was intended as an insult. A loosely bound braid of dark hair shifted to fall over one shoulder of the overlarge man's coat she was wearing. Her eyes were a truly beautiful gray, the color of woodsmoke before it dissipates in a breeze.

"I meant no offense, ma'am." He nodded toward the opened pack at his feet. "I was not going to steal anything."

This wasn't the first time he'd been on the wrong side of a rifle. He could usually talk his way out of a bad situation. All the same, his heart raced and a tiny thread of sweat trickled down his back. The autumn day was not unusually warm, but he welcomed the breeze that wafted up the hill from the Columbia River.

"So you say." The woman raised the rifle a bit higher. "If you weren't bent on thieving, why were you going through my pack?"

"I was looking for some identification, so I could return the pack to its proper owner." *I was looking to see if it had any information that I could use.*

Her eyes narrowed, as if what he was thinking showed on his face. He shifted his gaze to focus on her lips, avoiding direct eye contact. "My friend and I are private travelers on a tour of the Oregon Territory. Seeing the sights. Scientific exploration of the New World. Sketching scenic vistas. That sort of thing. While my friend was securing the boat at the landing, I decided to come up the hill to, er, see if I could get a view of the surrounding countryside. The leaves changing colors and all that. Charming, don't you know."

As he spoke, he relaxed his features into what he hoped she would take to be an expression of amiable fatuousness. "I was merely passing by when I saw the pack on the side of the road."

If he were being honest—which he mostly wasn't, considering all the lies he had just told her—"road" wasn't how he would have described a barely navigable trail through the woods. Still, this seemed to be one of those times when it would be as well to be diplomatic. The young woman might take exception to any criticism of the area. A local, by the look of her. Surely no female brought up in civilization would ever dress in an ill-fitting man's shirt and trousers, topped by an oversized coat. She wore the odd clothes with all the self-possession of Queen Victoria herself, though this girl could not have been much above twenty.

She looked as if she had forgotten how to smile. The corners of her lovely mouth seemed fixed in a permanent curve downward, but the charming sprinkle of freckles across her nose made her seem less forbidding, more approachable. Or as approachable as anyone could be while pointing a rifle.

"Do you suppose I could put my arms down? It's rather tiring to keep them up like this."

She ignored his question. "Where are you from? Nobody around here's got an accent like that."

"I come from Canterbury, in Kent. England, don't you know."

He tried that particular smile that he had used when home from school on holiday and trying to persuade Cook to slip him a few biscuits before afternoon tea. That smile had always worked on elderly English servants who had known him since he was born. It didn't seem half so effective on young American women who had just laid eyes on him. "Might I request that you point that excellent rifle in a different direction?" *I don't want to hurt you.*

"Hmph." The tone was dubious, but she did start to lower the rifle. *Thank you, Lord.*

Then Bradford, coming up the trail behind her, cracked a twig under his boot. She whirled, raising the gun and backing away to cover both of them. Geoff moved faster still, putting himself between them with his hands stretched out. "No. He's a friend." *And my superior officer. Bit tricky to have to write a report explaining why he's been shot.*

Geoff took a step toward the woman, just one, and stopped. "I'm not your enemy." He held her gaze, willing her to believe that lie, the greatest one of all. "Could you perhaps put the rifle down?"

"And do you always wander through the woods with a primed rifle?" Bradford asked from behind Geoff.

The woman answered Bradford's question while keeping her gaze fixed on Geoff. "I was tracking a bull elk. I nearly had him when you came up the track and scared him off."

At least she didn't seem inclined to shoot now. He took a step to the side. Then another. The woman's eyes flickered between Geoff and Bradford. *Yes. Pay attention to him while I take a step to the side.*

As if she had heard Geoff's thoughts, the rifle shifted to point directly at him again. "You keep trying to creep up on me, we're going to have a problem here."

He stopped, spreading his hands out to indicate he was harmless. He wanted her to put the rifle down. He wanted her to trust him. Most of all, he wanted her to stop frowning at him.

"I can prove that we're on a sketching tour. The drawings

are down with our belongings, by the boat." He looked at Bradford. "Unless you brought your sketchbook with you?"

Bradford raised his eyebrows. "No, I don't have it with me. I came up here to see how you were getting on with your... er, how you were getting on."

"Well then, we'll have to show you back at the camp." Geoff would probably never see this woman again. It couldn't hurt to leave her with a good impression of him. Even if the last thing he needed was for her to know who he really was.

THE TALL ENGLISHMAN give his friend a nod, a barely noticeable inclination of his head. Lia frowned. Something was going on here, and she was missing it. The tall Englishman was dressed like a prosperous trader, in buckskin trousers and frock coat, but he was clean-shaven, his brown hair neatly trimmed. He stood with his shoulders back, and his spine was as straight as a soldier on parade.

The man had a face that, if she were feeling polite, she would describe as plain. A better description might be rough-hewn. He was weather-beaten and somehow indomitable, like a mountain of granite. Yet he'd moved swiftly to come between her and his friend, as surefooted and quick as Lia herself.

She could not pin down exactly what was wrong. Subtle discrepancies nagged at her. The muscles around his mouth were too tense when he smiled, the charm a bit too forced. For all his easy flood of words, his eyes were cautious, gauging her reaction.

He was skillful; she had to give him that. His act would have fooled someone who had not learned from childhood to read people as well as animals by the language their body spoke. Curious to see his reaction, she lowered the gun. His hands fell to his side, but the lines around his mouth did not relax and there was still that tension in the way he stood.

Having a gun pointed at him could make a man nervous. But why was he still so tense after she lowered it? Then, like a puzzle that is just a collection of fragments until the last piece slots into place, something shifted in the back of her mind, and she recognized the look in his eyes.

It was the watchful gaze of the outsider. A look she saw every time she faced a mirror.

When Maman died, Pa and her brother Pierre had escorted her over the Rockies to a mission school in the Red River Valley. Pa had told her to be a good girl and study hard. Pierre had told her to have fun.

Then they left her there.

She had stood outside the school and watched the two of them ride off. The table-flat prairie stretched out until the horizon met the sky, and she stood there for what felt like a large slice of eternity watching the last of her family diminish against the immensity of sky and grassland, until finally she had to strain her eyes to see them. Then they were gone, and she was on her own among strangers. Lia had never been able to shake off that feeling of being set apart, even after she'd grown up and Pa had summoned her to come back. She no longer belonged here. Or anywhere else, either.

This man surely had no reason to feel that way. He was male, and he was English. The English ran the Hudson Bay Company, and the Company ran the Territory for hundreds of miles in any direction. He was top of the world as far as the trappers and the natives were concerned. It didn't make sense. Her initial alarm began to ebb. She didn't think he was a threat, but she had to make sure.

Lia took a step back, reaching one hand down to sling the pack over her shoulder while keeping the rifle ready with the other. "All right. You show me these precious sketches, and I'll take back my calling you a thief."

She followed the men down the path, walking softly, as Pa had taught her to do when hunting. The tall man moved like a cat in the woods, but the blond man's heavy boots clomped down with each step, probably scaring off the game for miles around.

At the bottom of the hill, the land flattened into an isthmus of level ground that connected the wooded peninsula to the land. The river lapped against the shore a few feet away. The men had not made much attempt at setting up camp, just a few packs thrown on the ground, with bedrolls next to a campfire laid ready to be lit. A dark-haired young man was crouched down, going through one of the packs.

"Here!" The blond man strode forward, outraged. "I say, you, get off out of that!"

The young man—no, a boy, really—looked up, and Lia stopped in surprise as she saw his face. Her nephew's dark brown eyes showed no alarm as he dropped the pack to the ground next to his own pack. "Hunting men now, Lia?"

"Henri, what are you doing? You were supposed to wait for your uncle down by the creek. Or—did he already come and then go again?" A brief ray of hope lightened her mood. If Henri's uncle had come and gone, and Henri was still here...

"The question is, what was he doing with my pack." The handsome blond man had turned pale, and his hand twitched toward the pistol at his belt.

The tall man laid a hand on his friend's arm. "Perhaps we should put this on a more social level. My name is Geoffrey Montgomery. This gentleman is Phillip Bradford."

"This is Henri Griggs," Lia said.

Bradford looked from Lia to Henri. "Is he with you? He's Indian, isn't he?"

"My brother is his father," Lia said coolly. Occasionally, she did encounter people who were surprised to find she and Henri were related. They might not look alike but he was family. If anyone had a problem with him, they would have to deal with her as well.

Mr. Montgomery murmured, "And you're Lia. That's a pretty name."

Still holding the rifle, she made an awkward attempt at a curtsey. "Amelia Elizabeth Griggs."

Bradford's blond eyebrows crimped together into a frown. "Someone should have taught you how to curtsey properly. It would help if you were wearing a dress."

"A *very* pretty name," Mr. Montgomery cut in. "I like it."

"What do my clothes matter? Makes no sense to wear a dress in the woods."

Mr. Montgomery took a step between them, as if she and Bradford were pointing guns at each other instead of glaring. "You're right. There's no need of formal rules of dress and etiquette out here. To return to the point, why was your nephew going through the pack?"

"Stealing, evidently," Bradford said.

Henri's fists clenched. "I was looking to see if you had any food, but I was going to *borrow* it, not steal. I was going to make it up to you later. I can catch Chinook easy this time of year, but it takes time to build a fire and cook it. I am hungry *now*. That don't make me a thief." He stood up and tossed the pack at Bradford. It slipped out of

Bradford's grasp, scattering papers all over the muddy ground.

Bradford cursed and knelt down to start picking the papers up. He peered at them. "Looks like everything's here."

"Better make sure," Henri said, stiff with dignity.

Bradford began shoving the papers back in the pack. He handled them roughly, stuffing them in without care, except for one portfolio, which he opened and rifled through with more respect. He offered a paper to Lia. "Here. One of the better sketches. Cape Disappointment. It's well named. Someone tried to sell it to us, except he didn't actually own it himself. Look, there's one of the volcanoes in the background."

Lia spared the watercolor a passing glance before returning it to Bradford. She turned back to Henri. "So—no sign of your uncle?"

"He's late, and I got hungry waiting. I was sure you'd come back with game, so it wasn't *stealing*, it was *borrowing*." He looked down at Bradford, still collecting papers from the ground. "And you can see for yourself that I'm not hiding anything that doesn't belong to me!" He picked up his own pack and turned it over. Various objects rained down around Bradford and onto his papers: a dip net, a Bible, a tinderbox, a spare shirt. Still clutching papers, Bradford raised his hand to shield himself.

Mr. Montgomery moved over to a smaller pack close by, where the wood was stacked ready for the evening fire. Extracting a small bundle, he extended it to Henri. "Here. Hunger can put an edge on a man's temper."

Henri unrolled the cloth. "Jerky! Thanks, mister!" He wrenched off a piece and put it in his mouth before crouching down to pick up his belongings and thrust them into his own pack. As usual, he stuffed these items into his pack in a haphazard fashion, without even bothering to roll up his extra shirt or neatly place his other belongings.

He pulled out a stray drawing from under the net and held it out toward Bradford. "That fell out of your pack." Bradford snatched the paper from him and went back to collecting the scattered papers.

Henri bit off another piece of meat. "This is tasty jerky. I really can catch salmon for you, if you want. It's good eating. My uncle showed me how, when I was down here last year. He's my great uncle, actually, my mother's uncle. My mother and baby sister died the last time the bad fevers came, and I went to stay with my pa's father. He was working up at the trading post near Waiilatpu. And he sent for Lia to come back from school out east to stay with us. He's dead now. My grandpa, I mean. Pa's a trader. He sails down to San Francisco and over to Owyhee and all over the place."

"Henri, there's no need to tell them all our business." It was better not to tell people anything about their background. Less chance that they'd get curious and pry.

"I'm going to be a trader too, once I'm old enough," Henri added.

"Only if your pa agrees."

Henri ignored her comment. "My uncle is going to come meet with me down at the mouth of Kekemarque creek up there." He pointed to the creek that came down just east of the point. "But he's late and I got hungry. And borrowing ain't the same as stealing."

When Henri felt defensive, he would refuse to back down, not even an inch. Lia had never been able to persuade him to let an argument go.

Mr. Montgomery picked up the Bible off the ground and

handed it to Henri. "This book has some good advice on 'borrowing,' as you put it."

Henri put the Bible into the pack with more care than he had shown for his other belongings. Head down, he mumbled, "I don't read so good."

Lia said, "He's learning, though. He'll be reading his Bible perfectly by spring. And at least he wasn't going through your belongings to see if he could find some form of identification."

Mr. Montgomery turned his head to meet her gaze. One corner of his mouth quirked up. "Touché." His eyes were the deep blue of the sky at mid-summer. Then his smile faded, replaced by a more intense expression. A whole new world lurked there in his eyes, waiting for her to explore.

Except, of course, that she had other issues demanding her attention. Such as Henri, who was looking from one of them to the other, a faint frown line between his eyebrows.

Bradford broke the silence. "There. That's all the papers stowed away."

Mr. Montgomery blinked. "Oh yes. The papers. All secure? Excellent." He turned his head sharply, his attention caught by movement behind Lia. He stood up, his hand going to the pistol at his side. Then he relaxed. "Not armed."

Lia turned and caught sight of a newcomer. The man had halted by the mouth of the creek, some fifty paces away, and stood watching them. "That's Henri's uncle. We need to talk to him."

Henri touched Lia's arm. "I'll just go talk to him in private first, all right? You won't mind, will you?"

"Oh. No. I guess not. I mean—of course not."

Henri patted her arm before going off.

Bradford's eyes gleamed. "I've not seen a native wearing that style of headdress before. A cap made from a fox's head with the ears remaining! Marvelous." He reached for the sketchbook. "If I sit by the fire, I can get his profile with the river in the background. I need to make a record of this." Without another word, he moved a few paces away and settled down, sketching with broad strokes.

Lia frowned. "Why is he drawing a picture of Henri's uncle?"

"He's always doing things like this," Mr. Montgomery told Lia smoothly. "Starts sketching. Stops talking. Stops listening. He becomes lost to the world when he sketches. I remember once..."

Something about this speech didn't ring true, but she couldn't concentrate on that puzzle at the moment. The sight of Henri's uncle had stirred up what felt like a horde of butterflies in her stomach. Or maybe it was angry bees. Something sharp and unsettled. Her future was being discussed, as well as Henri's. She turned her back on Henri and his uncle and looked out at the river.

Mr. Montgomery stopped babbling, his bright blue eyes intent upon her. "Is something wrong?"

She shook her head automatically. Silence was the safest course.

But... this man was a stranger; she would never see him again. It would do no harm to tell him the truth. Not the secrets buried in her past, just her present dilemma. Surprisingly, she *wanted* to tell him. She suspected he would make a good listener. "The fact is, I don't know what to do with that boy." It was a relief to say the words out loud. "Truly, he did not think of taking your food as stealing. He has a good heart. The problem is, he's too impetuous. He acts first and then wonders if he did the right thing."

"He's a boy trying to figure out how to be a man," Mr.

Montgomery said. "I don't think you can teach him that, no matter how much schooling he gets. Is he so very wild?"

"He's a normal thirteen-year-old boy." Even to her own ears, she sounded defensive.

"So that's a yes, then."

Too worried to smile, she looked down at the ground and kicked a stone so that it arced up and splashed down into the river. "He's growing up so fast. I know it's selfish, but I want him to stay a child just a little longer." *I want him to stay with me a little longer.*

She did not know what she would do with herself if Henri decided to go live with his uncle. Would she be welcome in the native village as well? Though her mother was part native, Lia had never spent much time with her Métis relatives. If Henri's relatives wanted her nephew to live with them, but they didn't want her to stay as well, where would she go? The thought of being on her own was terrifying in its loneliness. She did not know how she would face it.

Lia glanced up to see the tall Englishman watching her closely. She would have supposed that such a rough, weathered face would look forbidding, but she saw nothing but sympathy in his expression. "Did you raise him?" he asked gently.

"Only for the past couple years. When Maman died, Pa sent me off to get educated. I guess he didn't think a girl would be useful out west." The old pain was still surprisingly sharp. "Pierre goes off for months at a time, trading. Henri's mother died while Pierre was away, so Pa brought me out here to take care of Henri while he worked for the Hudson Bay Company. And then this past winter, Pa died. It's just the two of us, until Pierre gets back."

"And you need to find a place to stay until then."

Lia nodded. "Henri's uncle sent word that he wanted Henri to stay with him in his village, but he didn't say anything about there being a place for me. And I promised Pa that I'd take care of Henri until my brother comes back. I know he's going to leave me one day," she added. "Being a trader is all he's ever wanted to do. But I just want him to stay with me a little while longer." *I want to belong somewhere, with someone.*

Mr. Montgomery was silent. It was as if he were listening to the words Lia had not spoken aloud. Then he said, in his deep voice, "'In my Father's house are many mansions.' That's what the Bible tells me. I should imagine there's a place waiting for you. If the Lord went to all the trouble of creating a world so beautiful, with so much attention to the smallest details, do you think he would have neglected to pay a little attention to what happens to you?"

"Sometimes it doesn't seem like such a beautiful world." Lia refused to turn around and see Henri discussing his future with his uncle. Deciding her fate. She would not look. Instead, she turned to look up at Mr. Montgomery, this enigmatic man who could quote scripture but who was clearly hiding something from her.

Mr. Montgomery took a few steps down to the water lapping against the shore. He crouched down and plunged his hand into the river. A quick scoop, then he was up again and striding back toward her.

He opened his hand. On his palm lay a collection of pebbles that glittered like jewels: gold-flecked rose quartz tumbled in with carnelian, topaz, and jade-colored stones, all glistening with water and sparkling in the sunlight.

"Beautiful," she murmured. The tension inside her began to ease. She wasn't sure why exactly—his obvious concern perhaps, or the warmth in his eyes as he stood there looking at her. There was still something about him that she couldn't quite figure out. Even so, she felt better.

Hands as large as his should have been bumbling and awkward, but his fingers deftly plucked an arrow-shaped stone, red as a rose, out of the pebbles and handed it to her. "As a memento of our meeting."

He gave her a bow, like a gentleman from back east. The courtly gesture was so incongruous in this wild land that her lips curved upward.

"Ah, you *can* smile," he said softly. "Beautiful indeed." His gaze flicked behind her. "Your nephew is waving at you. I think he wants you to join his discussion." He went back to where the campfire was laid, next to the busily sketching Bradford, and set about starting a fire.

HENRI'S GREAT-UNCLE, Djaqi'lxida, had the frail-boned look of the very old. But his body was wiry and strong still. The dark eyes that met Lia's were bright with interest and—could that be pity? She stiffened. Whatever he had come to say, it was not going to be good.

He spoke Kalapuyan laced with the Chinook Wawa, the creole language used by tribes and traders. Henri translated the words she did not understand. "Since the sicknesses came, there are few left in my tribe."

Lia said, "I can help. I can hunt. Or I can teach the children. I was teaching at the mission school at Waiilatpu, but that wasn't enough to support me and Henri both. That's why we have to find a place to live."

Djaqi'lxida listened as Henri translated her words, but then he shook his head. "You may be Métis, but when the *cheechako* look at you, they see a woman from their own country. It would cause trouble if you came to live with us."

Every word he said was true, but it still hurt to hear it. Her mother had been the daughter of a French trapper and a Cree woman. She had come from a Métis village that lay over a thousand miles away. There was no place for Lia among the native tribes here. And she did not fit in with the American settlers either, no matter what she looked like. The only time she ever felt that she was where she belonged was when she was with her family and other trappers. But trapping was dying out as a way of life in the west, and Henri was the only family she had left, until Pierre returned.

The old man went on, serene and implacable. "There is much unrest in this land. The Americans, they say the land belongs to the people from beyond the mountains. The British, they say the *Hyas Klootchman Tyee* rules over all the people here."

"I doubt Queen Victoria cares one way or another if I stay with you," Lia said wryly. "The Hudson Bay Company surely doesn't. The whole reason Pa started to work for them was to provide us with a place to live. But once he was gone, they wanted us to leave the trading post. They didn't care that we had nowhere to go. And the Americans and British are always squabbling, but it's never changed anything as far as I can see. Why should we concern ourselves with their quarrels?"

"There is talk of war between them. We do not want to give them cause to make war with us." Djaqi'lxida put his hand on Henri's shoulder. "The boy could stay."

Henri took a step back, shaking his head. "I'm the only family she's got left. I need to look after her until my pa gets back in the spring." Lia started to speak, and he gave a short sigh. "I know. You think I'm a child. But I'm nearly as tall as you now, Lia. I can work."

"You're going to get an education no matter where you live," Lia said firmly. "I promised Pa before he died that I'd see you get some book learning."

"Then I cannot help you," Djaqi'lxida said.

As she watched Djaqi'lxida walking away, she should have felt sad. Instead, a sense of relief filled Lia's heart. She was not going to be left on her own. Henri was going to live with her until her brother Pierre came back from his trading voyage to live with them both.

Now all she had to do was make sure he got some education in him. She suspected he would hate school as much as she'd had. Sitting indoors all day with strangers who had never tasted the freedom that came from roaming the wilderness.

But it was worth it, now. She could teach Henri herself, if they couldn't find a school for him. The trouble was, she needed to find a way to put a roof over their heads and food on the table while she was educating him.

There was no work for them in Astoria, a scanty collection of cabins huddled on a little spit of land between the river and the Pacific Ocean, where the wind blew constantly and the seagulls uttered their mournful cries.

"All right. We'll leave word at Astoria for your pa so he knows where to find us." She picked up her pack and heaved it over her shoulder. "In Oregon City."

As he worked to get the campfire going, Geoff kept one eye on Lia talking with her nephew and his uncle. Whatever the meeting had been about, it was soon over. The older man nodded to Lia and Henri, then walked away, heading back up the creek into the hills. Henri and Lia spoke to each other for a moment longer before coming over to Geoff. The campfire was burning well, and the delicious smell of roasting meat drifted over from the cast-iron pan.

"Will you stay for a meal? We have some salt pork left over from our stay at Fort Vancouver, and I can make some tea."

He thought that the young boy, Henri, looked hopeful. But Lia shook her head. "We need to be on our way. Good day to you."

Geoff got to his feet. "So, have I proved my innocence in the matter of your pack? I am not a thief."

She tilted her head up to study his expression. "Now that, for some reason, I can believe. I'm not sure what you're up to, and it's none of my business, but it's not robbing. Just as well. They hang thieves in these parts."

"I will bear that in mind, should I ever feel the inclination to go through another pack," he said solemnly.

Another smile, transforming her sober features into warmth and beauty. Really, she was astonishingly pretty when she wasn't frowning. He watched as she and Henri made their way downriver. Lia turned her head and gave him one last look before she disappeared into a grove of trees. Then she was gone, and he could not escape the feeling that he had just let an opportunity slip through his fingers.

Which was utterly foolish. He could never pursue any kind of friendship with Amelia Elizabeth Griggs. Especially when he considered her parting words. If that was the way they treated a thief in these parts, he hated to think how they would treat a spy.

CHAPTER 2

Out in the middle of the south channel, the wind whipped the water into a sea of whitecaps. This far down the Columbia, only a few miles from the Pacific Ocean, the river was immense. Geoff could just make out that low, sandy spit of land on the opposite bank —Chinook Point—that had been their last campsite. Cannon placed there could sweep the whole of the north channel.

Bradford looked at him. "They're well on their way. Your report, Lieutenant."

Geoff stiffened. Even out here, with nothing but the wind stirring the river, that was a reckless comment to make. "We are gentlemen of leisure on a scenic tour. Always. Even if it seems safe, you should never lower your guard. You should have secured the papers in the secret bottom of the pack, not left them loose inside."

"Yes, yes, of course." As usual, Bradford did not sound concerned. The son of a well-to-do family, he had been sent out to Canada to serve as aide-de-camp to his uncle, the commander in chief of all forces in North America. Geoff would have considered that a good reason to work twice as hard to prove that he could do the work, that it wasn't a sinecure. Bradford, on the other hand, regarded the position as simply his due. "I don't think we need to take elaborate precautions to hide the paperwork every time. For one thing, the majority of the people out here can't even read. That careless boy didn't notice anything odd."

Geoff turned away and looked out over the river again. He could not afford to lose his temper with Bradford, not as this juncture.

Britain and the United States both claimed the Oregon Territory. The British Colonial Office had decided that an artist and an engineer would be the perfect officers to send into the Oregon Territory to prepare a report on its defensive capabilities. Their orders had stressed the importance of keeping their activities secret from the populace, so they posed as private travelers. Geoff evaluated locations for possible fortifications, and Bradford sketched them.

The army had given Geoff a structured life and a sense of purpose. When he joined the army, he had given a solemn promise to do his duty. To obey the orders he was given. It didn't matter how he felt about them.

All his life, he had considered himself a plain-speaking man, who had walked in the way of the Lord and kept to the truth and tried to do the right thing. Now he was being asked to lie, in the course of his duty and for the sake of his country. Guilt gnawed at his conscience.

But if he *did* have to be a spy, then he was going to make a proper job of it. It was dangerous for Bradford to leave papers lying about. He turned back and said, as mildly as he could, "It's the principle of the thing."

Bradford merely shrugged. "What did you conclude on your survey?"

"I'd recommend a battery of heavy guns on the west side, overlooking the shipping channel. Put a defensible barrack on this side and dig a ditch across this neck of land. With cannon placed at Chinook Point as well, the army could control the river traffic to the Pacific."

"All right. Write it up and we'll cross Tongue Point off the list. What's next?"

Geoff considered. "Based on what I learned at Fort Vancouver, we've checked all the possible sites on the Columbia River. Up the Willamette, there's Oregon City. I need to draw up a plan to occupy it, in the event that the government decides on a show of force."

"We need to stop there anyway. It's the only populated area of any size for hundreds of miles. I fancy some time in civilization again, or as much of it as we can expect in an American village."

"But you're not going to go carousing while we're on duty."

Bradford smiled. "Of course not." The man smiled easily and often. Geoff had to walk a delicate line here. One did not reprimand one's superior officer. So long as the papers were secure, the mission was not affected.

"I'm not so concerned with the outlying areas; the population is not concentrated enough to concern armed troops. For my report I need an estimation of the populace clustered around Oregon City. As accurate as possible."

"They can't expect miracles."

"This is the Colonial Office you are talking about."

"Good point," Bradford conceded. "They probably will expect miracles."

"The Colonial Office will expect us to finish the mission. No matter the obstacles." The alternative would be to fail at his mission, fail in his career as an army officer. He was not going to let that happen. No matter how he felt about spying on people he had no argument with and telling lies to lovely women.

"Well then," Bradford said. "Oregon City it is."

Lia stared about her in bewilderment. Oregon City really was a town, not just a few log cabins hastily thrown up on a muddy strip of land by the Willamette River. She had been there before a couple years ago, when she first came out west. She didn't recognize the place now.

The cacophony of noise overwhelmed her senses: men hammering on the roof of a new building, the jingle of harness from horses trotting by, women chatting as they walked along the sidewalk and behind it all the constant, muted thunder of the waterfall upriver. She could smell freshly sawn lumber and the pungent odor of horse droppings on the dirt street.

She was completely lost. She could track anything in the woods, but here, there were no natural landmarks. Buildings rose taller than trees all around her.

It wasn't just the surroundings that confused her. It was the people around her. She understood natives and trappers. Settlers were a new breed, outside of her experience. They even looked different. The men all wore their hair short, with no long, ragged beards. The women were dressed in what were probably the latest fashions. It was overwhelming. She had come here with her father once, when he wanted to visit some friends, former trappers like himself. But she did not see anyone she recognized now.

She could tell Henri was overwhelmed as well. He angled his head back to take in the building across the street, an entire building made out of brick. He narrowed his eyes against the sun, reading the sign above the building across the street. "Mer-can-teel-ee?"

"Mercantile," Lia corrected. "When the 'e' at the end of a word is silent, you treat the vowel before it as a long vowel." At his blank look, she added, "You pronounce the vowel the way you do when you're saying the alphabet."

"Why?"

"That's the rule for spelling."

"Huh. School is all about rules."

Lia mustered up all the enthusiasm she could. "There will be loads of other boys here, I'll bet."

Henri looked around, frowning doubtfully. "Settler boys are probably still helping with the harvest. Bet they're just as ornery as the boys at the mission."

Lord, please send a teacher who knows how to deal with Henri! It wasn't that Henri was dull. He had a quick wit, but it was matched with an equal measure of impatience. If a topic interested him, well and good. If not, then it was like dragging a mule through mud to get him to work through the lesson. When the teacher at the mission in Waiilatpu had tried to teach him to read, Henri had gotten frustrated with her rigid teaching approach. He had declared that reading was boring and stopped doing his lessons. He reacted to the problem with the emotional response of a child and the independent spirit of an adult.

That was the problem: he was no longer a boy but not quite a man. And he was her problem, whether he wanted to be or not.

She and Henri finally tracked down where her father's old friends had stayed, only to find that it had changed too. The spot down by the river where they'd lived was now occupied by a whitewashed clapboard house next to a new gristmill.

She smoothed down the white bib that ran down the front of her dress. It was the only dress she still possessed, one she'd worn at school. That had been a few years ago. The skirt was shorter now, the bodice snugger. And probably no one had worn a dress in this style in several years. *Lord, you accept me as I am, with all my faults. If it is Your will, they will too.*

At her knock, an American man opened the door. His welcoming smile faded into suspicion when he saw Lia standing in front of him.

"Er... Hello. Good morning. I am looking for Phillipe Lascaux. He used to live hereabouts."

"That old trapper? He took off for French Prairie, last I heard. Lot of the trappers and half-breeds moved down there."

Lia tightened her grip around her pack. She ignored the sinking feeling inside her. "I need to find a place to stay and some work to do. He was my father's old friend and I was hoping he might know of someone who was looking for help."

The man looked her up and down, still frowning. She could imagine what he saw. She'd had no chance to get the creases out of her dress. Lacking any hairpins to put her hair up, she had braided it neatly this morning but let the plait hang down her back. She had the sense he was not quite sure which box to assign her to, trapper or newcomer. He wouldn't put her into the box marked "native," though. No one did. She didn't look the part.

"I'm not afraid to work," she added a bit desperately. "I can read and write. I know how to do sums. And I can sew." She was throwing in everything she could think of. She had to find a way to make her way in this town. If she didn't, she would have broken her promise, failed her father and her brother both.

She wasn't sure if her desperation showed in her face, but for whatever reason, the man's forbidding expression softened. "Do you know Mrs. Whitlow? She runs a laundry, rents a couple of rooms sometimes if she likes the look of people. Make a good impression on her and you'll go a long way toward getting in good with the townsfolk. You'll need that if you want to find respectable work." He added, "I do hear they're looking to replace the schoolmaster. Seems he's feeling poorly. People were saying that there are going to be interviews for the job today. You might want to go see the superintendent, down on Main Street." He turned away.

"Thank you!" Lia called after him. He shut the door before she could ask the man for directions, but it didn't matter. She had a chance now.

Back on Main Street, Lia looked around for someone who might give her directions. Everyone seemed to be rushing by, intent on their own affairs. She watched a smartly dressed young matron making her way down the sidewalk. Her fair hair, under the dainty bonnet, was curled and crimped, and she walked with her ruffled skirts held fastidiously clear of any dirt. She stopped a man about to push open the double-doors of the saloon. "If my brother Edgar is inside, would you ask him to come out? I'll wait."

The woman looked respectable enough, though a thin line of worry creased a line between her brows. Lia crossed the street, carefully avoiding a pile of horse droppings, and stepped onto the plank sidewalk in front of her. "Could you tell me, please, where I might find the school superintendent?"

The line between the woman's brows deepened. She looked Lia up and down, her gaze lingering on every wrinkle in the outdated dress before coming back to her face. "What do you want with him?"

"I hear that the schoolteacher is sick. I was thinking he might need help at the school."

The woman's eyes dropped down to Lia's dress again. "From *you*?"

Lia stiffened. Before she could reply, the door of the saloon flew open. A man barged through the doorway, knocking her off the plank sidewalk. She landed on her hands and knees, splashing a brown streak of mud down the front of her dress. *Oh.* Lia wrinkled her nose at the stench. That brown streak wasn't mud.

Henri was at her side, helping her up. The man who had knocked her down, a thin man with hair the same blond color as the young matron, frowned down at Lia. "You all right?" He slurred the words.

"This lady wants to take your place as the schoolteacher," the matron told him.

The man huffed a dry laugh. "She's welcome to it! Ignorant little ruffians. Here, you've got a streak of... something on your dress." He offered Lia his handkerchief. She tried brushing the front of her dress, but that only smeared the stain further into the fabric.

The man pulled a silver flask out of his jacket pocket and uncapped it. "This'll take that stain out." And before Lia could stop him, he had splashed the alcohol down the front of her dress. The man peered closer. "Well, it smells better, anyway. This whole town stinks. That's a joke, get it?"

"I can't say that I do, actually." Nothing struck her as funny just then. She looked down at her only dress. Ruined. Would the superintendent even consider her for the position if she wore her old, comfortable hunting clothes? Probably not. But she had no choice.

"That's the problem with people around here," the schoolteacher mumbled. "No sense of humor." Politely, Lia held the handkerchief out to him, but he waved it away. "Consider it a gift."

The matron linked her arm in his. "Your sense of humor is too playful, dear. Not everyone has your sensibilities. Come along with me now. I told everyone you were too ill to attend to your duties today. What would people say if they saw you here? You'd better lie down for a spell." To Lia, she said, "I'll tell my husband there's a woman wanting to speak to him. He's the superintendent, you know. I don't think you should come to the house. That combination of aromas is rather strong. No, I'll tell him you're waiting for him outside the saloon. I'm sure you'll make a memorable first impression. Come, Edgar. You need to rest. You'll feel better."

He might feel better, but Lia couldn't see any way to avoid things getting a lot worse for her. *Lord, what can I do now?*

"WELL, THAT WENT WRONG IN A HURRY." Peter Ogden was a short man, and his weathered face had spent too much time outdoors to show a flush of anger, but even though he stood half a head shorter than Bradford, he could still direct an impressive glare from under his bushy gray eyebrows. When he frowned, the extra creases lent weight to his displeasure.

He'd spent years working for the Hudson Bay Company in the Oregon Territory, so he passed among the local Americans without comment. Unlike Geoff and Bradford.

Bradford retorted, "It's not my fault if the men in this town get suspicious when they see an Englishman. What can you expect of uncouth Americans?"

They had rented rooms above a newspaper office in Oregon City. Ogden had gone with them to the local livery stables, to introduce them and help them procure a couple of horses. Now, Bradford sat on one of the beds, laying out his clothes. Geoff should have been doing the same, but he was too restless. He prowled around the room, stopping occasionally to look out the window at the street below.

Ogden picked up a bottle of scent that Bradford had acquired from the stores at Fort Vancouver. He sniffed and then wrinkled his nose in disapproval. "The most important men in the whole town, and you"—he put the bottle down and thrust a finger at Bradford—"managed to antagonize them within a few minutes with your British superiority. And it didn't help that you'd doused yourself in oil of roses until you smelled like a whole bouquet."

"A gentleman likes to make an impression," Bradford said.

"Oh, you did that, all right. And you," Ogden turned to Geoff, "weren't much help."

"What did I do wrong?" Geoff stopped pacing, surprised.

"It's not what you did, it's the way you act, like a soldier on parade. You might as well be wearing your army uniform. This disagreeable puppy here," he indicated Bradford, "needs to stop exuding British superiority, and you need to cultivate an air of relaxation. You're too upright. You'll never stop irritating the Americans if you don't adapt."

"It's not as if it's much of a town," Bradford grumbled. "A muddy strip of insignificant houses clustered along a river."

"It's the biggest settlement for hundreds of miles," Ogden said. "It's got four dry goods stores, three literary societies, two churches, and a schoolhouse. What did you expect, Paris?"

"I expected... less mud."

Geoff rather liked the town. There was an energy in the streets, a sense that anything was possible with hard work. These people had created a town from wilderness and imbued it with a sense of optimism so strong even he could feel it. "Do you have an idea of how many Americans there are here?"

"They tell me over five hundred wagons came over the passes this year. Maybe two thousand Americans in the area as a whole. That's a guess, but even so it's twice the number of last year or the year before. We are already outnumbered."

"If we block trade from the ocean and occupy this town, we might be able to keep the Territory. But we still need to get an accurate estimate of the population." Geoff turned to look out the window again.

From this vantage of the second story of the building, he had a good view of the town and the surrounding area. Oregon City stood at the farthest point a ship could sail up the Willamette. Above the town, a horseshoe-shaped ledge spanned the width of the river, creating a powerful waterfall.

On either side, hills covered in dense brush rose to tall ridges. *Waterfall about forty feet wide, not navigable. Would need to build a portage road to move troops and supplies around the falls.* Geoff eyed the ridges on either side of the river, automatically determining the best place for artillery to control the river both above and below the waterfall. A cannon placed just *there* would be ideally situated to rain down death and destruction on this bustling town, its new wooden buildings smashed into splinters... He closed his eyes for a moment, as if he could shut out the sight in his imagination.

What right did he have, did a government on the other side of the world have, to tell these people how to live? Granted, these people had come along and displaced the natives, telling them how to live. Even so, duty was harder when you could put a face and a name to the enemy.

He watched the people passing by on the street below. Decent, everyday people. Not hardened soldiers used to battle and its bloody aftermath. He tried to picture these people crouching behind palisades, fearing a random sniper shot, and felt sick to the pit of his stomach. He had been in battle before, smelled the smoke of cannon fire, heard the screams of the horses as they fell, the moans of the wounded men dying on the blood-soaked field. He'd forced himself to endure, to concentrate on the job he needed to do. His duty.

This time, duty felt more like betrayal.

He was lying to people, day in and day out. He was good at it. Maybe he was stiff, as Ogden said, but even so people believed his stories. Each time another smooth lie fell from his lips, part of him wanted to demand, *Can't you see the lie? Can't you tell it's not true?* He could feel the lies like a physical pain, each one like a barb hooked in his skin.

Worse, lying became easier the more he did it. Each time he spun a cover story, he was taking yet another step off the path a righteous man should walk. He wondered if he would even recognize himself once this mission was finished. Yet he could not just quit. He could not walk away from his duty.

He used to like army life. It was straightforward: you had your duty and you did it. No ambiguity. And he did not fear getting caught. With adequate precautions, it should be possible to avoid any suspicion. Bradford did have a tendency to leave papers about as if they were safely back in Fort Vancouver, but Geoff knew to look out for that by now, and he always made sure they were safely stowed beneath the false bottom of the knapsack.

No, what he feared was losing a part of himself. Every time he had to look one of these Americans in the face, decent, honorable people for the most part, and tell them a lie, it felt as if he were undermining the very foundation he had always stood on. He read his Bible every night, praying that the Lord would help him find a way to make this burden easier to bear.

He clenched his hands into fists so tightly that his fingernails dug into his palms. Then he made a conscious effort to relax his hands. "All right," he told Ogden. "I will make more of an effort to be friendly toward these people, if that's what it takes."

"You two are going to have to come up with a way to present yourselves that doesn't make them suspicious. Especially if you plan to stay for any length of time."

"We need to soften them up," Bradford decreed. "Get to know them. Once they get a chance to know us in a social setting, they'll come to see that we're really quite delightful fellows after all. Give 'em a few glasses of whiskey and that'll loosen their tongues, sure enough."

"I am not going to buy drinks for anyone," Geoff said. "We'd be better off going to the local church services, talking to people who can give us sober answers instead of talking wildly about anything that strikes their fancy."

"You might be right," Bradford said, a bit sadly.

"We want them to see us as respectable people who are interested in the area," Geoff reminded him. "The best way to do that is to make them think we are serious about learning more about the people and the places."

Ogden made a *harrumph* sound. "The question is, how do you two propose to start this campaign of friend-making? It seems to me as if you have already managed to annoy or strike suspicion into most of the people around. The men, at any rate. Not a fine start, I must say. You can't return back over the mountains until spring. I can't always be around to rescue you from the locals. You two should spend the winter at Fort Vancouver in the bachelors' quarters."

Bradford rolled his eyes. "Three months looking at palisades in the rain."

"It's not as fancy as Montreal." Ogden grinned, showing crooked teeth. "No ladies to flirt with. Just a bunch o' sailors, if the Navy feels like sending a ship upriver."

"We couldn't really make any progress on our mission at Fort Vancouver," Bradford mused.

"What mission?" Ogden flung his hands wide. "The Colonial Office is filled with dreamers. There are three times as many Americans in this Territory as there are British. And more are coming each year. Mark my words: this is the beginning of a flood. There's no way we can defend the passages against them. It's folly to even suggest it, and you're not fools. You're going to go back and hand them the facts, whether they like 'em or not, and your work is done."

Bradford said, "I still think we should get to know the people here. We could study the weaknesses of the city as a potential occupation site. We just need a convincing explanation for our presence if we're going to stay. Three literary societies, eh? I could go see if there's any useful information to be picked up there. Bound to be one or two good-looking ladies there eager to be impressed by a cultured British gentleman."

"We can settle that later," Geoff said. "Right now, we need to take care of the horses. We can't leave them tied to the railing out there." He stopped speaking, his attention drawn to a commotion on the plank sidewalk outside the mercantile store. A man and a woman standing on the sidewalk, with a boy crouched down to help someone else get to their feet. A small figure with a dark braid falling over one shoulder. Geoff sighed and headed for the door. "Excuse me, gentlemen."

HENRI LOOKED AT LIA. "What can I do to help? Do you have another dress?"

Lia shook her head. She wanted to run back into the woods and never come back to this horrible town, but she could not do that. There was nothing she could do. "I'll have to face the superintendent looking like this." *Lord, help me. I cannot see what to do.* "My reputation in this town will be ruined. I'll never find work."

"A bath?" Henri looked around the street as though expecting to see a bathhouse appear. "There must be something I can get you."

"A parasol," came a deep voice behind her.

Lia turned around. The tall man she'd met in the woods, Mr. Montgomery, stood there. He extended some coins to Henri. "There's one in that store window across the street. Get it for me now. Run!"

Henri jumped to obey. Mr. Montgomery grabbed her by the elbow and swung her around. "Start walking," he said in a low voice. "People are watching. Start walking and don't look back."

CHAPTER 3

Geoff guided her down the plank sidewalk in the opposite direction from the one the matron had taken. Years of experience dictated that the first line of defense was to choose the battleground. Lia was in no position to deal with the townspeople until she could get cleaned up. He marched with decision down the sidewalk.

Lia muttered, "What are you doing? I need to speak to the school superintendent. He's supposed to meet me there to discuss the schoolteacher position."

He released his grip on her elbow, transferring her hand into the crook of his arm. "Right now, you're going to make a bad first impression on everyone you meet. Let's fix that first, then deal with this superintendent. Act natural. People are watching."

"Who is watching?"

Her voice was soft, but he could feel tension in the way she gripped his arm. He patted her hand. "Several men by the livery stables. They saw you fall. A few women by the dry goods store looked this way when that blond man knocked you down, but they've gone back to talking amongst themselves. If any of the townsfolk are watching now, they will merely see us strolling down the street like any idle couple. I think you're too far away for anyone to notice details, but let's not attract any more attention. Laugh. As if I have just made a joke."

Obediently, she laughed. It sounded hollow to his ears, but no one else seemed to notice. A couple passed by. The man nodded to the two of them. The woman wrinkled her nose. She said to her companion, "They really should do something about these streets. The smell is awful."

Lia murmured, "If the superintendent comes and I'm not waiting for him, what is he going to think?"

"We need to get you out of sight. That's the first thing. Worry about the rest later. We just have to get you off the main street."

"I can't go into one of the stores. People will see me. They'll *smell* me."

"True," Geoff conceded. "At the moment you're... memorable. And it's a long, straight block, wide open. I'll think of something."

He couldn't think of anything at the moment, but his tone must have carried conviction. He had dashed out to help her on impulse. Something about the way she had stood, trying futilely to tidy her soiled dress, had touched him. It wasn't right that she fight this battle on her own. He put his hand over hers and gave an encouraging squeeze. Her grip on his arm relaxed.

Her nephew dashed up with a parasol, brown silk with a long fringe. "It was the first one I saw," he panted. "Is it all right?"

"Exactly right." Geoff gave the boy a reassuring grin. "That will be a great help."

He unfolded the handle and opened the parasol, positioning it over Lia's head to shield her face from passersby while they walked.

Henri jogged alongside, taking two steps for every one of Geoff's strides. Lia herself had to hurry to keep up. Geoff slowed his steps. Henri said, "Can I do anything else? There must be something else we can do."

Geoff flicked his fingers unobtrusively toward a rangy chestnut gelding tied up a few stores down in front of Abernethy's Mercantile. "That's mine. Untie him and see if you can distract that woman if you see her coming back this way." To Lia, he added, "We just need enough time to slip down an alley. The nearest one is several stores down, but I think we'll make it."

He risked a glance behind them. "She came out of a house and is walking down the street in this direction with a man. He's walking fast. Looks a bit impatient. We need to walk a bit faster."

"I'm already stretching my legs as it is. I think it will draw attention if I run."

"True. In that case, perhaps we need to—Ah, excellent."

Henri came riding the horse down the street at a fast trot. Lia started to look behind her, and Geoff gave her a discreet nudge with his elbow. "Look in that store window to your right. You can see the reflection behind you." In the reflection, Henri was riding the horse straight down the middle of the street. Then he veered toward the matron and her male companion. Henri shouted at the horse, as if it were out of control. To an outsider, it would look like a complete coincidence that the horse's fast pace churned up chunks of mud as it passed. The matron stopped with a cry of dismay and started to brush off her dress. Her male companion stopped with her. Geoff could just make out what he was saying. "Now, Sally. If you hadn't insisted that I come out with you... I've got a lot to do today—now *don't* get upset with me. We can go back home and you can show me whatever it was that was so important later."

"That's done it," Geoff said, his voice rich with satisfaction. "While they're standing there arguing, we have time to slip down this alley—right here, past the watering trough—and, there." He drew her down the alley and around a corner. He stopped then, still holding her arm. "There. They won't see you now."

LIA WAS STILL BREATHING QUICKER, recovering from their fast pace. "Do you think you could let go of me now?"

"Oh. Of course." He released her arm and took a step back. "My apologies."

Lia looked around. A row of prosperous-looking houses, but few people. Perfect. "I have to thank you. That was quick thinking, sir."

"Think nothing of it. Though perhaps, if I could ask it as a great favor—my name is Montgomery, rather than sir."

Lia laughed, a little ruefully. "It is a good name, Mr. Montgomery."

His smile came on slow, but it transformed his features. He wasn't plain at all, not in this moment. Gentle warmth spread through her body, setting her at ease, telling her everything was all right. She was safe. That other man, his friend, had been handsome pretty, but this one was far more interesting. Whatever he had been hiding from her when they met, here was someone she could trust. He could never be her enemy.

Now that she was able to relax, she became aware that

he was almost close enough for her to touch him. One step would bridge the gap between them. His gaze fell to her lips.

Abruptly, he looked away, and she noted the red flush on his cheekbones. Odd, that such an imposing man could be as shy as she was. He had been confident enough when decisive action was called for. She cast about for some way to set him at his ease. "I really do appreciate your help."

"It was my pleasure."

"I'm not sure what the superintendent will think about me, though. I mean, if his wife told him I was waiting for him and I wasn't there."

"I would simply go see the man. If he doesn't ask for an explanation, don't offer one. If he does, you were called away, and came as soon as you could. Or write him a note. Get your young lad to deliver it. Tell him that you were delayed and you would be glad to call upon him in an hour if that's convenient."

"You're full of ideas."

He gave a half bow. "Madam."

"I do wish you'd stop calling me that. But no." Lia straightened. "I have to find a place to stay. And I need to clean this dress."

A passerby directed Lia and Geoff to Mrs. Whitlow's place, a couple blocks farther down on Main Street. Geoff reconnoitered up and down first. No sign of the superintendent or his wife, so he waved Lia to join him. With the parasol strategically poised to hide her face, they walked on. Mrs. Whitlow's house turned out to be a white house with crisp muslin curtains hanging in the windows. Mrs. Whitlow was of middle height, brown hair growing gray, and an uncompromising line to her lips. "Well. Ben Wallace sent his boy over to tell me he'd recommended a young woman to board with me." She looked Lia up and down.

Then she nodded. "I've got rooms you can use. I rent by the week or the month." She named a sum, her eyes running over Lia's bedraggled appearance. She looked stern, but her voice was not unkind when she added, "You'll need to change into another dress if you want people in this town to look upon you favorably."

"I don't have another dress." Lia kept her gaze steady on Mrs. Whitlow. She felt as if she were back at school, facing an unexpected quiz. She made sure to keep her spine straight, shoulders back, her eyes steady on the older woman. "I can find work without getting a vote of approval from everyone I meet, can't I?"

Mrs. Whitlow snorted. "Not in this town. It's too small and there aren't many things a woman can do, or at least not if she's respectable and all. You are, I can tell."

"Well, thank you," Lia said, somewhat mollified. "I think." She fingered the coins in her pocket, the last of Pa's legacy. "I can pay for lodging for the next month or so, for myself and my nephew. But I'm going to need to find work, and soon, if we want to eat as well." *Whatever it takes to get Henri an education and put a roof over our heads.*

She indicated the brown streak down the front of her dress. "Do you know of a way I can get this stain out? I need to call on the school superintendent, to see about the schoolteacher position. His wife already hates me. I don't want to make things worse."

Mrs. Whitlow's eyebrows shot up. "Have you made an enemy of Sally Mason? She's silly and spoils her boy something rotten, but she's not evil. What did you do to rile her up so?"

"I asked if I could take her brother's job."

"Aye, that might do it." Mrs. Whitlow pursed her lips doubtfully. "We could try soaking the dress in vinegar. I doubt it will make a difference, though. You'll probably end up having to dye it."

Lia frowned. "Then I'll need to wear my old trapping outfit."

"Men's clothing? That's all you got to wear?" Mrs. Whitlow shook her head. "I've got a better idea. Come inside."

Mr. Montgomery said, "I should be going now, see what happened to your nephew and my horse."

Lia offered Mr. Montgomery the parasol. "Thank you so much for loaning me this."

He refused the parasol with a flick of his hand. "Consider it yours. It's not really the style for a gentleman to use one of these things."

Mrs. Whitlow said, "You can just take that back to where you found it. The girl can't go about accepting gifts from men. It would cause talk."

"Well," Mr. Montgomery said reasonably, "I can hardly return it back to the store. That would cause more talk."

Henri came riding down the street. He halted the horse beside them and slid off. The horse snorted, stepping to one side. Geoff restrained it with one firm hand on its bridle and soothed it with his deep voice. Lia wasn't surprised when the horse calmed down.

Henri grinned at Mr. Montgomery, who gave him an approving nod before turning back to Mrs. Whitlow. "Besides, technically, the parasol was a gift from her nephew. I gave him money in exchange for exercising my horse. All fair and proper, ma'am."

"Hmph."

Lia introduced Henri to Mrs. Whitlow. Mr. Montgomery bowed to Lia and Mrs. Whitlow equally. "If you ladies will pardon me, I need to rejoin my friends. Good day to you,

sir." He tipped his hat to Henri and strolled off, leading
his horse.

Mrs. Whitlow looked at her. "That young man of yours
has a quick tongue."

"He's not *my* young man," Lia said.

"Hmph," Mrs. Whitlow said again. She turned to Henri.
"All right, youngster. Let's see what we can find you for
supper."

"Supper?" Henri perked up. He followed Mrs. Whitlow
indoors without another word. Lia lingered outside, looking
down the street to where Mr. Montgomery was striding
away. She felt his absence with an almost physical sense of
loss. It was as if she had been leaning against a granite
monolith and its support had just been withdrawn, leaving
her bereft.

A cold breeze whispered down the street. It was only her
foolish imagination that made her think it had a lonely
sound to it. She lifted her skirts out of the mud and followed
Henri and Mrs. Whitlow indoors.

GEOFF REJOINED Bradford and Ogden in the room they'd
rented above the newspaper office. From the look in Bradford's eye, the man had seen most of Geoff's encounter with
Lia. Geoff went on the offensive immediately. Take your
ground from the start and hold it, his military instructors
had always said. "She needed my help. You're supposed to
help ladies in need."

"Well, quite." Bradford almost managed to keep the
amusement out of his voice. There was no reason to feel so
defensive, but Geoff glowered at him. Bradford went on,

"And I believe I've found an excuse for our lingering in Oregon City."

"And what might that be?" A dark suspicion took hold in the back of Geoff's mind.

Bradford beamed at him. "Dalliance."

CHAPTER 4

"No." Geoff folded his arms.

Bradford lowered his voice to a persuasive, wheedling tone. "I don't mean seduce her, man. Use your charms to jolly her along, sweet talk her until she agrees to help us."

Geoff did not budge. "Help us do what?"

"It's very simple. All you need to do is get her to agree to let you spend time with her. I, of course, will spend time with you both. As a respectable chaperone."

"You?"

"Don't sound so surprised. It's not flattering. You'll be seen to be courting her, and that will give us an excuse to stay in town. You'll need to take her out to see the surrounding countryside... all the strategic areas..."

"In the pouring rain..." Ogden sounded doubtful.

"And when the weather is too inclement, then you'll be forced to keep company with her indoors, where all the Americans will gather to socialize. You'll become so familiar it'll be as if you are part of the wallpaper. They'll start to see you as one of their own, a man who's planning to settle down here. They'll lower their guard and tell you all kinds of things. It'll be simple."

"Things always seem simple to you. I do not think it would prove to be so simple in actual fact."

Bradford waved a hand. "Even if they don't spill all their secrets, no one will question your presence with such a pretty excuse to dally."

Geoff turned back to the window and took a deep breath. Back in Montreal, the commander of the Royal Engineers had made Geoff's instructions quite clear. Colonel Halloway himself had expressed his particular desire that the two lieutenants act together and with cordiality. All the same, there were limits. He turned back. "One does not trifle with a lady's affection."

"Our orders were to use any means at our disposal."

Ogden sat down at the desk, stretching out his legs with a weary sigh. "You've been in the army for years. Why is this mission any different?"

"I wasn't befriending people to betray them. Any piece of information I get from these people goes into my report. I can't treat a lady like that."

Bradford said, "We can't go back with our report until spring. We can either spend the winter cooped up in Fort Vancouver doing nothing, or we can use the time to further our investigation. Which do you think our superiors would be most impressed by?"

Ogden nodded at Bradford. "I know you would much rather spend your time with brandy and opium, given a chance."

Bradford flashed him a quick grin. "I'll make my own fun, thank you. But it won't hurt our chances if we can provide a good explanation for our presence here for so long. That girl is a heaven-sent opportunity, and you'd be a fool if you didn't take it. Who would it harm if you took the time to get to know her better? Perhaps you could start small. Take her out on a picnic. What could be more innocent?"

"I don't like it," Geoff said. Even if Bradford *was* senior to Geoff, that did not mean he could order him to make the girl think he was in a position to court her. He was leaving in the spring. It wasn't right.

LIA REGARDED herself in the small mirror that hung on the wall of Mrs. Whitlow's front room. The deep blue dress was made of fine wool that felt incredibly luxurious to the touch. It held the faintest scent of lavender, probably from the trunk the garment had been stored in. The bodice was tightly fitted and the corset underneath was tighter still, but if the other women in town could bear it, she would too. Below the waist, the skirt billowed out in yards of fabric that swirled around her as she moved. That was going to take some getting used to. She had hoped that dressing like the other women in town might make her feel as if she were one of them, but it didn't. Instead, she rather felt like a fraud, someone playing dress-up and pretending that she belonged. She looped the little matching reticule onto her wrist.

Mrs. Whitlow handed her a straw bonnet trimmed with a broad blue ribbon. "Here. No woman in town would set foot outside without a bonnet. Otherwise, you'll end up as brown as an Indian!"

Lia dropped the bonnet. "Sorry," she said, a bit breathlessly, kneeling down to pick it up. "So clumsy." *Foolish. Mrs. Whitlow didn't mean anything by the remark.* She had to be more careful. She couldn't risk anyone finding out. Part of Lia wanted to protest that there was nothing wrong with looking like a native. And part of her wanted to just keep quiet and hope that she could be appointed schoolteacher without anyone discovering her ancestry.

Nervously, she waited while Mrs. Whitlow walked around Lia, inspecting her closely. The older woman nodded her head, satisfied. "Now you look like you belong in a town."

"It's lovely," Lia said. "You truly do not mind my wearing this?"

"The dress used to belong to my dear daughter. She'd not begrudge you wearing it." There was a suspicion of moisture in Mrs. Whitlow's eyes, but she blinked quickly. "It's not in the latest fashion, but only a silly fool like Sally Mason would care about that. You look respectable enough, and that's what matters." She gave a short nod. "Yes, you'll do."

Lia let out her breath in relief. "I just hope the superintendent agrees with you." She gathered up her courage and moved toward the door.

Henri followed her out onto the street. "I don't see why you have to go be a schoolteacher anyway. I'm the man of the family. I should be the one working."

When Henri pushed out his lower lip, he looked like a little boy still. But he was as tall as she was now, and likely to grow taller still. She had to be careful not to hurt his feelings. "Maybe Mrs. Whitlow could use your help with the laundry, after school. It would help repay her for the dress." Lia looked hard at Henri. "But only after school. I promised Pa you'd get an education."

He scowled down at the ground. "Maybe I'm too dumb

to learn. That teacher in Waiilatpu didn't think I was too bright."

"Oh, Henri, that wasn't your fault! She was too set in her ways. It might be a struggle to learn, but it'll be worth it in the end. You'd like to be able to read your Bible."

He shrugged, shoving his hands in his pockets. "I s'pose."

This was useless. She wasn't getting through to him. *Lord, what am I doing wrong? I want so much to help him. Please show me the way.* "I need to go see the superintendent now. There must be other people who want this position."

THERE WERE INDEED other people who wanted the job. The door had been opened by a young blond boy, around Henri's age, who looked supremely bored. When Lia had said she'd like to speak with the superintendent about the teaching position, the boy had jerked his head toward the chairs lined up against the wall and then slouched off to the back room.

Lia looked around. The parlor stretched the full width of the house. She had already felt intimidated just walking up to the imposing house, two stories tall. Even with her borrowed finery, she did not belong here. A clock over the mantelpiece ticked loudly, emphasizing the quiet.

She sat on the edge of her chair, eyeing the two people. A young woman sat on the farthest chair, her head tilted down so Lia could only see her enormous black bonnet. She did not look up or acknowledge Lia, but kept her gaze fixed on her hands tightly clasped in her lap. The young man next to her did give Lia a nod. He opened his mouth to speak. Then he doubled over, coughing into his handkerchief. Lia clasped her hands in her lap and sat up straight. She tried to compose herself. Success came from confidence. No one would hire her if even she didn't think she could do the work. And without a position, she couldn't find a way to put a roof over their heads.

She hated feeling homeless. At the end of the day, everyone needed a place where they could shut the door on the outside world and be themselves without judgment.

On impulse, she put her hand into her reticule and pulled out the little red stone that Mr. Montgomery had given her back by the river. She wasn't sure why she had taken it with her when she changed into this dress, except that when she looked at it she could hear his voice... "In my Father's house are many mansions..."

She turned the red stone over and over. Its smooth reflection gleamed in the light from the windows. The stone had been polished by water and force as it tumbled down the river. The Lord had created beauty out of chaos. Everywhere she looked in nature, she could see His works. *All I need do is look for it.*

The door to the back room opened. The boy stood in the doorway. He pointed to the young woman with the enormous bonnet, and jerked his thumb into the back room. The young woman got up and went inside. The door shut behind her.

The young man sitting beside Lia gave her a weak smile, then subsided into another fit of coughing.

It seemed a long time, but probably was only a few moments before the door opened and the young woman returned to her seat. At the boy's signal, the man with the cough went into the back room. The boy followed, shutting the door after him. The ticking of the clock sounded louder than ever. Lia closed her eyes. *Lord, please make this come out all right. If I am meant to get this position, I will. All I have to do is do my best and accept Your will.*

After a few minutes, the door opened, and the man with the cough came out. Still wordless, the boy pointed at Lia. She went inside.

The boy shut the door behind her and went to lean against the wall by a side door.

The superintendent was seated at a desk, with a chair placed across from him. He was younger than she'd expected, with a neat little goatee, and dressed with all the formality of a fancy gentleman back east: frock coat, fancy waistcoat with a bit of silver embroidering on it, starched shirt and intricately knotted tie. He wore his clothes with an air of self-consciousness, as if being fashionable were a duty. She was more thankful than ever that she hadn't met him while wearing that old, ill-fitting dress. The man did not look like he was in a very good mood. He held his shoulders tensely, as if very conscious of carrying a burden, but he got to his feet as Lia entered the room.

"Good afternoon. My name is Sam Mason."

"I'm Amelia Griggs."

He took a pocket watch out of a fob and consulted it. "Are you the last person out there?"

"Yes, sir."

Tucking the watch away, he indicated the chair in front of the desk. "Please, sit." He waited until she sat down before seating himself. "I don't believe we've met. And you're new to town." It was not a question. "I'm not sure what the townspeople would think about someone they don't know teaching their children. I've got a reputation in this town. People expect me to act in their best interests. Who are you? Would I know your family?"

"My parents are dead. My brother is away on a trade

ship at the moment, but he's returning back to the Oregon Territory come spring." There. Enough detail, but not too much. That was safe enough. Keeping silent wasn't the same thing as telling a lie.

Or not very close to it, anyway.

"Hmm." Mr. Mason frowned. He picked up his pencil, tapping it idly against the paper on the desk. "What makes you think you could be a schoolteacher?" His tone was neutral, his brown eyes giving nothing away of his thoughts.

"I spent six years at the mission school in Red River. I learned reading, writing, arithmetic, geography, history, and embroidery. After I turned sixteen, I obtained a teacher's certificate and began teaching the younger classes."

Mr. Mason stopped tapping the pencil. "Well. That's more experience than the other two have. You've got something to back that up? A certificate or some such?"

"Yes, sir, I've got my diploma."

"All right then." He placed a slate on the desk in front of her. "Let's see what you know."

Lia parsed sentences on the slate while Mr. Mason hovered over her shoulder, checking her work. He paced up and down, throwing out questions on arithmetic and geography. The questions were simple enough, but Lia raced to answer them before he fired off the next question. She didn't think she made any mistakes, but she could get no idea of whether she was impressing him or not. His expression did not give away anything. Finally, he stopped and came back to settle in his chair opposite her.

He leaned back. "Very well. You've got the book learning. Can you pass it on?"

"I think so, sir."

"What would you do if one of the boys started acting up in the back row?"

Promptly, she said, "Shoot 'em." The instant the words were out of her mouth, she wished she could take them back. It was the sort of thing her father used to say, but he never *meant* it. No one took him seriously when he said it, or stared at him as Mr. Mason was staring at her now.

"Er... that was a joke. I would get their attention. Show them who's in control of the situation. A pack of wild dogs needs to have a leader. Then everything settles down. Not that I'm saying a crowd of young children is like a pack of wild dogs..." She was floundering now. She could feel her cheeks beginning to redden.

Mr. Mason was still staring at her. One corner of his mouth quirked up as though he were trying to repress a smile. "I have a good sense of people," he said reflectively. "You seem like a fairly sensible young woman. So perhaps you'll understand my dilemma. I need to find a replacement schoolteacher as soon as possible. The children of this town are running wild. They need education, and they need a firm hand. My choices are a man so frail he might not last the term, a young woman so shy she could not look a child in the eye, or you—who would be perfect if it weren't for the fact that no one knows where you're from, who your people are."

My father was a trapper. My mother was a Métis woman he met in a native village. No. That probably would not impress him. "We're staying at Mrs. Whitlow's place," Lia threw in. Maybe that would make her look more respectable in his eyes.

"Hmm. Mrs. Whitlow wouldn't have let you stay with her if she didn't approve of you." He stood suddenly, startling her. "If you could please wait outside for a moment?" The boy opened the door to the front room.

"Of course." She scrambled to her feet awkwardly. The

skirt was so full it was easy to get lost in its yards of fabric. She smoothed down the dress and left the room.

The ticking on the clock in the front room sounded louder now. Even the man next to her had stopped coughing. She did not hear a sound from the young woman on the other side of him. There was a faint murmur of voices from the back room, but too low for her to distinguish words. She sat down in the chair again and closed her eyes for a brief, intense prayer. She had done her best. It was out of her hands.

It seemed an eternity before the door to the back room opened again. The superintendent came out into the front room. This time, the fashionably dressed matron that Lia had run into on the sidewalk came out with him. She must have been lurking behind that side door the whole time. She did not look happy; her face was flushed and her lips were pressed into a flat line.

Mr. Mason spoke abruptly. "Thank you all for coming. The sad fact is that the school board can only afford one schoolteacher. After careful consideration, I have come to the conclusion that Mr. Harris is the best candidate for the position."

Lia felt as if the floor had dropped out from beneath her. She had no idea what she was going to do now. *Lord, if this is Your will, then I accept it. But please help me find a way to support Henri and myself.*

The young man rose from the chair, the handkerchief still in his hand. His face was flushed with delight. Or so Lia thought, until he bent over in another spasm of helpless coughing. He coughed so hard that when he finally straightened up, Lia saw spots of blood on the white handkerchief.

Mr. Mason clearly saw them too. He looked at his wife and shook his head. "On the other hand, it is clear that Mr.

Harris' health is too precarious to risk at this time. I have decided to appoint Miss Griggs as the new schoolteacher." His wife let out her breath in a short huff, but said nothing.

Lia tried to control her delight; she didn't want to crow over the others. But from what Lia could see of her face beneath the enormous bonnet, the shy young woman looked relieved as she left. The young man was regretful, but resigned. "Good luck to you," he said to Lia. He was coughing again before he was out the door.

Lia looked after him. "Oh, the poor man. Is there any way to help him? Aren't there any doctors in town?"

"Of course there are," Mrs. Mason snapped. "People still get sick, even so. Not the town's fault."

Mr. Mason said, "Can you start Monday? We'll try you out. I'll expect the full curriculum, mind. Spelling, geography, mathematics, history."

His wife coughed, a refined, ladylike *ahem*. "I should perhaps mention one thing more. My brother Edgar is an excellent scholar, but he is a trifle delicate. Sensitive. He suffers from the occasional indisposition. That's why my family sent him out west, so I could take care of him. My husband wants Edgar to rest until he regains his health." Her gaze lingered on Lia. "We won't be needing your help after that."

Mr. Mason nodded. "You've got the position *pro tem*."

"Yes, sir. If I may ask, how long does this *pro tem* period extend?"

Mr. Mason glanced at his wife's frowning expression and shook his head, very slightly. "For the rest of this term. Until the New Year. After that, we'll see."

"I'll take it," Lia said. It would be enough to last her to Christmas, and if she saved up her funds carefully enough —and found a way to feed Henri's insatiable appetite on low funds—then they might have enough to last them through to spring and Pierre's return.

Guilt tugged at her conscience like an impatient child. Should she have told the superintendent about her parents? Her mother's ancestry? It might not matter to him... but then again it might. She hesitated, and the moment was lost. Mrs. Mason came up to her. "I'll see Miss Griggs to the door." Her husband nodded and went back into the inner room.

As soon as the door shut behind her husband, Mrs. Mason turned to Lia. "Edgar will be well enough to go back to teaching in a week or so. It is absurd to talk about keeping you on for the rest of the term. He has his bad spells, but he always recovers and then everything is fine again. That Mr. Harris would have been perfect. He would not have expected to stay in the position very long. And you are a complete interloper. No one knows who your family is."

Lia lifted her chin. She had earned the right to this job, and she was not going to be intimidated by this woman, no matter how influential she might be. "Your husband said I had the job until the end of the school term. Unless he has a problem with my teaching, I'm staying until then."

"If my husband saw that you weren't fit to do the job, then he'd *have* to ask Edgar to come back." The matron leaned closer to Lia. "I'll be watching."

LIA STRODE down the plank sidewalk, putting as much distance as she could between herself and Mrs. Mason. She had thought that once she had been appointed school-teacher, her problems would be over. But that last encounter with Mrs. Mason had shaken her confidence.

The voluminous skirt hampered her efforts to take a full stride. She missed the freedom of wearing trousers, as she had in the woods. Women who lived in town apparently thought it was important to wear clothes that stifled them. It didn't make sense. Every lady she passed took little, mincing steps. They wore gloves, and shielded their faces from the sun. When they looked at her, she could see a question in their eyes.

She was not one of them. She did not want to be. Upon leaving school, she'd joyfully slipped back into the comfortable old men's clothing that was so much more suitable for riding or trapping or hunting. It had felt like returning to the freedom of childhood, when she and her brother had travelled with Maman and Pa in the mountains.

She'd traded that freedom for the duty of taking care of Henri, and she'd never regret that decision. But living in this town would mean trying to blend in.

Lia slowed, considering. The superintendent cared what other people thought. Making a favorable impression on the townsfolk would count in her favor.

Book learning was not enough if she were going to succeed. Nor was simply dressing like the women here. A thought crept into her mind. She would look as respectable as any other woman if she were walking down the street on the arm of a tall man with a kind heart and fine manners. A man who doubtless knew all the little mannerisms that a proper lady would employ.

All very logical, but that didn't stop her from feeling nervous. It was simple enough to find out where Mr. Montgomery was staying, but as she climbed the outside stairs that led to the room above the newspaper office, the butterflies in her stomach began their agitated dance again. Her nerves were partly from the awkwardness of having to ask for help. If she were being honest, the thought of seeing Mr. Montgomery again unsettled her as well.

In Lia's experience, men fell into three categories: family, friends of her father or brother, or strangers. Most of the men she'd met before were trappers, like her pa. Lia had never felt any inclination to get attached to one of them. Her pa had married her mother, but he was the exception. It was not unusual for a trapper to live with a native woman for a few years, and then go back east and marry an American woman, leaving the native woman and any children to fend for themselves. Lia had decided early that she wasn't going to go down that road herself, so she had avoided becoming close to any of them.

She wasn't used to a man who actually listened to her when she talked, who helped her when she was in trouble and didn't ask for anything in return. Having a man as a friend or ally was a new notion and not an entirely comfortable one. She did not know what to expect, or what he might expect from her. She was venturing into unexplored territory.

At the head of the stairs, Lia paused. She could hear a murmur of deep voices inside the room, though she couldn't make out the words. Taking a deep breath, she knocked before she could reconsider. The voices stopped. A moment of silence, then she heard the creak of floorboards and footsteps coming closer. The fluttering butterflies redoubled their agitation. She clasped her hands together and clenched them tightly for a moment, then deliberately relaxed. She could do this.

"Why, hello there!" The handsome blond man—Bradford—beamed at her. Behind him, she could see the tall figure of Mr. Montgomery leaning against the wall with his arms crossed.

He was surprised to see her, that was evident, though his arms relaxed to his sides as he straightened up. Pleased to see her too, she thought. But though his lips curved up in a hint of a smile, the gladness in his eyes was tempered with caution.

AS BRADFORD USHERED the young woman into the room, Geoff tried to squash a feeling of unease. He knew what the others were expecting from him, but he did not want to do it. However intriguing she was, it did not seem right to use the girl for his own ends.

"How did you find me?" His voice came out harsher than he had intended, but she did not seem offended. He stopped and cleared his throat.

"I asked people passing by. There aren't too many Englishmen in this town."

"That's true enough," Ogden grumbled from his seat by the table.

Geoff tried to make amends for his original abruptness. He pulled a chair forward. "Please, take a seat."

"No, thank you all the same. I would rather stand."

She was not as relaxed as he'd first thought. She stood stiffly, with her hands clasped together. He decided to probe. "How are you doing? I gather you survived your encounter with the school superintendent."

"Yes. He's offered me the position of schoolteacher. Only for a couple months, but that's long enough to get on my feet in this town."

"That's good," Geoff said cautiously. "Isn't it? Is there a problem?"

"That's why I came to see you." She clasped her hands

together and took a breath. "I need your help. You were right, what you said about not needing formal etiquette out in the woods. That sort of thing belongs in town. I can hunt and trap and live off the land, but I'm lost when it comes to sipping tea in fancy dishes and acting all dainty." She stopped, a red flush warming her cheeks.

"Have the townsfolk been treating you as if you don't belong?" It was bad enough that he was an outsider here. At least he came from another country, far away. Did they have to make Lia unwelcome as well?

"Not all of them. Some. The ones that matter, unfortunately. I was thinking maybe you could help me out, give me a few lessons in how fancy people behave." She looked at Bradford. "You're going to be in town doing your sketching, or whatever it is, for a few days, aren't you?" He nodded, and she turned back to Geoff. "What were you planning to do while he was sketching?"

"I have not quite decided yet," Geoff said firmly. Bradford frowned at him, but he pretended not to see it. "But if the people here do not accept you as you are, then the problem is with them, not you. You don't need to change your ways."

Lia shook her head. "If you look different, people don't trust you. Not at first. And I don't have time to earn their trust. The only way I'm going to keep this job is if you help me learn how to pass myself off as one of them."

He looked at Lia standing there, lovely and stubborn, determined to find a place in the world for herself. "You can change how you dress, how you talk. Others may see you differently. But if you feel one way but act another, you'll end up thinking of yourself as a fraud. That's not a good position to be in."

She raised her chin, defiance personified. "I don't care. If it lets me keep this job, I'll do it. Will you help me?"

Bradford shifted, restless. Geoff recognized the signs. If he didn't get on with the job at hand, Brad would blunder in and do it for him.

It would not hurt to spend one afternoon with her. He could help her with her plan. That might assuage his guilt over the position he found himself in. Using a beautiful woman to further his country's aims.

"My friend Bradford mentioned that he wanted to do a sketch of the town from the escarpment above." He took a breath and spoke quicker, forcing the words out. "We could have a picnic, after church tomorrow. Bring your nephew along. Nothing could be more proper. We could enjoy the scenery and see if we can't find a solution for your difficulty."

She was frowning again, as she had that day they first met, and he was seized with the sudden conviction that she knew he was not telling her the full truth. But then she nodded. "All right then."

As soon as the door shut behind Lia, Bradford looked at Geoff and raised his eyebrows. "It's perfect. She needs your help. And we need her."

"One picnic," Geoff said unhappily. "I'll do it. But I don't have to like it."

"Oh, I don't know," Bradford said, the note of cheerfulness back in his voice. "You might find that you like it very much indeed."

CHAPTER 5

The next day, Lia attended church with Henri and Mrs. Whitlow. She'd checked her appearance in Mrs. Whitlow's mirror and decided that she looked presentable enough, wearing the blue dress and with her hair pinned up under the straw bonnet. Nothing that would make her stand out. It wasn't enough to give her confidence. Spreading out her skirt carefully, she sat down in the pew. Then she put her hands in her lap and gripped them together. Tightly.

The superintendent and his wife were two pews ahead of her on the left. The bored blond boy sat next to them, his hair plastered down, looking too innocent to be believed. Henri eyed him curiously. Lia felt something closer to dread.

She would have to go make polite conversation after the service. Just for a minute or so. Show them she had good manners and wasn't some unsuitable hoyden. Her mouth was dry. It took an effort to rise with Mrs. Whitlow and Henri to sing the final hymn. On the way out of church, she saw Mr. Montgomery moving down the aisle with the rest. There was no sign of his blond friend.

Outside the church, people fanned out in all directions: some heading home or in the direction of the docks, others standing about in groups and chatting. Mr. Montgomery hadn't made it past the church steps; the pastor was talking with him. He nodded at Lia as she passed.

The superintendent and his wife were standing under an elm tree, deep in discussion. The bored blond boy Lia had seen at the interview had gone over to investigate a gathering of boys playing a game of tag. Henri turned his head to follow the game.

"Maybe you can go play with the other boys," Lia suggested. "I need to talk to the superintendent and his wife. It's only polite."

Her tone must have lacked conviction, because Henri did not move. "It's okay, Lia. I'll go with you to talk to these people you want to impress."

No matter how much he wanted to act like a man, sometimes he was still just a sweet boy. She wanted to give him a hug, but doing so in public would embarrass him dreadfully. "I'll introduce you to them." Lia straightened her spine, put her shoulders back, and started to march over to the Masons. Then, mindful, she corrected her pace to a decorous stroll. "Good morning. That was a fine sermon, was it not? Allow me to introduce my nephew, Henri Griggs. He will be attending school this term."

A faint frown had formed between Mr. Mason's eyebrows. "You plan on sending him to school with the other boys? I don't know what the townspeople are going to think about that. There's talk of sending Indian orphans to boarding schools. Teach them to be proper Americans instead of heathens."

Lia put one hand on Henri's shoulder. She felt the tension in his muscles and squeezed his shoulder to remind him to keep still. "Henri is not an orphan," she said, as pleasantly as she could manage. "His father is off on a trading voyage, but he will return in the spring."

Mrs. Mason wrinkled her nose. "We may be in the wilderness, but that is no reason to be uncivilized. I see no need for my Eugene to associate with savages."

Lia had been hearing comments like that all her life, but somehow the sting never faded. Still, practice had given her the ability to keep calm in such situations. She wasn't so sure about Henri keeping his temper. Under her hand, she felt him taking a deep breath, as if about to speak. To fend off the impending explosion, she said firmly, "My nephew is neither a savage nor a heathen." Lia tightened her grip on Henri's shoulder. *Let me handle this.* She kept her eyes level on the matron and did not flinch.

The other woman's eyes flicked back and forth between Lia and Henri. "That may be, but his mother must be an Indian."

So was mine. "Who his mother was is not going to stop him from attending school."

Mrs. Mason looked as if she smelled something unpleasant. "If things were properly arranged, it would."

"Well... if his father's American... I guess the townspeople would accept that." The superintendent didn't sound as if he were convinced of that fact, but Lia decided to let it go for now. So long as Henri could stay in school.

Bradford came strolling down the street, whistling a cheery tune. He had a sketchbook tucked under one arm and held a hamper with the other. "Good morning." He bowed toward Mrs. Mason and Lia equally.

Mrs. Mason's expression changed to a sweet smile. She practically simpered as she introduced Bradford to her husband. "We met at the literary society meeting last night. He's come all the way from England!"

Mr. Mason shook hands with Bradford with all the enthusiasm of a man encountering a rattlesnake. "Hello." He dropped Bradford's hand as soon as he could.

Bradford handed the picnic basket to Henri. "Here. You can carry this."

"Why should I?" Henri bristled. He seemed glad of the chance to take out his mood on someone. "I don't take orders from you."

Mrs. Mason sniffed, as if her worst suspicions had been confirmed.

Lia wanted to groan. Henri was not helping the situation. She would have to talk to him later. "He's usually much more polite," she told Bradford.

The blond man did not seem perturbed. "I've heard much worse." To Henri, he said, "The hamper contains all our food for the picnic."

"And you trust me with it?"

"Henri, he knows you're not a thief."

"I trust you with it," Bradford said gravely. "I apologize for any insinuation that might have implied otherwise. That was a misunderstanding. Let's start over."

"Well, all right then." Grudgingly, Henri took the hamper.

Out of the corner of her eye, Lia saw Mr. Montgomery detach himself from his conversation with the pastor and stroll over. "All present and correct?"

With the arrival of Mr. Montgomery, Mrs. Mason's face lit up with a smile. Her husband looked at the two Englishmen suspiciously, but she positively simpered. "Good morning! I'm so pleased that you are here. My husband and I have decided to hold a supper party, just a small affair with dancing afterward. I wondered if you gentlemen would be able to come. It would be a nice opportunity for the Americans and the English to get to know each other better."

Her husband grunted. "I've been reading all the talk in the papers about the English. That prime minister of yours, Peel, keeps rattling his saber about the Oregon Territory."

"Just as your Mr. Polk has been doing," Bradford said. Lia saw Mr. Montgomery give his friend a sharp glance. Bradford added, in a more conciliatory tone, "But certainly, a festive gathering would be welcome."

"I agree," Mr. Montgomery said, and he turned to Lia. "Miss Griggs, perhaps you would honor me with a dance?"

Mr. Montgomery evidently credited Mrs. Mason with enough courtesy not to discuss an engagement in front of Lia that she was not invited to. There was a short, uncomfortable silence. Mr. Mason opened his mouth to say something, but his wife smoothly interceded. "I was just about to invite Miss Griggs. This would be an opportunity for you to get to meet all the members of the school board and their wives. I am sure they would find your quaint mannerisms most... *novel*."

Lia ignored the insult. Panic was rising in her like an inexorable tide. A fancy dinner surrounded by folk who had known from infancy which fork to use and how a lady should curtsey. A dance where everyone else would know the steps. If she made enough of an embarrassment of herself, would the superintendent reconsider offering her the position of schoolteacher? She managed to choke out, "How delightful."

"Well, the day's getting on," Mr. Mason said. He nodded to Lia and the two Englishmen. "Good day, ma'am. Gentlemen. Come, Sally. Let's collect Eugene and head home."

Henri, surprisingly, controlled his response until the Masons were out of earshot. "I'm not sure I want to go to this stupid school. If all the other kids are from back east, I'm not going to have anything in common with them."

"You are all there to learn," Lia said. "That's something you have in common. And I need to learn too. I need to learn how to make them think I'm one of them. It can't be that hard."

"There is always a price to pay," Mr. Montgomery said.

BRADFORD HAD ARRANGED for a boat to take them across the river. Then he led them up a rough trail that led upward toward the top of the ridge. Geoff stepped over a rotting log and extended a hand to help Lia over it. "Bradford, are you planning to have a picnic in the middle of the woods? Not much of a view."

"Have faith," Bradford said.

Lia tripped over her full skirt. Why did women willingly put up with these impractical garments?

Geoff extended a hand under Lia's elbow to support her. She did appreciate his firm hand, but she would have preferred for him to see her as a woman who could take care of herself and didn't always need rescuing. She nodded her thanks, concentrating on keeping her skirts out of the mud.

Bradford said, "It'll be worth it once we get to the top. A local assured me that this trail leads to a lovely vista."

Sure enough, after a few minutes of steady climbing, they came out into a clearing on the top of the escarpment. There had been a forest fire here, evidently, some years before; the space was denuded of trees, leaving nothing but tall grasses waving gently in the wind. They had climbed high above the town; the vista of the river in its narrow valley spread out before them, the waterfall, the hills with their fall colors, and the great snow-tipped peak of Mount Hood rising in the background. The wind lifted the ribbon on Lia's bonnet and trailed it behind her. She felt as if she were on top of the world.

"Bird's eye view," Bradford said with satisfaction. "All the details of river navigation and the points of access to the town laid out like a map. Perfect."

"Points of access?" Lia looked at Bradford, but he was busy setting out his pencils and did not seem to have heard the question.

She turned to Mr. Montgomery. "What is he talking about? Why does he want to draw a map?"

Almost imperceptibly, Mr. Montgomery stiffened. Then he smiled, and his tone was light and unstudied. "Pay no attention to him. Artists talk like that, don't you know. All those funny terms that only mean something to other artists. Points of access. Light and color. Form and balance. I once had to wait a whole day in this uncomfortable spot halfway up a mountain just so he could paint it at dawn. Something about how the early morning light had to strike the rock face at just the right angle..."

There he was off again babbling, that fake smile on his lips but tension tightening the corners of his eyes. What was the problem with the man? He was no fool. So why was he pretending to be one?

On impulse, she put a hand on his arm. He stopped talking at once. Looking up at him, she was suddenly conscious of how close they stood. "Come, take a walk with me. Henri, could you lay out the picnic basket?" Henri eagerly began taking the food out of the basket while she and Geoff walked back down the trail to the edge of the trees.

Once they were out of earshot, she turned to face him. "Stop doing that."

"Doing what?" He had dropped the smile, but tension still lurked in his eyes.

"Stop playing the fool." She had thought of him as an ally, maybe a friend. He was comfortable to be around. So she didn't understand why he was putting up barriers between them now. "If you're trying to protect me from some unpleasant truth... well, don't. If you don't want to tell me something, fine, you have as much right to privacy as anyone else. But I am not an idiot. Stop lying to me."

There was a silence. The wind stirred the pine boughs. He was ramrod stiff, and very still, but the look in his eyes was odd, a mixture of—could it be shame? And admiration? And some kind of pain. She softened her tone. "You're good at it. Too good. You must have had a lot of practice lying to people."

The corner of his mouth twitched, as if in pain. "Sometimes it is necessary to tell people what they want to hear."

"I want to hear the truth," Lia said. "If you keep making things up, you're going to forget how to tell the truth."

"I hope not." He looked as if something were bothering him. He hunched his shoulders as if to ward something off. Then he put his shoulders back, like a soldier. "It's not always possible to tell the truth."

More gently, she said, "If you can't be honest, then don't tell me lies. Just don't say anything. Silence isn't the same thing as telling a lie outright."

He raised one eyebrow. "Isn't it?"

She was supposed to be asking him for his help, not

arguing with him. "It just bothers me when you tell me something I know isn't true."

"Point taken, madam." He gave a half bow.

She just looked at him.

"Ma'am. I meant to say ma'am."

Lia had to smile. "Better. Let's go eat, shall we?"

GEOFF ESCORTED Lia back to the others, careful to keep his expression neutral. He only wished he could calm his racing heartbeat. He'd been successful for so long at fooling people that it was disconcerting to have someone see through him. He would have to be careful around Lia.

Henri had spread out a red-and-white-checkered cloth and was laying out bread, cheese, smoked salmon, and fruit. Bradford was still lost in his sketch, muttering under his breath. Henri gave Bradford a doubtful look. "Should we wait for him?"

"No need," Geoff said. He spread out a blanket for Lia. Bradford finished up his rough sketch, scribbled a note on the side, and then came over to join them. "Are you finished already?" Geoff asked.

"Oh, I'll go back over it again later, but I've got the basic points covered." Bradford hefted a jug and poured out liquid into a cup. He wrinkled his nose. "Water."

"Do you suppose the Masons will serve something stronger?" Lia hunched her shoulders. The wind teased a lock of hair out of her pinned-up braid, and she tucked it behind one ear.

Geoff settled down on the blanket next to her, sheltering her from the breeze. He cut a slice of bread and put it on a plate with some cheese. "Here. I don't think you need to worry. I am sure they will serve something suitable for ladies. The Masons care about what the people of the town think of them. They will want to set a good example."

Her shoulders relaxed a bit as she took the plate from him. "That's true. Do you think you'll be spending a few weeks in Oregon City?"

Bradford said easily, "Oh, I think we'll be staying longer than that." He ignored Geoff's warning look and went on, "Montgomery here is writing a book and I'm sketching illustrations for it."

I'm doing what? When Geoff had to spin a web of lies, he was careful not to spring his story on Bradford without warning. He really wished Bradford would extend him the same courtesy. But this wasn't the time to ask Bradford to stop. Lia was looking at him. It felt as if those clear gray eyes were seeing down into his soul. She had the ability to strip away his barriers and see the real man hiding behind. He had to walk a fine line between telling the truth and exposing his real mission.

"What made you decide to write a book?" Lia asked.

Stick to the truth as closely as possible. She could spot an outright lie, but it was harder to detect an untruth if it were mixed in with the truth. "I never considered writing a book until I came here," he said with perfect honesty. "Bradford and I used to be in the army. I was an engineer. I enjoyed building things. Now... I want to make something that will last longer than the next battle. An army engineer tears things down as often as he builds them up, and for what? So some desk-bound official in London can get a boost in his pay grade?" He stopped. Where had that thought sprung from?

Bradford looked at him sharply. Then he turned to Lia. "Miss Griggs. Why don't I sketch your portrait?"

"Me?" She sat back, startled. "Well... I was hoping I could talk to you gentlemen about learning all that fancy etiquette they expect from ladies at dinner parties." She was looking at Geoff as she spoke, but Bradford responded.

"It doesn't interfere with my sketching if you talk. Just don't move about." He positioned Lia so that she was sitting with her back to the river valley. "Just... there. Perfect. I can just get in the view from upstream in the background."

Lia took off her bonnet and laid it aside. The breeze tossed a strand of hair across her forehead. She brushed it aside. Her hair was not as dark as he'd thought; in the bright sunlight, he could see gold highlights where the sun had lightened it. There was always something new to discover about this woman. A man could devote a lifetime to studying her.

She folded her hands in her lap. "So," she said. "We're at a fancy dinner party. The kind the Masons will be having." She looked at Geoff expectantly. "What do I do?"

"In a formal dinner setting, there will be several courses and several forks to choose from. The rule is to select the outermost fork for the first course, the next fork for the next course, and so on."

"Ridiculous!" Henri scoffed. "Fancy people have fancy rules for everything, even eating. Everyone who comes out west starts at the bottom, and even so, some people want to show they're better than everyone else."

Geoff shrugged. "In England, the lines drawn between the different classes are much more rigid. Everyone's put into little boxes from the start and expected to stay in them."

Lia tilted her head, looking at him as if she were hearing something in his voice that he hadn't meant to betray.

He'd buried his past long ago; there was no need to go revisiting old memories. Besides, he would rather learn more about the woman behind the piercing gray eyes. Purely in the interests of duty, of course. "Where are you from?"

"That's a simple question, for some people. Not for me." She shrugged.

"Don't move," Bradford said sharply. "Talk as much as you like, so long as you remain still." Lia resumed her former position, and Bradford went on, "I'm not sure Americans are less rigid about the different classes. Frankly, some of them are terrible snobs. Last night at the literary society, for example. It was amazing how many of the women there had unmarried daughters. And most of them were convinced that they wanted an Englishman for their son-in-law." Bradford shuddered dramatically. "I had to resort to some fancy evasive maneuvers to escape unscathed."

"How fancy?" Geoff asked suspiciously.

"Ah. Well. I've noticed that some matrons, especially ones with unmarried daughters, are rather concerned with social rank. The more titled relations a man has, the more eligible he is. I might have embroidered the truth a little, just to divert their attention. Anything to avoid having to chat with these ladies again."

Lia frowned. "You lied to them?"

"Just added a few artistic touches here and there. Nothing too serious."

Bradford was looking far too innocent. That usually meant it was something that Geoff would have to deal with sooner or later. But he'd spent the past several months dealing with Bradford. He'd rather concentrate on Lia at the moment. "Could you tell me more about yourself? For my book. Your life will sound very exciting to readers back in England."

She squinted at him. "Really? Doesn't seem all that exciting to me."

"Even so. What was it like growing up?"

"My father was a trapper. When I was little, we stayed in a trading post in the Red River valley with my mother when my father was off trapping. Then, when we got older, we would go along. Maman taught us to live out in the wilderness, finding roots and berries that were safe to eat. Pa taught us to shoot and trap."

"So that's where you learned to be so comfortable in the woods."

"After my mother died, he sent me to a mission school at Red River. He let my brother Pierre stay and help him with trapping. But a daughter... well, I guess he didn't think I could be useful."

Geoff could see the tension in the way she held herself, the thin line creased between her brows. He could reach out his hand and smooth it out. He didn't move. "Do you look like your mother?"

The question was an idle one, designed to relax her with a change of subject. But instead she tensed, like a soldier on a battlefield who hears a warning shot. "Not really, no." She looked down at her hands.

"Don't tilt your head," Bradford snapped.

Lia sighed, and resumed her original pose.

Interesting. The lady has things to hide as well. He probed further. "Then your brother came out west and settled down?"

"He came out west, yes, but he didn't settle down. He met Henri's mother, started a family, but he started going off trading up and down the coast. He goes all over, up to the Russian Territory and down to San Francisco to sell lumber. Even out to Owyhee. Pa came out and got work with the

Hudson Bay Company, up near the mission at Waiilatpu. When Henri's mother died, Pa asked me to come out here so Henri could stay with us while Pierre was away trading. Now that Pa is gone, Henri is my responsibility. Well, until Pierre comes back. He said this is going to be his last trading mission for the Company. He's planning on setting up a store instead."

"I can look after myself, Lia." Henri had wandered off to look at the view over the river. Now he turned back, frowning at Lia. "I can look after you, too. You need someone to do that." Lia frowned back at him.

"Ahem," Bradford said.

Lia sighed but stopped frowning.

"Pierre and Henri... are you French?" Bradford asked.

She stiffened. "Maman was French. Well, half French. Oh look. There's a boat coming downriver."

Geoff put a hand over his eyes to shade them against the sun. "Indians."

"It's late in the season for catching eel," Henri said. "They're probably looking to trade."

"I thought they didn't mix with the settlers much."

"They don't," Lia said sadly, "not really. Things are changing now. When I was a little girl, we'd go to the Rendezvous, where all the traders and natives got together for trade. And everyone got along. Now trapping is dying off and everyone is divided into groups. And I don't belong in any of them. It's like you English with all your little boxes."

"Don't fidget," Bradford said. "In fact, perhaps you shouldn't talk after all. You can't seem to hold a conversation without moving your hands."

That was part of what made her so lovely to watch, the way her body expressed itself in a language all its own. Surprising that an artist like Bradford couldn't see that. "If the superintendent doesn't appreciate you as you are, then find another job where you can be yourself. I'll help you."

Bradford cocked an eye at him, and then went back to sketching, frowning.

"I'm good enough for myself, but I'm not good enough for them." She reached her hand out to touch a fold of her skirt, then self-consciously she put her hands back in her lap before Bradford could chide her. "I can't help worrying that I'm not going to be a success. I'm not used to small talk and fancy clothes. If I want to pass as one of these people, I've got to know how to play at being a lady. I need some lessons on blending in. Etiquette and fine manners and such."

Still sketching, Bradford said to Lia, "It sounds like you've got a lot of experience traveling around the area. You would be a perfect subject to interview for our book. In fact, we were thinking of spending the whole winter here in Oregon City."

"We were?"

"Much more lively place than Fort Vancouver," Bradford said firmly.

Lia said, "So maybe I could help you with your book, and you could help me pass as a lady. What do you say?"

It was his fault that she was in this situation. He had been annoyed when Mrs. Mason had been rude to Lia, so he had maneuvered the matron into issuing Lia an invitation to the dinner. But the panicked look on Lia's face at the mention of a formal setting had struck at his conscience. "I could do that. Give you lessons. But... it changes you, you know," he said slowly. "Passing yourself off as something you're not."

"I don't care. Just show me." She fixed her gray eyes on him, and he felt pierced through.

That was part of the attraction, perhaps. He would not have expected being called out for lying to have such an effect, but it was a heady sensation. She saw *him*, Geoff. Not the army lieutenant or the gentleman of leisure, but himself. He was tempted to linger near her, savor the experience.

After his mother died, his father had lost himself in books. He would emerge occasionally from his study to give Geoff a coldly puzzled look, as if not sure why this child was trying to engage his attention. Joining the army had given him a purpose and a way to prove himself worthy of notice. But with Lia, he did not have to justify himself. She just liked him.

Of course, if she knew the truth about why he was here, she would turn away from him in disgust. He had to find a way to help her without betraying himself.

All the same, he hesitated. "By the time you're done pretending, you might not be able to find your way back to yourself."

The stubborn lift of her chin indicated her opinion of this advice. He chose another approach. Perhaps he would have better results if she started thinking of him as a friend.

"Could I ask you a favor? Mr. Montgomery sounds so awkward. Do you suppose that you could call me Geoff?" *Say yes.* Suddenly, he was eager to hear his name on her lips.

She met his eyes. For a moment, Geoff did not move. He did not breathe. Lia's cheeks began to flush a delicate red. She looked down at her hands and nodded.

Bradford threw down his pencil. "Montgomery, my dear fellow, could you possibly take yourself off for a while? Go admire the view. Count the number of boats on the river. Do something that does not involve distracting my model."

Geoff would rather have stayed—he really did want to hear Lia say his name. It seemed important. But Bradford was his superior officer, and that had sounded very much like an order. He got to his feet. "I can take a hint."

Henri stood up as well. "I just want to talk with this man." Henri indicated Geoff. "I won't take a minute."

"Yes, go. Then she won't talk and I can finish this sketch."

Henri walked to the edge of the ridge, just out of earshot. Then he turned, squinting up at Geoff. "You interested?"

"I beg your pardon?" Henri's expression was intent, serious. Had Geoff made a slip?

One of the problems with being a spy was the uncertainty. You could never be absolutely sure that you were undetected. Was Henri sensing something wrong? Logic dictated that he should be safe. But even so, there was always the possibility that he had made a mistake.

Henri jerked his head in Lia's direction. "I see the way you look at her."

"I'm not sure I understand where this conversation is headed."

"I'm going to become a trader like my pa," Henri said, impatience clear in his tone. "But first I need to find a good man to take care of my aunt Lia."

Geoff relaxed. This was not a suspicious American, just a well-intentioned boy. His concern was touching. A child acting like an adult. Except that out here, children grew into adults early. Henri had had a hard life and he was trying to do what he thought was right according to tradition, just at Geoff would have in his situation. But there was no need. "Your aunt is the most competent woman I've ever met. She can take care of herself."

"No, she can't." Henri's dark eyes were fixed on Geoff. "She needs to feel useful to someone. I saw how sad she got last winter after Grandpa died while Pa was away. Pa told Lia he's planning to come back and set up a store, but I can't see him staying in one place. He loves traveling too much. So do I. And I can't leave her if she's going to be alone. I really do want to go to sea. So." Henri crossed his arms, looking at Geoff. "You interested, or what?"

The boy was barely taller than his aunt; his voice still broke into a treble occasionally. But he clearly wanted to step into the role of the man of the house, defending his womenfolk. All the same, there were limits. "That's not the sort of question a gentleman asks."

"Why not?" Henri squinted up at him. "There something wrong with her?"

"No! Of course not. I mean—I'm sure she's a lovely woman. But I hardly know her. I'm not in a position to press my suit, as it were."

Henri frowned. "You sure do talk funny. Nobody's asking you to press nothin'. I'm looking to find her a man to marry her off to, respectable and all."

"I think she is more than capable of finding a husband on her own—if she's looking for one, that is."

"She's too ornery. She doesn't know what she needs, or if she does she's just being contrary for the sake of it. You listen to her, you'd think she was able to survive on her own. But she's not. So, you saying you're *not* interested?"

Geoff hesitated. As much as he hated to acknowledge it, Bradford was right. He was on a mission. Lia provided an excuse for their lingering in the town. Too firm a denial would drive Henri away, and Lia with him. On the other hand, too much enthusiasm would land him in even greater difficulties. He was going to leave when his mission was completed. It would be wrong to become involved if he could not commit to anything serious. "I barely know the lady. I am sure she is all that is lovely, but I need a longer acquaintance with her before I can state whether I would like to develop a deeper friendship."

"That's a whole lot of talk, but it sounds like it all adds up to 'no' to me."

"Not at all. I'm simply saying 'not yet.' Let's get to know each other a bit better before making any decisions, shall we?"

Henri gave a grudging nod, and Geoff felt he'd had a narrow escape. There was no way he could be honest with the lad, and the alternative wasn't much better. If he didn't analyze the emotions Lia was stirring up inside him, then he wouldn't have to deal with them. For there was no way he could have any kind of relationship, not an honest one based on truth. When his mission was completed, and the passes were free of snow, he was going to leave. If he got involved with Lia, he was going to hurt her.

CHAPTER 6

W hen they got back to the boarding house, Mrs. Whitlow handed Lia a key. "Mr. Mason came by, dropped this off."

"Oh, good. I wanted to look over the schoolroom before school starts."

"We'll come with you," Bradford said promptly. He nudged Geoff, who jumped.

"Oh. Yes, that would be delightful."

This time, Lia did not call him out for speaking an untruth. She was worried about him. He had been silent all the way back down the hill after the picnic. Maybe she had pushed him too hard to get him to help her. But she could think of no reason why he'd come along to the schoolroom unless he really wanted to. The man was a puzzle. She told Mrs. Whitlow, "Mr. Montgomery is going to give me lessons in etiquette, fine manners and such."

"Is that so? I don't see the need. You're wearing a dress. You look respectable."

"I agree," Geoff said quietly. "You don't need to change to please anyone else."

Lia did not want to open the argument again. "Henri, are you coming to see the school?"

"I'll see it soon enough." Henri put his hands in his pockets, looking glum.

Mrs. Whitlow said, "Well, in that case, young man, you want to start earning a wage? I've got some chores I need a man's help with."

The words acted like a tonic on Henri. He straightened up, and his chin came up. "Yes. Of course." Maybe it was her imagination, but even his voice sounded deeper. He waved a hand at Lia and followed Mrs. Whitlow inside.

Lia looked up at Geoff. "He wants so much to be a man already."

"That's normal, at his age." Geoff held out his arm, and she took it.

His words were gentle, not judgmental. But she wasn't sure if he was just being kind. She needed to know. For some reason, his opinion mattered. "I don't know what to do about Henri. I need to make him see the value of getting an education."

"One thing at a time," he said. "Let's go look at this school."

The one-room schoolhouse, or "shed" as Bradford put it, was tucked away behind the church. The sun was low over the western hills across the river, and the late afternoon sunlight seemed to pick up every flaw in the clapboard building: the cracks in the weathered wood, the sagging roofline, a gutter that drooped at one corner.

"At least they whitewashed it," Lia said, trying to be fair.

Bradford snorted. "Gray washed, more like."

Geoff said nothing. He walked around the outside of the building, frowning. Lia could practically see him calculating the strength the beams would bear, measuring the way the flooring had been laid across the foundation, figuring ways to make it more level. He came out of whatever daydream he had been occupied with and caught Lia watching him.

His expression changed, the frown vanishing behind a wall of pleasant neutrality. And yet—there had been that split second when he had looked at her, and she would have sworn he felt unhappy. What was troubling him? He surely didn't see her as an enemy.

The next moment, she wondered if she had imagined the whole thing. Geoff spoke in a perfectly friendly manner. "It'll do. I think the builders were a bit hasty; you can see where the floor's a little uneven because the ground in that one corner settled down. But I think it'll survive until the end of the year without falling down."

"Even if it's filled with thirteen-year-old boys?"

"Even then." His tone was serious, but the corners of his eyes crinkled in a delectable fashion when he smiled back. This wasn't the time to be thinking thoughts like that. She could not let herself get too close to this man. Henri was her priority. He had to be. "Well, let's see what the inside looks like."

The inside was plainly furnished. Rows of desks on either side of an aisle that led up to the teacher's desk and a blackboard hanging on the wall. In the corner, a cupboard held textbooks for various grades.

Lia moved to the teacher's desk and riffled through the desk drawer. There were a few pages scattered about inside, and she laid them out on the desk. She sighed. "I was hoping he might have left some notes on lesson plans, but it doesn't look like it. I'll have to check with the superintendent." She bit her lip.

Geoff studied her, his head tilted to one side. "You sound worried. You shouldn't be. The Lord is with you, whether standing on a battlefield or standing in front of a room full of restless children."

"Much the same sort of thing, really." Bradford wandered off to peer out the window on the side of the room.

"It's important that the superintendent think I'm competent. I can't stop being nervous. Not just about tomorrow, but about the dinner on Friday as well."

"You've got the basics of etiquette down already," Geoff said. "And after dinner, if you don't want to make conversation, there's always dancing."

"Dancing!" Lia turned to face him, eyes wide. She hadn't thought of that. "I can't dance."

"Can't? Or won't? One of those can be remedied. There's enough space right here. We could practice."

"I mean, I don't know the steps." And she was afraid. She had seen couples dancing, but she had never wanted to try it herself. Dancing had always seemed so intimate: a stranger taking her hand, putting his hand on her waist? Guiding her around the room? She couldn't see how she could avoid putting a foot wrong, literally, and revealing how little she belonged here.

As he had before, when they had first met, Geoff seemed to understand what she felt without her putting it into words. It was enormously comforting to be understood. "Your secret is safe with me."

Bradford turned around to stare at Geoff, then returned to peering out the window. Geoff kept his gaze focused on Lia. What would it feel like, to have him touching her? The blush began instantly under her skin, hot and far too revealing. She turned away, idly straightening the papers on the desk. "I wouldn't even know where to begin."

"Will you trust me?" he asked, very softly.

She was looking down at the floor, at the students' desks, anywhere but at him. "Mr. Montgomery, it's not about trust."

"I THOUGHT you'd agreed to call me Geoff." He kept his voice low, persuasive, as he extended his hand to her and waited. He was not going to force her into this. She had to want to come to him. But he wanted her to. Suddenly, with all his heart, he wanted to forge a connection with her. Right here.

Slowly, not looking at him, she slid her fingers into his open hand. The friction of her warm skin sliding against his created an intense wave of sensation throughout his body. The woman was touching *him*. Geoff. Not the army officer, not the spy. Not, thanks be, the babbling fool of a private traveler that he was supposed to be passing as. Geoff himself.

He placed his other hand on her waist. "Put your hand on my shoulder. Now, I start with my left foot, and you with your right." He guided her through the steps and tried not to notice the faint sweet scent of lavender that clung to her. Loneliness welled up inside him, bringing to the surface feelings that he had submerged long ago in favor of duty. This woman was pulling him back to tender emotions, bringing him back to life. And it hurt.

He stopped abruptly and took a step back. "Well. I think you've gotten the idea."

"Yes. Thank you." She was still looking in any direction but at him.

"What do you think about this window?" Bradford fiddled with the sill, jiggling it up and down. "I'm no engineer, but this sill looks like it's about to fall off."

Geoff crossed the room and inspected it. "That sill is not

going to last the month." He turned to Lia. "I need to ask around, but I'm sure that I can find the tools I need to fix it. It's going to be too dark to get it fixed this evening."

"Could you come look at it tomorrow? It might look good if I took the initiative and had someone fix it before the rains start. Better than if I'd started out the term by complaining. I don't think I need to worry about your presence being a distraction for the students. Tomorrow's going to be chaotic even without that. I'm going to have to spend the morning testing their abilities and making sure they've got the correct schoolbooks for their grade."

"I'll be here tomorrow morning," Geoff said.

"We'll be here," Bradford corrected. He was looking at Geoff in a way that Geoff did not like at all.

Bradford waited until they had said goodbye to Lia and started back to their room before he spoke. "'Your secret is safe with me'? It's all very well trying to get her to trust us, but you sound like you're starting to lose your objectivity."

"You are giving me a lecture on the necessity of caution? I have this situation under control." He wasn't sure if he was trying to convince Bradford or himself.

THE NEXT DAY, Bradford insisted that he would be delighted to come along and help Geoff fix the window. Geoff ignored him as he worked. He kept his eyes on the windowsill, but his attention was fixed on the front row of desks, where Lia was bent over the youngest children, evaluating their reading abilities. He listened intently, trying to catch every word.

"What are you doing?" Bradford spoke in an indignant whisper. "Aim the hammer at the nail, not my thumb. You need to focus. This is exactly what I was talking about last night."

"If you think I am losing my objectivity, I could stop spending time with her," Geoff said, equally low.

Part of him hoped that Bradford would say yes. It was an active fight not to get closer to the woman, give in to the urge to get to know her better. There were so many mysteries hidden behind those gray eyes.

"You do realize there is no room for sentimentality on this trip, don't you?"

You were the one who wanted me to squire the woman around in the first place. No. Not the most diplomatic remark to make to a superior officer. Geoff hammered in a nail, not looking at Bradford. "I know that. I can't afford to get involved with the woman. I'd only end up hurting her. And getting involved with her would be a distraction from the mission."

"You put the mission as the second priority. Were you aware of that?"

"If you think it's a risk associating with the woman, we could leave. Go back to Fort Vancouver." It would be the safest course. This woman was dangerous to his peace of mind, if nothing else.

"No. She's the best excuse we have for staying here. No one will question it if we linger. Besides," Bradford's voice lowered to a more persuasive tone, "I think she might need a bit more polish."

"She doesn't need anyone's help. She's fine as she is." He *was* losing his objectivity where this woman was concerned. He had a connection to Lia, a closeness that he hadn't felt since he was a very young child. He wanted to protect that. Preserve it. But he could not afford to get close to this woman, not if he wanted to keep his focus on completing the mission. "Look at her. It's her first day, but you'd never know it."

It was true. While Geoff and Bradford worked on the window, Lia had been going from row to row, making sure each child was in the correct grade. She had started with the youngest children in the first row and worked her way toward the back. The younger children were all reading quietly now, or copying letters Lia had written on the blackboard.

The older children, however, were a different matter. The last row was where the largest boys sat, including Henri. Geoff could hear a constant whispering coming from the back row. It stopped every time Lia straightened up and looked at them, but it started right back up again as soon as she went back to the younger children.

"Pay attention to what you're doing, man." Bradford's voice held a note of barely concealed exasperation. "That hammer nearly hit me that time." He shifted his hold on the sill, keeping it in place against the window frame. "Try it again."

Geoff went back to his work. He'd heard that children with native mothers were accepted in society here. But apparently that referred to areas run by the Hudson Bay Company, where many of the men had native wives. In Oregon City, it was a different matter. Henri was a novelty. Not a welcome one.

From his position, Geoff was able to catch phrases. "Have you ever scalped anybody?" "Do you wear war paint?" "My pa says the only good injun is a dead injun."

Geoff darted a quick glance at the back row. Henri was sitting with his arms folded, glowering impartially at everyone in the room. He was controlling his temper, but Geoff could see his skin reddening. He had no authority here. He couldn't interfere, and it would not help Lia's authority if he took matters into his own hands. She had to deal with this on her own. All the same, his hands slowly curled into fists.

She reached the back row. "Is there a problem, boys?"

The tallest boy, with white-blond hair and a sunburned face, turned an innocent face up to her. "Why no, ma'am. Thank you kindly."

"Could you tell me your names, please, and what grade you are in?"

The boys turned out to be Eugene Mason, Clarence Brewer, and Horace Dobbs. Eugene, the blond boy, had perfected the art of looking innocent. You could always count on at least one of these troublemakers in any regiment. He had learned not to trust them.

One by one, Lia asked each boy to read and gave them the appropriate textbook for their level before returning to her desk at the front of the school. As soon as her back was turned, the whispering started, louder than ever.

"Can you shoot with a bow and arrow? My pa's a crack shot with a pistol. He can shoot an eagle out of the sky without looking twice."

Standing at the teacher's desk, Lia had her back to Geoff. He could see her take something out of the pack on the desk. She was doing something with it, but he couldn't make out what. He tried to crane his head to look, but Bradford hissed at him to get back to work. Behind him, he could hear the voices in the back row more clearly now.

"That's nothing! My pa shot a grizzly bear when it was charging straight at him!"

"Hey, injun, you ever wrestle a grizzly bear?"

Crack.

Dead silence in the schoolroom. Everyone froze, staring

at Lia and the pistol in her hand. The smell of powder lingered in the air. Slowly, Geoff turned his head to look behind the boys in the back row. The pine knot in the board above the door had a hole drilled straight through it.

Lia lowered the gun. "Now that I have your attention," she said sweetly, "might I request you begin reading the assigned lesson?"

Bradford looked at Geoff. "Still think she doesn't need polish?"

"Well, it worked. Look at their expressions! A mixture of respect and awe."

"They respect good marksmanship, true. But do you think their parents will see it in quite the same way?"

Lia had evidently been thinking the same thoughts. After she dismissed the children for lunch, she came down the aisle toward them. Her shoulders were hunched together, apprehensive. "I suppose that might have been a bit impulsive."

Bradford opened his mouth, then shut it again. Lia was looking at Geoff. Her lovely mouth was pinched close at the corners.

He said gently, "I think I can find some putty to fill that hole."

The relief in her face startled him. It mattered to her, what he thought of her behavior. It mattered a lot. He felt a strong urge to reach out and pull her close.

He clenched his hands into fists. Duty pressed down on him like a heavy weight. There was no escape from it. He could never get close to Lia without telling her the truth. And that was the one thing he could not do under any circumstances.

∾

AFTER THE TUMULT of the first day, Lia found the rest of the week at school went smoothly. Geoff had come by Mrs. Whitlow's house a few times, always accompanied by his friend Bradford, and she had practiced dancing with him. It had gotten easier to stand so close to him. She didn't blush nearly as much as she had at first. It helped that usually Mrs. Whitlow and Henri were in the room watching.

When they were alone together, he had opened up, shown what he really felt. Now, with other people around, his real emotions were hidden, with only tiny changes in his face to indicate what he was thinking. She had to watch closely to catch clues to his mood. He could not hide the way the corners of his eyes crinkled when he was suppressing his smile, or the way he hesitated before taking her hand, as if her touch affected him even through gloves. His subtle body language fascinated her, even though she did not have time to study him properly. It was tricky to manage these voluminous skirts and the intricate steps at the same time. She was getting better, but she still needed to concentrate.

Henri seemed to find her efforts at becoming refined very amusing, especially since they had to practice dancing without any musical accompaniment. Mr. Montgomery was reduced to counting out the time as they circled around the room. Then he bowed, and she curtsied like a fine lady.

"You're getting better at curtseying," Bradford said. "See? I was right. Wearing a dress does help."

Mrs. Whitlow pursed her lips in thought. "But all the other ladies at this dinner will be wearing evening dresses. I have another dress you can wear." She went off to her bedroom.

Bradford said, "The woman seems to have a lot of spare dresses lying about."

Henri spoke in a low voice. "Mrs. Whitlow told me she had a daughter who died a couple years ago. She had married a factor at Fort Vancouver, and he had given her lots of fancy clothing. But she died of a fever a couple years back, and her husband went back to England. I guess Mrs. Whitlow likes to keep the dresses to remember her?"

"Then I probably shouldn't borrow them," Lia said, troubled.

"Nah." Henri shrugged. "I think she likes helping you. Makes her feel useful or something."

"An evening dress will help you look respectable," Bradford said. "Especially after your performance on the first day of school."

"I knew she wasn't going to hit anyone," Henri said loyally.

Lia smoothed down the smooth wool of the blue dress. "It would've worked with a gang of trappers," she muttered. "And maybe that's more proof that I need more polish."

"That's what I said," Bradford muttered.

Mrs. Whitlow returned with her arms full of a gauzy white material. "This was the dress my daughter wore when she went to a dance."

Lia took the dress, shaking out its folds and holding it up against her. The material was silky, so light she could hardly feel the weight of the skirt. She was dying to try it on, but she hesitated. "It's lovely. Are you sure—?"

Mrs. Whitlow cut her off. "Yes. Wear it. Not doing anybody any good lying in a trunk."

Geoff nodded in approval. "I could get you some hair ribbons to go with the dress."

"People will think we're courting." He had been kind, spending time with her to try to help her blend in with the townsfolk. That didn't mean anything. He was the sort of man who wanted to help people. It wasn't as if he'd ever try to hold her hand, apart from dancing. He'd never tried to kiss her, not once. Lia didn't have much experience of being courted, but all the men she'd known who'd wanted to get involved with her had tried to kiss her at least once. Maybe Englishmen were different. She wished she knew how he felt about her.

"They're going to think that you two are courting already, all the time you spend hangin' around," Mrs. Whitlow warned.

"Ah well." Bradford had been sitting in the corner, sketching them as they danced. He put down his pencil. "What does it matter if they do?"

Lia frowned at him. "Gossip won't bother me, but I don't want to encourage them to believe something that is not true. If they ask, I'll tell them that you're helping me because you want to talk to me about your book."

Mrs. Whitlow nodded. "Take care with your reputation. In a small town like this, gossip can hurt you." She took the dress back from Lia. "I'll hang this up and get the creases out."

"There's one more thing you might want to practice." Bradford got up, grabbing a book from the side table and placing it on Lia's head. "Here. Try walking with this on your head. It's to teach you balance, posture, that sort of thing. At least, that's what our old dancing master insisted it did. Posture does make a difference in people's attitude." Bradford gestured. "Now, if you could actually manage to walk across the room with the book balanced on your head?"

Lia tried. To walk without the book sliding off her head, she had to walk with a more measured, mincing step, like Mrs. Mason, rather than her usual free, swinging walk. It felt silly and affected.

And she must not have been doing it right anyway. Geoff was scowling. "That's not you," he said abruptly. He crossed the room and took the book off her head. "That's not going to convince people that you're one of them. It's not how you carry yourself. It's about what is going on inside your own mind. You can convince people that you are who you want them to think you are. But you have to believe it *yourself* first."

She was startled by his fierce tone. The more she practiced acting like a fine lady, the more he seemed to hate it. Wasn't that the whole reason he was helping her? Sometimes, the man didn't make a bit of sense. "If prancing around with a book on my head or using the correct fork makes me more acceptable to these people, then I'll do it."

"You're never going to be good enough for that sort of person. It wouldn't matter if you possessed every virtue and grace a woman could have. Even then the superintendent's wife would not like you."

"That's probably true," Lia allowed. "But she would not be able to cut me down, either. As things stand, she has enough power in this town to stop them from keeping me as the schoolmistress, even temporarily."

"So we'll have to work around her, get on the good side of the other people in this town," Geoff said. "She can't be the only one who has a say in matters."

"She isn't." Mrs. Whitlow had come back into the room without Lia noticing. "Sally Mason's all puffed up because her husband owns a couple of gristmills. He's a hard man, Sam Mason is, but he's fair. He'd be more likely to want to know if you can teach his young fool of a son to sit still long enough to have some learnin' drilled into his thick skull."

Geoff gave Mrs. Whitlow one of his formal, courtly bows. "You, dear lady, are a font of information."

Mrs. Whitlow flushed. "Don't you go tryin' your charms on me, young man." But she was smiling as she said it.

Geoff still held the book she'd been balancing on her head. He rotated it until he could read the title on the spine. One corner of his mouth twisted up in a bitter smile. For a moment, she had a wild thought that he was going to throw the book across the room. Instead, he laid it down on the table gently, positioning the book so that it aligned with the edges of the table. His eyes still on the book, he said, "You shouldn't have to pretend to be someone you're not. It's not a good idea. It changes you. You end up feeling like a spy in enemy territory."

Bradford bounded to his feet. He said, too heartily, "Well, I think we've had enough practice for today. You look the part now, and you've learned enough to pass a cursory inspection. You're ready."

Lia looked at Geoff, waiting. Finally, he raised his head and met her eyes. "Yes. You're ready."

CHAPTER 7

That evening, just as the clock on the mantelpiece chimed the hour, a knock sounded at Mrs. Whitlow's front door. Henri put down the slate where he'd been copying out his spelling words, but Lia jumped up before he could. "I'll let them in. You keep on with your homework, Henri."

"I don't mind a distraction," Henri said. "I've been doing this for hours."

"More like twenty minutes," Mrs. Whitlow observed. Henri made a face, but dutifully turned the page. Lia smiled at them both. Despite his protests, she knew Henri was becoming fond of Mrs. Whitlow, as Lia was herself.

Geoff and Bradford stepped into the room. Geoff bowed formally. He was impeccably dressed in a new frock coat of dark blue wool. She had to admit that he looked good all spruced up. Even so, she was troubled by the look on his face. His expression looked somber, distant and austere. "Is something wrong?" she asked.

"No." He shook his head and forced a smile. "You look lovely tonight."

Bradford sighed. "Sometimes, I despair of you."

"What am I missing?" Lia looked down at the pretty white dress. The fabric was so light and delicate, she felt as if she were wearing a cloud. Even though the skirts were at least as voluminous as the blue wool, they were easier to manage. Perhaps she was becoming accustomed to dressing fashionably. It was hard to resist the urge to swish the skirts as she walked. Geoff had not only gotten her hair ribbons, he had obtained a pair of fine ladies' shoes from the trading post at Fort Vancouver. Mrs. Whitlow had let her borrow a pair of white gloves, and she had piled her hair up on the top of her head in a style similar to what the ladies in town wore. She looked at Bradford. "What is wrong?"

Bradford raised his eyes up to heaven as though seeking patience. "He's escorting a pretty girl to a dinner, and he looks like my Aunt Griselda at her cat's funeral. Relax! That's an order."

"You can't order me to enjoy it," Geoff muttered. At Lia's look, he added, "It's not that I dislike the idea of escorting you to dinner. I dislike being obligated to go. Life should be about more than duty."

"Life should be about more than homework," Henri said.

"But you're still going to finish that lesson tonight, aren't you?" Lia ruffled his hair affectionately. He ducked away, reddening. "Aw, Lia!"

Bradford said, "Well, *I* plan to enjoy myself. I'm going to infiltrate the men's conversation and stay as far away as I can from the ladies. I had enough of their inane chatter at that literary society. Our hostess tonight has a laugh so shrill it could scrape a chalkboard."

"Ah." Geoff nodded. "So *that's* why she invited us to attend this dinner. It must have been your conversation with her at the literary society meeting. I was wondering about that."

"I might have sung your praises to her. I needed to divert her attention from matching me up with one of the young ladies of the town."

"'Might have'? What exactly did you tell her?"

Mrs. Whitlow said, "You folks plan to stand here all night and argue?"

Geoff held out his arm. Lia placed her gloved hand on the fine cloth of his sleeve. She swallowed. Now that the moment had come, all her doubts had returned full force. "You really think I'm ready?"

"My dear girl," Bradford said grandly, "after all my tutoring? You are as well prepared as any woman could be."

"You'll do fine." Geoff spoke the words softly, but they cut through Lia's nervous tension, and she straightened. She might have to go through this baptism by fire, but she was not alone.

WHEN LIA AND GEOFF ARRIVED, with Bradford trailing behind, the superintendent and Mrs. Mason were greeting their guests by the front door. The superintendent beamed when he saw Lia. "I am so glad you were able to come tonight. I wanted to tell you how impressed I am with what you've done. The change in Eugene is amazing. He's actually looking forward to going to school. He says you're the most interesting teacher he's ever had. He's actually articulate about it."

Interesting. That was one word for her impulsive actions. Lia supposed it could have been worse.

Mrs. Mason looked as if she had bitten into a pickle. "Eugene is perfectly articulate, when he wants to be."

"Aye, when he *wants* to be. The trouble is, he rarely wants to be. And trying to get him to open a book and study is worse than pulling teeth."

Mrs. Mason opened her mouth to retort, then shut it again. The superintendent turned to Bradford, escorting him across the room to introduce him to a pair of prosperous-looking businessmen.

His wife ignored Lia completely, turning her attention to Geoff. Forcing a smile, she said brightly, "I understand that you've been hiding a very important secret!" With her hand still on Geoff's arm, Lia could feel him go rigid, as if turned to stone. For a moment, she had the impression that he had stopped breathing altogether. The matron went on, shaking a gloved finger at him playfully, "You came here under false pretenses. I hadn't realized, when we met, what a distinguished visitor you were!"

"Distinguished?" Geoff said slowly. He had the oddest expression on his face, as if he wasn't sure if the woman were serious or not.

"Oh yes," the matron went on, smiling. "I met your friend Mr. Bradford at the literary society meeting, and he told me *all* about your older brother being a baronet. I understand that he has no other brothers? And you are his only heir?"

"My brother the baronet." Geoff paused. "Well. I will have to speak to him about this." He nodded to the matron and they moved on to greet the other guests, a collection of staid businessmen and their fashionably dressed wives. Lia eyed the other women's dresses. She was no expert, but the dress Mrs. Whitlow had loaned her seemed just as fine as anything they were wearing. It didn't erase the tension inside her, but it helped a little.

One man stood out from the rest. A short, round-faced man dressed in rough, unfashionable clothes was introduced as Reverend Willett, a traveling preacher who was staying with the local pastor. Lia liked the look of him; something about him reminded her of Geoff, with his ability to put her at ease.

Lia had just greeted the man when Mrs. Mason was back at Geoff's side, telling them that dinner was served. The woman seemed to expect Geoff to escort her into the dining room, but Geoff kept his hold on Lia's arm. Bradford, looking slightly abashed, took the matron in ahead of them.

MRS. MASON and Bradford led the way into the dining room. The long table was laid out with a snowy white linen tablecloth. Crystal wine goblets and gold-trimmed china plates glinted in the light of the many-branched candelabra. "Oh my," Lia said, so softly Geoff doubted that anyone else had heard her. He gave a brief squeeze of his hand, smiling down at her. She straightened her spine and lifted her chin.

"My dear husband suggested we do away with place cards and adopt a more informal approach to seating." Mrs. Mason indicated the chair on her right. 'Mr. Montgomery, won't you sit here?"

Geoff gave a half bow. "I would not presume, madam. I know my dear friend Bradford would feel cheated if I denied him the pleasure of your company." Geoff drew out a chair in the middle of the table and held it for Lia as she seated herself. Bradford did the same for Mrs. Mason as the other dinner guests filed in. Bradford gave Geoff a telling look. "I can't tell you how much I appreciate your thought-fulness, Lieutenant."

"Lieutenant?" Reverend Willett's head came up like an infantryman hearing the first shot of battle. He had a surprisingly deep voice for such a short man.

"We served in the army together," Geoff said smoothly. "Old habits die hard." *Stick to the truth as much as possible.* "Bradford and I were stationed in Montreal."

The reverend's deep-brown eyes held an unexpectedly shrewd expression. There was no way to tell whether he believed Geoff or not. "What did you do in the army?"

Geoff felt the faintest breath of suspicion, which raised the hairs on the back of his neck. The man looked harmless enough, with his receding hairline and a cherubic face reddened from too much time in the sun. But there was an intelligent look in his eyes. He could not decide if the reverend was a threat or not, but something about the way the man was looking at him sent an alarm bell ringing in the back of Geoff's mind. He reminded Geoff of Lia, with her ability to discern when he was shading the truth.

"Administrative affairs," he said vaguely. He could sense Lia gazing at him, hearing the discrepancies between the story he'd told her and the one he was telling now. He did not look at her. He must not appear uncertain. Confidence was key when portraying a role. His foot touched hers, very gently, under the table, trying to reassure her.

The reverend did not shift his attention from Geoff. "Why did you leave the army? Do you miss it?"

Geoff shrugged, taking a sip from his water goblet before offering up his cover story. "I received a legacy when an uncle died. Bradford had long wanted to travel, and I had been thinking about writing a book. It seemed like the ideal time for us to resign our commissions and head west."

Bradford chimed in. "Yes, Montgomery is writing up an account of our travels and I draw the illustrations."

Reverend Willett was focused on Geoff. That level of concentration was rather unsettling. Geoff forced his features into a façade of slightly bored amiability. Finally, Reverend Willett said meditatively, "Indeed. How fortunate that your uncle's legacy enabled you to recognize your ambition."

"Your uncle?" Mrs. Mason sat up straighter. "One of your titled relations, perhaps?"

"My mother's brother," Geoff said dryly. "He was in trade."

"My brother Pierre is involved in trade," Lia said. "He's going to set up a trading store when he gets back home."

"Nothing wrong with that," a balding man with a neatly trimmed beard interposed. "Trade is what is going to make this Territory great."

"Aye, if the British will leave us alone," muttered another man with a shock of wild hair and a ragged beard. Geoff braced himself. If the issue of politics was going to raise its head, this dinner might become unpleasant indeed.

Mrs. Mason appeared to share this thought. She said hurriedly, "Well, let's not talk politics during dinner, shall we? I'm sure there are more congenial topics we could discuss. Mr. Lovejoy, have you decided what you're going to call that new town of yours?"

The balding man answered, "I'm afraid not, ma'am. I want to name it after my hometown, Boston. But Pettygrove here insists that we should name it after *his* hometown."

To Geoff, Mrs. Mason said, "Mr. Lovejoy and Mr. Pettygrove are platting out a new town a few miles downriver. Better access for ocean-going ships, I understand."

"Indeed?" Geoff made a mental note to add this to his

report. He and Bradford would have to make an excursion downriver to check out this new site. More evidence that the Americans were settling in and starting to claim this land as their own. Evidence that he would have to provide to his superiors, which might affect their decision on whether or not Britain should go to war over the Oregon Territory.

AFTER THE LADIES retired to the parlor for tea, the talk around the dinner table returned to politics, as Geoff had known it must. To maintain their pose as idle visitors, he tried to rein in Bradford's tendency to pontificate on Britain's right to expand its empire. Hopefully without overstepping his bounds as the junior officer on the mission. Tricky.

Mr. Lovejoy said, ominously, "Not much good building our new town if your prime minister, Peel, keeps talking about sending in troops to defend your country's interests."

"Your President Polk has been saying much the same thing," Bradford remarked, an edge to his tone.

Their mission was to gather information about the possibility of going to war. It was not to start a war all on their own. Bradford was glaring at Lovejoy, who was glaring back at him. Geoff turned to Mr. Lovejoy, spreading out his hands to get the man's attention. "If you can't come to a decision about your new town's name, why don't you and Mr. Pettygrove flip a coin to decide?"

Mr. Lovejoy raised his eyebrows. "I suppose we could try that." He fished out a coin and held it up. "Shall we say best out of three?" His friend nodded.

Bradford did not speak any more on the subject of politics, and Geoff relaxed. But not for long. Reverend Willett turned back to him. "I think I owe you an apology."

From the far end of the table, Geoff heard Mr. Lovejoy say to his friend, "All right, the first coin toss is yours. I'll flip this time."

The reverend went on, "I used to be in our country's army, before I devoted my life to the Lord. I had to obey orders whether I liked them or not, and sometimes those orders sent me far from home. I know what it's like to be a stranger in a strange land. It's not always a comfortable situation to be in. I hope we're not making you uncomfortable with this conversation."

Geoff wished he could tell the plain truth for once. They had made him far too welcome. He was seated at the table like a guest, as if he were one of them. No wonder he felt guilty. He was a spy in enemy territory, and the enemy was treating him kindly. That was because they did not know who he truly was. If they knew, he'd be out of town by the end of the day—on his own two feet if he were lucky, on a rail if he weren't. They would all turn from him in disgust. Even Lia.

Every constant in his world had been turned upside down. It was his duty to lie rather than tell the truth. He had to befriend men he would perhaps have to betray. The only good thing he could cling to was Lia. She saw him not as a soldier or a spy. Just as himself. That recognition was his lifeline, a reminder that there was a saner world out there. Once he completed his mission, perhaps he could come back and see Lia again.

But no. That fantasy exploded like a nine-pound shell shattering into pieces. Once he completed his mission and returned to Montreal with his report, word would get out to the Americans of what he and Bradford had been up to. It wouldn't be too difficult to connect their report with the pair of strange British men who'd wandered around asking questions. And Lia would know he'd been lying to her. She would want nothing more to do with him. Once she knew the truth, she'd never want to see him again. That thought brought with it a sense of desolation so intense it was almost physical pain.

He forced himself to focus on the innocent-looking man in front of him. He could not let himself get distracted from the work at hand.

Reverend Willett was saying, "Some of us haven't forgotten what it was like to come across the mountains after crossing the continent to get here. When we showed up in the Oregon Territory, we were hungry. Supplies were nearly exhausted, and winter was coming on. If John McLoughlin and the Hudson Bay Company had not stepped forward to offer Christian charity, most of us would have been hard put to survive that first winter."

The superintendent nodded at this sentiment. Apparently not listening to the conversation, Mr. Pettygrove said to Mr. Lovejoy, "All right, we're tied. One last toss."

Geoff wondered what the man expected of him. Perhaps it would help if he tried pouring some balm on the troubled waters. "My friend and I have no wish to see discord between our two countries. Nothing would please us more than to see an amicable relationship flourish."

"Well said." Reverend Willett looked satisfied. Geoff wasn't quite sure now if the man had posed a threat or not. If he had, the threat had evidently been diverted. For the moment.

"All right then," Mr. Lovejoy said to his friend. "You win. We'll name the place Portland."

Mr. Mason dabbed the corner of his mouth, and then tossed the crumpled napkin on the table. "Well, gentlemen. Shall we join the ladies?"

Geoff rose quickly. Lia was in the other room. He needed to see her, touch her hand, to get his bearings again. She was his one refuge, for as long as he could maintain the illusion that he was not her enemy.

LIA DID NOT RELAX until she saw Geoff's tall figure returning to the front room with the other men. She had endured what felt like an eternity sipping tea and chatting with the ladies. They were polite enough, but it was an endless source of amazement how they could talk for ages and yet at the end of the conversation manage to not have actually said anything.

The musicians, a couple of fiddlers and a man playing a concertina, began playing dance tunes. Lia had hoped that Geoff would ask her to dance, but she saw Mrs. Mason step forward and claim him almost as soon as he had entered the room. Lia tried to squash the disappointment, even a little jealousy. Never mind. She would dance with him soon enough.

She danced with Mr. Pettygrove and then Mr. Lovejoy. Dancing with strange men wasn't as bad as she had feared. They were polite, at least, even if they were reserved. She danced with Bradford, who kept up an amusing patter of observations on the dinner guests, and then with the superintendent, who was positively jovial about the effect she seemed to be having on the board members. It felt like an eternity, but finally, Geoff was before her. The relief was almost overwhelming. She stretched out her hands and he took them, smiling down at her. "You seemed to be enjoying yourself. I did not see a single stumble, apart from that misstep with Mr. Lovejoy."

"He put his foot down right on top of mine," Lia confided. "I'll probably be limping all day tomorrow."

His eyes crinkled as he smiled. "I'll try not to imitate him."

As if he could. The man moved her around the room with a sure and confident touch, guiding her through the other couples so deftly she doubted they noticed. The evening was almost at an end, and she had survived without making a fool of herself in public. Thanks largely to Geoff. Elation swirled through her, sweet as the music. She only had to get through the next few dances, and they could escape. Perhaps she could arrange to dance all of them with Geoff. She smiled up at him, and he smiled back.

When the tune ended, however, Mrs. Mason came up to them. "Now, you mustn't take up all of our Mr. Montgomery's time! A man in his position has many important social obligations, you know. Brother of a baronet! Such an important position."

What was it about this woman that always made her feel out of place? Out in the woods, she would simply disappear, find a quiet place where there were no awkward social obligations. She was conscious of the embarrassed flush warming her cheeks.

Geoff glanced at her, appraising. Then he turned to Mrs. Mason and bowed low. "My apologies, ma'am. I promised Miss Griggs that I would dance the next waltz with her. I can't break a promise, can I?" His deep voice, so close beside her, sent vibrations resonating deep inside.

"I see." Mrs. Mason bit off the words, two ominous syllables. She pressed her lips together in a thin line and glared at Lia. Well, it wasn't as if the woman were going to be her best friend after tonight in any case. At least the superintendent was pleased with her work at the school.

Geoff added, "But I do seem to recall that Bradford mentioned once something about dancing with Queen Victoria herself, at a dance at Buckingham Palace. Perhaps he might tell you about it, if you ask him."

And with that, he placed his hand on Lia's waist and whirled her into the dance.

She tilted her head back to smile up at him. "You are always rescuing me. Like a knight in one of the old tales. One of these days, *I* am going to rescue *you*."

"I only wish you could."

"What do you mean?" She must have misheard that, misunderstood him. He had spoken so softly she wasn't sure.

He had turned his head to look behind her. She darted a glance over her shoulder. Mrs. Mason stood on the side of the room, eyeing them both. Her mouth twisted into a wry expression before she went back to her conversation with one of the other wives. "I don't think she approves of you," Geoff said, low in her ear. "You've made her brother look bad."

"The poor man didn't need my help with that." She was finding it difficult to concentrate on conversation. All she could think of was how close Geoff stood to her, his lips a few inches from her ear. His warm breath tickled her skin. It was extremely distracting. "How much of that story you told her is true?"

"Very little," he admitted. "Bradford is the nephew of a general stationed in Montreal. I doubt he and Queen Victoria have ever attended the same ball, let alone actually been introduced."

"So you were lying?"

The muscles of his mouth tightened, and his brows drew together. "I am tired of listening to him make up stories about me. Brother of a baronet, indeed. It seemed only fair to tell a few stories about him instead."

"I can see you're doing it for a game," she said slowly. "All the same, it doesn't seem right. That silly woman believed you. That's dishonest."

"She believed what she wanted to believe." He sounded like a man trying to convince himself as well as her. "What's the harm in that? It's not real. Even she knows that, deep down. If she wants to tell herself lies, pretend they're true, that's her affair."

He whirled her in a turn, making her skirts flare out. "Let us continue this discussion in a more private location." He deftly maneuvered her, guiding her with light pressure through the dancers to the other side of the room, where they slipped through the open door into the superintendent's study.

The fire in the fireplace had died down into glowing coals. He left the door partially open. She could see through to the other room. Everyone was dancing. No one had noticed their absence.

He had kept hold of her hand, his other hand still at her waist. The dying firelight threw shadows across his face, leaving it half in darkness as he looked down at her. She could still see the penetrating look in his eyes, so intense that her stomach tightened with apprehension. His voice held a pleading note. "People like Mrs. Mason don't want to hear the truth. They would rather believe a made-up story. I'm making her happy by telling her what she wants to hear. Nothing wrong with that."

"But you need to be careful you don't lose sight of what is right." She stopped. His gaze—it was as if he were trying to communicate a message without using words. She softened her tone. "I know you only meant it for a game, and maybe you're right. Maybe she doesn't really believe it's true either. All the same, I don't want you playing any games like that with me. I want nothing but truth between us. No lies. If you keep lying to everyone you meet, you're going to forget what truth is."

He tightened his grip, his fingers sliding over the palm of her hand. Even through the thin kid gloves, she could feel his touch. She shivered, but she wasn't cold. That look in his eyes reminded her of that picnic that day above Oregon City, when he had looked as if he were hurting inside.

"That's what I'm afraid of." He turned his face away and his voice dropped to a whisper. "I need you to remind me of how the world is supposed to be."

It was so odd to see a big, strong man look so lost. Compassion and affection welled up inside her in a wave so strong that she did not pause to consider her actions. She rose up on tiptoe and leaned forward. She had meant to give him a light kiss on his cheek, but he turned his head and his lips met hers.

His whole body went still. Then his hands closed around her arms, and he pulled her toward him. The touch of his lips against hers was inexpressibly sweet, but somehow interwoven with desperation. He kissed her with the gentleness of a boy holding a butterfly, careful not to damage its wings, and the urgency of a drowning man clinging to a life raft. Abruptly, he let her go and stepped back, his whole body rigid as a soldier on parade.

They stared at each other. Then Lia began, "I didn't mean to—"

At the same time, Geoff said, "I should apologize for—"

And behind them, Lia heard Mrs. Mason's voice, with its smooth purr of satisfaction. "Why, my goodness! I had no idea the two of you were so well acquainted."

Lia spun around. The unbearably smug look on Mrs. Mason's face reminded Lia of a cat that had just pounced on a mouse. "Well, this is hardly the behavior I would expect of a respectable schoolteacher. Sneaking off with a man like this. Trying to trap a baronet's brother. Simply shameless. I don't know what my husband and the school board members will think when I tell them."

Geoff took a step forward, shielding Lia from the matron's view. "I think you have perhaps misunderstood the situation here. This lady is innocent of any wrongdoing."

"That's not what it's going to look like to the school board." Mrs. Mason slipped out the door and shut it behind her.

Lia put her hand to her mouth. Cold fear washed through her, followed by hot shame. "But we haven't— We weren't going to—"

Geoff turned back to her, his mouth set into a grim line. "That doesn't matter. Your reputation is ruined, or it will be as soon as there's a break in the music so she can talk without shouting."

That was all it would take. She would lose her position. Henri would never willingly go back to school on his own. She closed her eyes as if that would shut out the pictures forming in her imagination. She wanted to go find a dark corner to hide in. Taking a deep breath, she looked up at Geoff. "Well then. I will just have to face them all down. Maybe it'll blow over."

Geoff muttered something under his breath. His rough fingers gripped her hand, firm and sure, their warmth bringing a sense of comfort even at a time like this. He tugged her into the front room. "Come on. We need to outflank her before she can begin her attack. She can't start spreading the story until the dancing is finished. Let's seize the high ground." He towed her across the room to where the musicians were playing. He tapped a fiddle player on the shoulder. "Would you please stop for a moment?"

All the musicians stopped playing. In the hush that followed, heads turned in their direction. Geoff's voice rang out. "Ladies and gentlemen, I would like to make an announcement." Lia caught sight of the matron across the room, standing next to two of the biggest gossips in town. The matron's mouth hung open. She seemed to have understood the significance of Geoff's actions before Lia did.

Geoff took in a deep breath. "Ladies and gentlemen," he said again, "I would like to announce our engagement."

CHAPTER 8

"I had no other option," Geoff said, for what felt like the twentieth time. "My duty was clear. I could not remain silent and risk a lady's reputation being ruined."

It had been a quiet walk when they escorted Lia back to Mrs. Whitlow's after the party. Lia herself had spoken very little, merely telling him good night before vanishing into the house. Geoff had wanted to talk to her more, but he could not find the right words to say, not with Bradford standing there, arms crossed, glowering at them both. Geoff knew better than to ask him to leave them alone. Tomorrow. He would have to talk to her tomorrow.

Bradford had held his peace until they were out of earshot, and even then he kept his voice low, but the edge of his anger was all the sharper for having been repressed.

"It was inexcusable carelessness to let yourself get trapped like that."

Geoff could not agree. His announcement had been an impulse driven by the need to save Lia from shame and scorn. There was no way he could have stood by and watched while the matron ruined Lia. It was completely unfair. But the idea of actually being engaged to Lia did not seem foolish at all. Perhaps there was some way to make this new situation work out for everyone concerned.

He was consumed with a fierce, secret elation. It had felt *right* to stand in front of all those people and claim Lia as his. Why not? He and Bradford were bound to go back to Montreal and make their report, but afterwards, if he were to return here... might she welcome him back?

That line of thinking would not sway Bradford. "You told me that we needed her."

Bradford threw up his hands in the air. "I didn't tell you to ask her to marry you!"

"Keep your voice down," Geoff cautioned. A man passed them in the opposite direction, heading for the saloon, and Geoff tipped his hat to him. "Good evening." He waited until the man was out of earshot. "Lia was not trying to trap me." *Shift to the enemy's ground.* "And you didn't help, telling everyone I was related to a baronet."

Bradford had the grace to look abashed. He muttered, "It was those literary societies. I couldn't help it. Three of them! All filled with women who have marriageable daughters."

"Ah." Understanding dawned, along with amusement. "And as a bachelor, you felt threatened."

"They're relentless. The worst snobs I've ever seen. I'd always heard it said that Americans weren't class conscious. Don't believe it. They go after titles like a—like a lion going after a lamb. I had to do something to distract them from myself. I... might have accidentally given them the idea that you had a title in your family. I thought if I diverted attention to you, it would give me breathing space."

"You decided to throw me to the lions."

"Well, the lionesses."

"At least I can be sure Lia doesn't want me for my titled relations."

Bradford's mouth twisted. "What are you going to do? Abandon me and your duty and turn into an American?"

"No," Geoff said. "Of course not. I will complete the mission. There is no need to leap into marriage. We could tell everyone that we've decided to have a lengthy engagement."

"Would she agree to that?" Bradford sounded doubtful.

"This might work out to everyone's advantage," Geoff said. "We need to spend the winter in this town, so it would be as well if we look like we're supporting the American presence in the Oregon Territory. Our engagement will protect Lia's reputation. I'll make it clear to her that this is a temporary arrangement between us."

At least, if she wants it to be temporary.

The more he thought about it, the more the idea of being engaged to Lia appealed to him. It might be that come spring, after she got to know him better, she would be willing to wait. He would have to return to Montreal to report on their mission, but he could come back. Perhaps... if he explained the situation then, she might understand why he hadn't been able to tell her the whole story before. It was possible. She did like him. By spring, she might be willing to trust him.

Bradford caught up with him. "And in the meantime, our position here is secure."

"I'll talk to her tomorrow. Make sure we have an understanding."

"You do that." Bradford stopped walking and turned to face Geoff, letting his words sink in. "But make sure that you do not forget what the priority is here. We cannot get involved. No more than we have to."

"I understand." He would be honest with Lia—as honest as he could be under the circumstances. He would offer her the choice to stay engaged until spring or break their engagement instead. Or maybe even wait for him...? So long as he was upfront about what she could expect from him, she wouldn't be hurt. If she didn't want to wait for him... his own heart was another matter.

THE NEXT MORNING, Lia sat on the settee in Mrs. Whitlow's front room, trying to make sense of her life. She fidgeted with a pencil, pretending to look over the lesson plans that Edgar had left. But her mind was not on the work in front of her.

Over breakfast, Henri had been eager to know what had happened at the dinner the night before. Lia had answered his questions mechanically. She ate the food placed in front of her without noticing whether it was spicy or bland. Finally, blessedly, Henri's curiosity had been tempered by his need to collect the breakfast dishes and carry them back to the scullery. Lia could hear the *clink* of dishes as he piled them up by the sink as she escaped to the front room. She sat down by the table and tried to focus her attention on the vague lesson plans that Edgar had drawn up before he left.

Mrs. Whitlow had gone to bed too early the night before to hear what had happened at last night's dinner, so Lia was not surprised when Whitlow sat down next to her and said simply, "Tell me about your dinner party last night."

Lia raised up her head to look at the older woman, who had gathered up her mending and was preparing to thread her needle. Henri wandered in, holding a textbook as if he meant to study. Lia knew he was listening as she tried to explain what had happened the night before. Haltingly, she described the dinner and the dancing. "And then, he drew me aside and we talked. Then he proposed. In a way. Well, to be honest he didn't propose an engagement so much as *announce* one. I've never seen a less romantic moment."

She could not remember feeling this lost before, even when her pa had died. Trying to analyze her emotions was like walking on a loose bed of shale; the ground beneath her kept shifting. She felt elated, flattered, and embarrassed by turns. Her instinct was to go slow, test her footing before she took the next step. If she could figure out what he was planning, maybe she could get a grip on this situation. He had announced their engagement as a way to defend against gossip. But was that the only reason? The very idea of becoming engaged felt foreign to her. None of the men she'd met before had seemed to understand her, how she didn't have any place in this sort of world.

There was a lot she did not understand about Geoff. And he didn't know her either. If he really did want this engagement, she was going to have to be honest with him. It would be so much easier to say nothing and let things go on as they were, but that was no longer possible. The man needed to know the risk.

"How can a proposal of marriage be unromantic?" Mrs. Whitlow scrunched up her nose.

"Well, it's not as if I've ever been standing next to them when a couple got engaged," Lia conceded. "But I've read about it in books. It's supposed to be... well, he should have looked happy. He might as well have been going into battle. Surely, if he wanted to marry me, he would have been a bit more... well, he would have acted like it was something he wanted to do?"

Mrs. Whitlow paused in her mending to consider this.

"He is British. They're a standoffish sort. Or maybe he just can't say what he feels. That's a failure common with men all the world over."

Henri was sitting sideways in his chair with a copy of his geography book in his lap and his legs draped over the chair arm. Idly, he traced the outline of a map. "I knew he cared about you. He just didn't want to rush things."

"So he proposed only because he felt pressured into doing the right thing. He doesn't want to marry me." She slumped into a chair. "I don't know what to do about it all."

She didn't know what to do about Geoff. She liked him. She was attracted to him. But was that enough for a lifelong commitment? She just wasn't sure. She wished they had more time together before she made a decision that would affect the rest of her life. She tried to imagine her future, five, ten, twenty years from this moment, tied to a man who felt sorry for her.

No. That made it clear. She would tell Geoff that the engagement was off. He would probably be relieved, if he had only suggested it out of obligation. Somehow, logic didn't cheer her up. For a moment, when he first proposed, she thought it had meant that he cared about her, and the warm glow that thought had created had been slow to dissipate.

She sighed. "We didn't really have a chance to talk after the dinner party. His friend Bradford stuck to his side the whole way back." That was odd too. Wouldn't a man who'd just gotten engaged want to say good night to his fiancée in private? But no, Bradford had acted as if he were the one in charge, and Geoff had simply let him. He hadn't said a word to Lia except what was strictly necessary.

Perhaps he was already regretting what he'd said.

Henri turned his head, his attention caught by something outside the window. He stood up, tossing the book carelessly onto the table. It landed with a *thump*. "I just saw someone I need to talk to. When I get back, we can go see Geoff, if that would make you feel better."

She sat up straight, squaring her shoulders. "No. I need to talk to him now. I can't put this off. I think I need to go by myself, if you don't mind. It's going to be... awkward. I don't want an audience."

"Well... you'll let me know if you need my help." Henri patted Lia on the shoulder, and then he left.

Mrs. Whitlow tilted her head to one side. "You don't look like a woman planning to talk to the man she's going to marry. You look more like a woman going to a funeral. Do you care for the man at all?"

"I am not sure *what* I feel," Lia confessed. She had too many emotions roiling inside her to make sense of them. If he had only proposed out of guilt, then the worst thing she could do would be to marry him. Tie herself for life to a man who thought of her as a duty? No. She shook her head. "I hardly know the man. It's too soon to talk about getting married."

"That's rather the point of an engagement, isn't it? To give the couple a chance to be sure they're doing the right thing."

"I suppose," Lia said doubtfully. "But I can't marry a man because he feels sorry for me. I'll have to tell him that."

There was a knock at the door, and Lia jumped. At the sight of Geoff, his broad shoulders outlined in the doorway, she was struck with a vivid recollection of the precise sensation of his lips brushing across her mouth with exquisite tenderness. A rush of heat flooded her cheeks. She concentrated her attention on his chin, unable to look him in the eye. "Good morning," she mumbled.

"Good morning." He cleared his throat. "Could we take a walk? I think there are a few things we need to discuss."

"Yes, of course. I'll get my wrap."

Her sense of uncertainty solidified into a decision. She would give him the chance to get out of this engagement business. Otherwise, she would have to tell him the truth.

WALKING HELPED her regain her calm. They walked down Main Street and out along the riverbank toward the wharf. The breeze off the river cooled her cheeks. She still found it hard to look at him directly, but she stole the occasional glance as they walked.

Geoff matched his pace to hers, but he did not look at her. His shoulders were braced and his whole body stiff. She could not decide if he felt as shy as she did, or if he was regretting the situation his kind impulse had landed him in. She spoke quickly, before she could change her mind. "Thank you for your kind offer last night, but I cannot accept it. It would not be honest. You don't really want to marry me. I will tell the supervisor and Mrs. Mason that we are not engaged."

He stopped, swinging around to face her. Their eyes met. His gaze on her was intent, probing. "Then you will lose your position as a schoolteacher."

"That is not the point." She kept her chin up. "A married woman cannot be a teacher. But I could be engaged and still teach school. Or, I could be jilted and still teach. So if you're thinking that you should try to shield me from the consequences of my actions last night, don't bother."

"What if the story gets out that you were seen with me?"

"I'll say that we got engaged and then decided not to go

through with it." She avoided his gaze, but she took a deep breath and kept going. "I cannot regret what I did—what we did. I mean—" She was growing red now, she could feel it, but she forced herself to keep going. "I mean, I release you from our engagement." She took a breath and steadied herself. "I realize you were trying to help me and be a gentleman, but you didn't have to. Truly. I will set you free."

"I only wish I were free," he said cryptically. "Am I so repulsive to you? I thought we were friends."

"We were—I mean, we are. But you don't owe me anything. I know you only made that announcement because you wanted to save my reputation."

"It was my fault that you'd gotten into that predicament in the first place."

"You did not force me to kiss you. It was my decision. I will pay the penalty for my actions."

He said, very softly, "Was it that dreadful of a kiss?"

"What? No! Of course not. I mean—well, it's not as if I know much about these things, but I thought—well, I liked it." Her cheeks were growing redder by the moment. Was it supposed to be this difficult to break off an engagement? She didn't know much about that either, but she had always supposed it was a simple enough matter. "I know you were being noble and gentlemanly but it was my fault. I kissed you."

"I did not exactly fight you off."

There was a gleam in his eye. It was distracting, warming her through and making her feel flustered. She had to force herself to keep to the point. "However it happened, it doesn't mean you have to get tied to me for life. The truth is you don't want to marry me."

He took a step closer. "I know I essentially forced you

into this engagement. But I had no choice either. The whole situation was my fault. It's only fair that I make it right."

"It's not your fault. You shouldn't have to carry my burdens for me." She knew she was being stubborn about this. But even though she had never expected passionate declarations of undying love, a proposal should mean something more than just a way out of a difficulty.

"We don't know each other well, true. But you would be helping me as well as yourself if you agreed to this engagement. And as for getting tied for life..." He shifted his weight, looking uncomfortable. "As it happens, I was thinking that we might want to make this engagement... a temporary arrangement. A business arrangement, as it were. You need a fiancé to preserve your reputation, and I would find it convenient as well."

"A business arrangement, even a temporary one for our mutual benefit, is still a lie."

He softened his voice. "It's true that we've only known each other a short time. But I'm not sure it's a lie. For the moment, it will suit both of us to be engaged. I have to leave come spring. Let's not make any permanent decisions just yet. Perhaps... once we know each other better..." He did not put the rest of the sentence into words, but the look in his eyes spoke volumes.

She looked away, shy again. Life should be straightforward, everything set out plain and clear. But it was not a plain and clear world she found herself in. She could not expect honesty from him if she was not prepared to give him the same. It was the only way they could forge a path through this uncharted territory.

EVEN THOUGH IT RANKLED, Geoff could understand why Lia hesitated. She was in an awkward situation. If he hadn't indulged in a moment of weakness, let his guard down, Mrs. Mason wouldn't have seen them together. He had handed the woman the tool to destroy Lia. It was only right that he fix things. Naturally she was going to feel like an obligation. And he could not reveal the truth to her without betraying his mission. *The price I pay for doing my duty is that I have to stand before a woman I could love and lie to her.* Would it balance out the scales if he gave her what truth he could? "I have to leave in the spring. But... I could come back next year. If you would want me to come back."

"Sometimes," she said, "I don't understand you at all. There are parts of you that just don't make sense. I'm not sure I can promise to marry a man who is a mystery. You're not telling me everything, are you?"

He hesitated, then reached out and tucked a loose strand of hair behind her ear, keeping his touch light as a whisper. Her eyes widened, but she did not move. "I promise that I will tell you all the truth that I can, and never tell you a lie just for the fun of it. In all honesty, I cannot apologize for the kiss. But you need to understand—this is a temporary arrangement only. When the snow melts in the passes, I am returning back east."

She studied him for a long moment. "That sounds like the truth. I'm still not sure this will work but... if we're being honest with each other, there's something you need to know."

She looked around. "This isn't a good place to talk in private. Anyone could walk by. Let's walk down by the river."

He followed her in silence until they had left the town behind them and started down the trail that led along the river. By the riverbank lay a narrow strip of gravel just wide enough for them to walk side by side. Rocks crunched under her boots. The falls upstream created a constant rumble in the background. This was as good a place as any. No one would overhear their conversation. She stopped and turned to face him. Taking a deep breath, she got the words out before she could reconsider.

"I told you my mother was part French. That's true; her father was a trapper from Montreal. But *her* mother was Cree."

She waited. He smiled, his body language conveying polite expectation. She gave a short exhalation of impatience. "Don't you see the problem?"

"I'm not sure," he said cautiously. "Is it a secret? Your mother's background, I mean."

"It was never a secret, growing up. Not before I came out here. My mother was never ashamed of who she was. My parents loved each other. Everyone in the Red River settlement understood how things were. But here... everything is different. People know about Henri, who his mother was. Her family's tribe still lives in the Twallity plains, though they don't know how long they're going to be able to stay there. The Americans keep coming and keep coming, they say. But no one here knows about Henri being more than half native. And I don't want them to find out."

"Would it really make all that much of a difference if your grandmother was a native? It will affect how some people think about you, perhaps. But surely it will not stop you from living as you choose. They say Lord Liverpool's grandmother was of East Indian descent, and he rose to be prime minister."

She stared at him for a long moment. "Things must be very different in England," she said finally. "Around here, all it takes is one drop of your blood being Indian for you to be less of a person. And if you're more than half Indian, then you're *all* Indian and that's all they want to know about you."

He cocked his head, studying her closely. "But they hired you to teach at the school..." His voice trailed off, and then he nodded. "They don't know about your ancestry."

She looked away, studying the view of the river rushing downstream. "I wasn't sure when I first came here." Her voice was low. "I had taught the children at the mission, and the question of my ancestry never came up. But the more I know about these people, the more certain I am that even being part native would close doors for me." She swallowed. "And people around here know about Henri's mother being a full-blood Kalapuyan. If they knew about my mother, his grandmother, Henri would not even be allowed to attend the school. A half-blood might be allowed in. But a child who's more than half native would never get in. And he must attend. I promised Pa, and Pierre would want it too. No one can find out the truth."

Finally, she tilted her head up to gaze up at him, those light eyes pinning him as effectively as a butterfly pinned to a corkboard.

"Do you understand what I am trying to tell you?" she demanded. "No one must know about my background. It's vital. You must promise to keep it a secret."

"I promise," Geoff said. Her obvious distress awoke a protective response in him. He wanted to keep her safe. He wanted—so very much—to cover her hand with his, to reassure her that he would always be on her side. But he could not make a promise like that. He would have to break it when he left. "You can trust me not to tell anyone. I'm good at keeping secrets."

She studied him, and he knew she was looking for signs

of indecision. "Still thinking we should get engaged? Even a temporary 'business' engagement?"

"Perhaps being engaged will help them accept you," he said.

She smiled, just a little. "You are a determined man, I'll give you that."

"Come now. Let's make a pact. A business engagement for our mutual benefit." He put out his hand. "Shake on it." She shook his hand, and he added, "I'm not sure if this helps, but Henri doesn't want to make something of himself in this Territory." Her eyebrows contracted into a frown, and he said, "Yes, I know. I was just wondering how much he really cared about what other people think of him."

"I care," she said passionately. "No one is going to be showing disrespect to Henri because of me. So no one must know about my mother, who she was. *That* is why I need your help passing off as a lady, with manners as fine as any woman in a palace." More softly, "People are polite and courteous now, but if they knew about my mother, they would not smile and nod and act so friendly."

"Surely that's an overreaction."

"You think so? Mrs. Whitlow told me about Mr. McLoughlin. The most respected man in the whole Territory, but he still ran into trouble because Mrs. McLoughlin came from a native tribe. He actually came to blows over the matter."

He could not deny that story; he had heard it himself while he was at Fort Vancouver. Still, "That was some years ago, wasn't it? Perhaps things have changed."

"Yes," Lia said sadly. "They got worse." She sighed. "If they ask, I'll tell the truth. I'm not saying anything. I'm keeping silent. Not volunteering information. But I'm not hiding who I am. No one asked me if I have a mother who was half-native."

"You're letting them believe what they want."

She hesitated, then twisted around to look up at him. "Am I doing the same thing you were doing last night? Is it so wrong, when everyone is happier if I don't volunteer the information?"

Her eyes pleaded with him, asking for—what? An answer? Forgiveness? He had no idea what to tell her. The situation was beyond irony. He was the last person who should be advising her. *Lord, why did you bring this woman to me now, at this one point in my life when I cannot open my heart to her?*

CHAPTER 9

She shouldn't have told him.

Even if Lia had no practice reading body language, she could have read Geoff's mood. His body practically shouted the shame he felt. He held himself as erect as ever, but his shoulders were rigid with tension, his jaw set in a firm line, and his eyes shifted away to study the ground. He would not meet her gaze. He must be ashamed of her, of her ancestry. Her instinct to hide her past had been right after all.

She had never been ashamed of her mother's family. But other people never understood.

Lia started to withdraw her hand from his arm. He turned sharply, as if she'd drawn him out of his thoughts. "If we are engaged, let's start acting like it." He tucked her hand into the crook of his elbow. "Let us go back to Main Street and promenade. Show the world that we are united."

They strolled along the street at a decorous pace. Lia kept her head high, nodding at a couple passing by in the other direction. The woman nodded back to Lia, the man tipped his hat. That was a far different reaction than what she'd encountered the first time she'd walked down this street. Having Geoff at her side was enhancing her reputation already. Out of the corner of her eye, she slanted a glance at him.

If she was going to be linked with Geoff publicly, then she needed to understand him. She felt instinctively that he was someone she could trust, but for the first time in her life she wondered if her instincts were leading her astray. Why was he keeping his life a secret from her? There was so much about him that she did not understand, that she *needed* to understand. It was frustrating. There was a connection between them. She knew it. But he was still a closed book to her.

Several men standing outside Abernethy's store stopped talking as they approached. Could these men tell she didn't belong? No, most of them were watching Geoff as if *he* were the impostor. Reverend Willett was the only man she recognized. He nodded a greeting to them, and Geoff nodded back, as if he had noticed nothing, but she knew he'd seen the looks the other men were giving him. He was quick.

Maybe that was what was bothering him so, the attitude of the townsfolk and not their sudden engagement. Or maybe it was something else altogether. Reading his body language gave her clues, but the man himself was still a mystery.

Just as he had the day she had arrived in Oregon City, Mrs. Mason's brother Edgar came barreling out of Vandehey's saloon. But this time he was far less steady on his feet. He stumbled off of the plank sidewalk and swayed dangerously before regaining his balance. "I'm fine," he said to Lia, though she hadn't said anything. "Just wasn't expecting that drop."

The drop hadn't changed from the last time Edgar had

stepped off it, but Lia didn't see any benefit from pointing that out. She just smiled politely and hoped that would be an adequate reply. Edgar didn't seem to notice any hesitation on her part. He went on, "I heard you're getting married. I suppose that means you're leaving the school. I'll have to go back to teaching the brats."

"I might be engaged, but I'm not getting married before spring, at the earliest." She could feel the tense muscles in Geoff's arm relax at her words. "If you dislike teaching so much, surely there are other things you could turn your hand to."

"My sister thinks because I like reading books, I must want to teach others to do the same." Edgar leaned forward, as if to confide a secret. He was close enough that she could smell the brandy on his breath. "You can't force someone to like learning. I can't, anyway. I've tried."

"Maybe you should tell Mrs. Mason that. I'm sure she only wants what's best for you."

Edgar frowned, considering the idea. Then he shook his head. "There's no point bringing the matter up. There's no reasoning with Sally, not when she gets an idea in her head."

"Well," Lia pointed out, "if you don't try, you'll never know if you could convince her."

"I'm not sure." He rocked back and forth, chewing his lower lip. "I might... think about it."

Geoff said mildly, "On my way to call on Lia, I saw your sister down at the other end of town, asking for you outside of Verboort's tavern."

Edgar's pale face reddened. "I don't know what good she thinks she can do, asking around for me like a lost puppy. I'm a grown man. I can take care of myself."

"Indeed." Geoff's tone was neutral, but Edgar narrowed

his eyes. "And you need not look down your nose at me, sir! You English, always thinking yourself so superior. I don't care if you are the cousin of a duke, you're no better a man than I am."

"Cousin of a duke?" The corner of Geoff's mouth crooked upward. He murmured to Lia, "Bradford is getting out of control. Next, he'll be telling people I'm in line for the throne."

Edgar sneered. "Outmoded aristocrats! We're moving with the times here. We're a democracy. You'll see."

The reverend came down the sidewalk toward them. "Come now, sir." He addressed Edgar. "There is no need to quarrel. We are all out here in the wilderness together."

Edgar swayed on his feet, raising a finger to point at Geoff. "Look at him, so puffed up and proud. These English walk around thinking they own the place. They'll learn soon enough, him and the other English. We Americans are putting together a new set of laws. You'll see some changes 'round here."

The humor drained out of Geoff's face, leaving it closed and watchful. "What kind of changes, exactly?"

Edgar ignored him. He gave the reverend a ceremonious nod, and then he bowed to Lia, slowly and carefully, making sure of his balance, before walking off down the street as if Geoff did not exist.

"What was he talking about?" Geoff's gaze remained on Edgar's retreating back.

Reverend Willett frowned. "I'm afraid there's been some talk of gathering men from around the Territory together to talk about passing some new laws. The Organic laws that they set up down in French Prairie need to be updated, they say. Make it clear to the world that this land belongs to the American settlers and no one else. Especially the British." The reverend's normally placid face looked almost troubled. "I'm praying that they do not listen to all the exaggerated bluster that some men have been foolishly indulging in. Seeing as you are an English subject..."

"I shall take care not to wave the Union Jack around too prominently."

"And if I might suggest, your friend might be persuaded not to talk quite so loudly while discoursing on British superiority. Not a topic designed to smooth troubled waters."

Geoff nodded. Then he held out his arm for Lia, and they walked on. A thin line had formed between his brows. Lia watched him. Finally, she spoke. "Is this going to cause problems?"

"I'd thought it was idle talk, before. But if they're serious enough to start thinking about passing laws, then I truly do need your help. We can't return until spring. It would simplify my staying here if people believed we were engaged." He was preoccupied, his eyes hidden, withdrawn. Abruptly, he said, "I need to speak to Bradford."

Whatever it was that he was hiding, he hadn't wanted to share it with her. She had hoped that honesty would be met with an equal frankness on his side. Apparently not. The man had as much right to privacy as anyone else. Still, she had to wrestle with a reaction of disappointment.

She sighed, and he gave her a sidelong glance, seeming to understand her mood. With the air of a man eager to introduce a new subject, he said, "It looks like your nephew is finding friends in town."

"Pardon?"

He nodded toward the blacksmith's shed. "I just saw him head around the corner with another boy. The blond boy who sat next to him in the back row."

"I don't think they're friends." Behind the blacksmith's shed, they heard a scuffle, then a thud. "What on earth?"

She dropped Geoff's arm and raced for the corner of the shed.

Eugene's blond hair was covered with mud. He was lying flat on the ground with Henri straddling him. Henri spoke between gritted teeth. "Take back what you said!"

Eugene's response was lost in Lia's anguished cry. "Henri, no!"

Henri twisted around in surprise, and Eugene seized the opportunity to roll so that he was the one on top, Henri wriggling like an eel underneath. Geoff strode forward, grabbing Eugene by the collar and heaving him up onto his feet. Lia grasped Henri by the shoulder. "Up!" The schoolteacher voice had the desired effect.

The two boys glared at each other.

"You've got dirt on your shirt."

"Yeah? Well, *you've* got a bloody nose."

"What you've both got is, I hope, an explanation," Lia said briskly. "What were you boys fighting about?"

Henri drew himself up to his full height. He was just tall enough to look her in the eye. "It was a matter of honor. We needed to settle it like men."

Lia said, "I don't think Mrs. Mason will see it that way when she hears about this."

Eugene wriggled out of Geoff's hold on his collar and backed away, looking unsettled for the first time. "Don't tell my ma that I was fighting. She says it's unchristian."

"There are certainly better ways to solve a problem," Geoff said.

"I'm not going to tell her a lie." Lia resisted the urge to brush the dirt off Eugene as well. His white-blond hair was liberally streaked with brown, and there was a suspicion of a bruise at the corner of his mouth. Without his bored look, he looked very young. They both did. She relented. "I won't tell her if she doesn't ask me. So long as she doesn't know about Henri's role in this, she probably won't ask."

"I'll tell her I tripped and fell," Eugene said. "That's true enough." He looked at Henri. "I won't tell her it was 'cause somebody tripped me."

"I did not—" Henri stopped when Geoff laid a hand on his shoulder.

"You boys can argue about this later, but if you want your escapade to remain undetected, you should separate immediately. The longer you stay here, the greater the chance you'll be found out."

Eugene nodded and left. Henri shifted his weight to his other foot as Lia brushed the dirt off his shirt. "I could've beaten him."

"Winning the battle does not always solve the problems that led you to fighting in the first place," Geoff said. "It's a better approach to resolve the issue in a way that doesn't lead to bloodshed."

His voice was unusually serious. Henri looked up at him and nodded.

"Let's get you back to Mrs. Whitlow's," Lia said. "If people see you and Eugene both looking a sight, they're going to put two and two together."

"I'll duck 'round and go along the back alley," Henri said. "I won't be seen. Trust me."

Lia watched Henri run off, and shook her head. "I thought I was getting through to him. He hasn't been acting impulsively lately. I thought maybe he'd learned to think first. Now he and Eugene are going to be enemies."

"Not necessarily," Geoff said. He fell into step with Lia and they continued down the street. This time, he kept his hands clasped behind his back. "A matter of fisticuffs doesn't mean they can't patch things up later. Sometimes, boys need to use up all their excess energy. If they can't find anything else to focus on, well, there's a reason boxing is such a popular sport."

"I will speak to Henri." Lia sighed. "Though I don't know what I'll say. He needs to learn to control his impulsive nature. He can't go around making enemies."

"He's a good lad at heart. If you could find an outlet for all his excess energy, that would help. I'll come by later. Perhaps we can find a solution together." Even as he spoke, however, he glanced back at the men standing outside the mercantile store.

"I was thinking... If Edgar doesn't want to be a teacher, maybe I could persuade the superintendent to extend my contract."

"Hmmm."

"Do you think I should ask him?" She wasn't sure why she persisted. Some stubborn urge to get him to look at her, perhaps. Wherever he was in his head, it wasn't here.

"It couldn't hurt to ask." His eyes were hooded, his voice somber. And he still wasn't looking at her.

On impulse, she said, "Won't you tell me where you are right now?"

He looked at her then, his eyebrows raised. "I am reasonably certain that I am standing in front of you."

She shook her head. "That's where your body is. The rest of you is somewhere else. Won't you tell me what's bothering you? I shared my secret with you. It wasn't as hard as I thought it would be."

They arrived in front of Mrs. Whitlow's place. "I have to go now." He started to turn away.

"Having second thoughts about our engagement?"

"That is the least of my worries right now." He took her hands in his and gave them a squeeze. "Go talk to Henri. I don't think he and Eugene are mortal enemies or anything of the kind. Just a couple of young men with an abundance of energy and too much time spent cooped up indoors."

She tilted her head up to study him. "And you're not going to tell me what's bothering you."

His silence was its own answer, but she pressed on, driven by some obscure compulsion to understand him. "I shared my secret with you. It didn't hurt."

He looked down the street. Some of the men who had been talking in front of the mercantile went past. They were arguing fiercely in tones too low for her to distinguish the words. Geoff hesitated. "I can't talk now. I'll come by this evening."

She watched him go. Again, she had that sense of a support being taken away from her.

If she gave him time, would he learn to trust her?

GEOFF LENGTHENED his stride as he walked away from Lia and her questions. Life would be so much simpler if he could have gotten engaged to a less perceptive woman. But it had felt natural and right, walking down the street with Lia. As if she had belonged there beside him.

The next few months would be tricky. She was quick to spot a lie, and he didn't want to lie to her anyway. The best approach would be to find a way to occupy her mind and distract her from wondering about him. He had a hunch that he was going to be busy enough on his own. He did not like the sound of those "changes" that Edgar had been hinting about.

Geoff found Bradford at the newspaper office talking to Murphy, the proprietor. Well, not talking exactly. Arguing would be a more accurate description. Murphy stood in the doorway of the newspaper office, his arms crossed. "I told you before, Bradford, you're not getting a look at this paper until I'm ready to distribute it to everyone who wants a copy."

"Murphy, old chap. Be reasonable. You've never cared before if I saw the paper before it was distributed to the greater public."

"You British think you deserve special treatment around these parts. It's about time you learned otherwise. Things are changing 'round these parts."

That was starting to sound like a refrain. This was the first time the man had turned secretive about the information he printed, and Geoff didn't like the change. He caught Bradford's eye and gave a hand sign. Bradford acknowledged this with a barely perceptible nod. He stepped closer to Murphy, claiming his full attention.

While Bradford occupied the man in an argument, Geoff slipped around to the back of the newspaper office. The back door was not locked. Quietly, Geoff looked around. The newly printed newspaper sheets were stacked on the counter, ready for distribution.

The headline screamed up at him. "Fifty-Four Forty or Fight!" Dread filled Geoff's stomach like a lead weight. He scanned the article that took up most of the front page. "...it is our manifest destiny to overspread the continent allotted by Providence for the free development of our yearly multiplying millions." President Polk claimed America was entitled to the Oregon Territory all the way up to above the 54th parallel, where the Russian Territory began. The British would fight rather than agree to that. This article might rouse people to take up arms.

He read further down the page, and his hand clenched into a fist. These people were planning to rewrite the provisional Organic laws that a loose gathering of settlers and trappers had decided on a few years before, when English and Americans had first started moving into the Oregon Territory. The natives and the newcomers had lived together more or less peaceably under these laws. Now, the Americans were proposing to move all the natives off to reservations on the other side of the Cascades and send their children to boarding schools to learn to be Americans. Even part-natives had to leave, so long as they had more than fifty percent native ancestry.

Lia had been right. One drop more than fifty percent, and your blood was all native. It didn't matter if someone like Henri hadn't been raised in the native culture. All that mattered was his ancestry. These changes would affect Henri and Lia both. He had to warn her, prepare her for what was coming. He returned the newspaper to the stack, neatly aligning the edges so it would look undisturbed, and slipped out the back door. He walked briskly around the corner to the front to join Bradford as he stood in the doorway arguing with Mr. Murphy. "All right! All right. Keep your newspaper, you stubborn old scoundrel."

"You'll read the news as soon as anyone else," Murphy jeered. "You English need to learn you're not above the rest of us."

"For shame, Bradford," Geoff admonished him with perfect gravity. "Badgering an honest tradesman like that. Your pardon, sir." He tipped his hat to Murphy, who gave him a grudging nod in return, and urged Bradford up the stairs to their room.

As soon as the door clicked shut behind him, Bradford turned to Geoff. "Well? Did you read what was so secret?"

"An open letter calling for Americans to defend this Territory against perfidious Albion." Geoff settled at the table by the window so he could look out. "Pure rabble rousing. Written by a man who'd never heard cannon fire himself, from the sound of it. They want to make America's border well above Vancouver Island." Geoff did not trouble to keep the discouragement out of his voice.

"They can't be serious?" Bradford sat up straight. "The British government would never allow that."

"There was a call for a meeting tonight, to choose government representatives for the Oregon Territory. Establishing military forts so that they don't need to rely on support from their Navy to defend their interests. They're even talking about rewriting the Organic laws."

"I doubt they will just give us all the details of what they're planning. We shall have to employ stealth." Bradford tilted his head, considering all the options. "It could get dangerous. It might be safer to spend the winter in Fort Vancouver after all."

"No. If they're fomenting trouble, we need to be on hand to find out what is going on. The government will need to know every detail we can provide." He shoved his hands into his pockets and stared out the window at the men and women passing by in the street. Innocent people, who'd never had to face the full force of the British Army, the deadliest fighting force in the world.

Despite the talk over dinner, the threat of war hadn't seemed quite real before. This peaceful settlement, where the only blood shed had been the result of a trivial fight between a couple of boys, had lulled him into thinking that actual violence was a distant possibility. It had been diverting even, helping Lia outwit Mrs. Mason. But the truth was, things were getting dark. "We have to gather all the information we can, and report back without anyone figuring out what we've been doing."

The grim look on Bradford's face mirrored how Geoff felt inside. His mission was more important than ever. And so was the need to keep it secret.

CHAPTER 10

When Lia entered the front room, Henri got up from the chair, facing her like a criminal awaiting sentencing. "I can't say I'm sorry I fought him. It wouldn't be the truth."

He stood with his shoulders back, spine straight, in an unconscious imitation of Geoff, but with a little tuft of hair sticking up on top of his head as a result of his tussle with Eugene. He looked so much like a little boy trying to act like a man that Lia couldn't scold him, much as she would have liked to. She diverted her exasperation into another outlet. His pack was lying on the table, flap open, its contents all jumbled about. She poked at it with one finger. "Don't you ever clean this out?"

Henri ignored this, his whole body tense. "I am sorry I upset you, Lia."

"Oh, Henri." For a moment, she gave in to the impulse to reach out and gather him close. Henri hugged her back for a moment, forgetting his dignity. He even permitted her to tousle his hair, ruffling it so that more tufts stood up. "I just worry about you. Did you really have to fight him?"

"He told me the government was planning to pass a law, saying all Indian children had to be sent away to special schools. He said it was because I was an ignorant savage. Just because I don't read so good."

"What? That's absurd." She didn't have a high opinion of governments at the best of times, but surely no one could pass a law like that. "And you can read. I know you can. So I don't understand why it's hard for you to finish a reading assignment. It takes practice, but you can do it."

He stepped back, smoothing down his hair. "It's not the reading that is the problem, but that reader—"The cat sat on a mat." I read things like that and then I remember that the window's open and I can smell fresh grass and maybe there's a hawk crying overhead, and I start thinking that I'd rather be outdoors instead of sitting there reading some boring old book."

Lia could sympathize. It was hard, sometimes, to focus on teaching a lesson when she could be out in the woods exploring. She tried to make a joke of it. "So I should make sure the window is closed before I start teaching? Or perhaps we should change your reading material. When I was little, before Maman died, Pa used to read the Bible to us at night. Maybe we could start doing that after you finish your lessons at night."

"I guess." He was still brooding. "I don't think that Eugene reads any better than I do. He always leans back and acts like he doesn't care when it comes time to read, but he's quick enough with the answers when it's solving math problems."

Lia considered this. "And if he did have a problem, he wouldn't want to admit it. He'd be too embarrassed. Mrs. Mason is always bragging about what a great scholar her brother Edgar is. Oh, the poor boy."

"I don't feel sorry for him." Then he hesitated. "Maybe I am too stupid to learn. The other boys seem to pick it up quick enough. Not Eugene, but Clarence and the others. When one of the younger boys get something wrong, they make fun of him. I don't want them making fun of me."

Lord, please help me find the right words. "Well," she said finally, "there's one thing I know. If you can't see the whole road, you can at least take the first step and trust the Lord to guide you to the next step. I bet you can learn just fine if you have someone to help you when you get stuck. We can help you."

"We?"

"I meant to say I." She had been unconsciously thinking of Geoff helping her. She was growing too accustomed to him being on hand when she needed him. It might not be wise to get too attached to the man, no matter how natural it felt. He had gone on at some length about how he must leave in the spring, even though he had given no reason why he must go. He had told her very little about himself. It was time to start getting answers.

She said, "Tonight, let's take turns reading from the Bible. Do you want to try?"

Henri shrugged. "I guess."

It was not the most enthusiastic response, but Lia would take it. And pray that the Lord would guide her to the next step.

WHEN GEOFF CAME IN, Lia and Henri were seated in chairs in front of the fireplace, where a fire was crackling merrily. Henri was using a piece of chalk to scrawl something on his slate and Lia was leaning over to watch his progress.

Lia looked up and blinked. "I hadn't realized it was growing dark outside. We've been practicing spelling."

Henri asked, "Did you know that adding an 'e' at the end of the word changes how you pronounce the vowel before it? It's true! You take the word 'hop.'" Henri scrawled it on the slate. "Now, if you add an 'e' at the end, you pronounce it 'hope' instead. You see?"

"You're going to be a teacher yourself, next."

"Never!" Henri put down the slate hastily. "Once my pa gets back, I'm going to become a trader. Travel all over the place."

"Only if your pa agrees," Lia said.

Geoff lit the lamp on the side table and settled into a chair, stretching his legs out. The light cast a circle of warmth across the room, lightening the shadows and making the rough homemade furniture look cozy. A smudge of chalk dust covered the freckles across Lia's nose. Another smudge accented the curve of her cheekbone. It was distracting. Geoff wanted to trace it with his finger. He asked, "When is your brother due back?"

She shrugged. "I'm not really sure. He said he'd be back come spring, but Pierre was never good about keeping to a schedule."

"Well, the winds don't always blow when you want them to," Henri said, sounding defensive.

"It's not just the winds," Lia said wryly. She turned to Geoff. "Pierre is, well, I guess I'd call him 'easily distracted.' He's always going off on tangents. In a way, that's a good thing. He spends a lot of time exploring new trading ports. It makes him a successful trader. He's done very well with his voyages. He's going to set up a trading store when he gets back."

"Ah." A tension he hadn't been aware of eased a bit. Lia

would have a place to stay when he left. Her family would be reunited. She was going to be just fine without him. She didn't need him. That was a good thing. He should be glad. He *was* glad.

"Do you have any brothers?" Henri asked.

"No," Geoff said. "No sisters either. Just me, rattling around in a drafty old house with my father."

"That sounds lonely," Lia said softly.

He shrugged. "I was sent to school when I was still a young boy, and then I went into the army. I've spent most of my life surrounded by other people."

"Being in a crowd is not the same thing as not being lonely."

Impatient with this discussion, Henri picked up his Bible and began to leaf through it. "Are you ready to start the reading?" To Geoff, he added, "Did you bring your Bible?"

"No, it's back at my lodging. Should I have?"

"We're going to read a chapter from the Bible. Well, Lia's going to read out loud, and I'm going to follow along."

"I'm going to start," Lia said. "You're going do some of the reading too."

Geoff remembered her talking about Henri's difficulty reading. "If you're going to be doing this on a regular basis, I will bring my Bible along next time. We can take turns." Lia smiled at him before opening her Bible. The warmth of her smile was almost a tangible thing, like the fire crackling in the hearth.

A vague emotion that had been lurking at the back of his mind surfaced. A sense of belonging. This was what it felt like to be part of a family. Geoff leaned back in his chair, watching Lia and listening to the sound of her voice. Lia.

She was the source of his contentment. Just walking into a room and seeing her there made him feel as if he had just opened the door to his home after long wandering. He was home.

He was warmed by her presence more than any fire. It was a relief for the moment not to play the spy, simply to be himself.

Henri opened his Bible and was following along, one finger tracing the words as Lia read them aloud. Then Lia stopped and nodded to Henri. Haltingly, he began to read the next section. Geoff's gaze lingered on Lia's dark head as she sat there listening. "Excellent!" Lia said. She lifted her Bible and extended it to Geoff. "I think it is your turn."

He was part of the family, just for this evening. If he weren't bound to his duty, he could have a life like this. He could picture spending his summers traveling through this region with Lia, then spending the winters in some snug little cabin while the snow piled up outdoors. So long as the two of them were together, everything would be right with the world.

It was a fantasy, of course. It could never happen. Bradford was right: he needed to break off this engagement as soon as it was safe to travel through the mountains. But he didn't have to leave just yet. He could still savor this time with Lia.

Henri took over reading again. He read slowly, sounding out the unfamiliar words. Lia helped him when he faltered, but for the most part she sat there listening, her eyes on the boy. After a little while, Henri stopped and Lia continued the reading. Mrs. Whitlow slipped in with her knitting and took a chair in the corner.

Lia came to the end of the chapter, and put down her

Bible. Henri was sitting back, ineffectively hiding an enormous yawn. "Bedtime for you, young man."

"I s'pose."

"This was an excellent start. I think if we make this a regular routine, you'll get better at reading and it won't take so much concentration."

"Maybe. I don't think it's going to make that Eugene like me any better."

"Or his mother." Lia sighed. "We need to find a way to convince them that you belong here in school. If we could put on an exhibition, like they used to do at the end of term at my old school, you could stand up and *prove* how much you've learned in this school. That would show them. You could read out loud from the Bible."

Henri looked doubtful. "The school term is going to end at Christmas, isn't it? I'm not sure that's enough time. I mean, I'm not... I'm not quite ready."

Mrs. Whitlow spoke up. "That reminds me. The superintendent came by this afternoon. He told me he'd like to speak with you after church tomorrow."

"Oh, no. What if he decided that our getting engaged wasn't good enough? Maybe he wants me to stop being the schoolteacher right away."

Geoff said, "You won't have to face him alone. I'll be there with you." He saw her shoulders relax. His presence made a difference to her. That pleased him far more than it should have.

Mrs. Whitlow said, "He didn't sound as if he were upset. It's probably nothing serious." She got to her feet. "It's getting late. I'll say good night." Her gaze flicked to Geoff and back to Lia. "I'll leave you to escort your young man to the door." Henri followed the older woman out of the room, still yawning.

"She's not subtle," Geoff said. "But I'm glad to have a chance to talk to you in private."

Lia laid the Bible carefully down on the side table. "That sounds serious."

Quickly, Geoff told her what he had learned about the proposed changes regarding the native people in the Oregon Territory. Lia listened intently, her light gray eyes fixed on him. When he finished, she said quietly, "This is going to change everything for Henri. I don't know what to do."

Geoff leaned forward. His hand covered hers and he gave it a squeeze. "I'll help all I can. But it may be just as well if he becomes a trader. Not that that will help all the other natives."

"I was thinking of Henri's uncle. He's lived here all his life. I can't imagine what it would do to him to move off his land."

"I don't see a way to stop the Americans passing these laws. Well, unless the British take over the Territory. I can't see that happening without a fight."

"And anyway, the British government isn't any better." She sounded scornful. "My father worked for the Hudson Bay Company for years. But when he passed, the British kicked Henri and me out of the cabin we were living in. It didn't matter to them that we had nowhere to go. No compassion." She sat there, cheeks flushed, clearly still resenting the slight.

Geoff suddenly realized he was holding her hand. He let it go. "I hadn't realized you were so anti-British."

She started to reach out her hand to him, but he stood up and she let her hand drop. "I'm not against British people. It's the British government that I don't approve of. Not that I am in favor of governments as a whole, really. They seem to spend most of the time telling people what to do and not letting people get on with their own lives. But I don't think the Americans would have kicked us out, seeing we had no place to go."

"I'm sorry." The words felt inadequate, but they had to be said. He was sorry for more than the hardship she had faced. He was a fool to think that she would ever want to spend a lifetime with him. It was just as well he hadn't asked her to consider making their engagement more than a business arrangement. Clearly, there was no way she would want to be the wife of a man who worked for the British government.

And he didn't know what he would do if he left. He tried to picture himself working behind a counter, or teaching at a school, and he couldn't do it. No. It was safest to stick to what he knew, and that was the Army. "I should say good night."

Lia made no move to get up. She tilted her head up to meet his gaze. "I was thinking. You know so much about me. My mother, Henri's problems at school, what Pierre is like. I've told you things I've never told anyone who wasn't family. But I don't know anything about your background. Other than the fact that you come from Canterbury and don't have any brothers or sisters. You never talk about your past. Why did you promise to go back to Montreal in spring? Are you going to go back to England when you finish writing your book? Who are you, Geoffrey Montgomery?"

"You want to know all of that tonight?" He stretched. *Act relaxed. Like a man with nothing to hide.* If he were free, he could tell her what was in his heart. But he had no choice.

She got to her feet. "I'd settle for knowing what you're thinking. What is going through your mind right now?"

I want your face to be the first thing I see when I wake up and the last thing I see before I close my eyes. "I'm thinking it is getting late. I should be going." He bowed and made his escape.

She wanted to understand him. He only wished she could. He could not afford to let her know too much about what led him to the Oregon Territory. She was too quick, too perceptive. But he did not know how he was going to keep her from finding out the truth about him without rousing suspicion.

BRADFORD WAS WRITING in his notebook when Geoff returned to their room. He looked up as Geoff entered. "All well?"

Geoff nodded. "I'll be escorting her to church tomorrow."

"Excellent. The townspeople will get used to seeing you with her. They'll start to see you as belonging here. Looks like you got engaged just in time. If you can play the part of the besotted fiancé who wants nothing better than to please his lady love, they'll be bound to see you as aligned with the American interests."

"I don't know how to act besotted. It sounds ridiculous. I will just act friendly."

"You might be able to lead the school superintendent to confide in you. His brother-in-law knows a lot about what's going on. He's got to be getting that information from someone. You could try chatting with him."

"Chatting." Geoff could not face the prospect with any enthusiasm. At least if he had Lia with him, it might not be so bad. Except that he must be careful not to start to believe the lie that he belonged here.

"The people of the town can't suspect why we're asking

questions. It would only inflame the situation. You want everyone in town to be convinced that you are head over heels in love with the girl. Including her. You must convince her of your affection."

"You were the one who was concerned that I was getting too involved with her."

"That was before," Bradford snapped. "This is too important to worry about hurting her feelings. Use your charm, man. Be attentive. Compliment her."

"She is sharp enough to suspect something if I pour on the endearments. But I'll escort Lia to church tomorrow," Geoff said. *And pray that I can find a way to be around her without getting in too deep.*

AT THE CHURCH service the next day, Reverend Willett rose to give the sermon. He spoke on the need to accept your neighbor, as the Lord has accepted you.

Lia felt the words like red-hot arrows directed straight at her. Mrs. Mason sat two rows ahead of her, as usual. Going into church that morning, she had directed a narrow-eyed gaze at Lia that seemed almost like an attack. Lia's first impulse had been to glare back, but thinking of the verse, she restrained herself.

After the last hymn had been sung, Geoff escorted her out the door. Outside, the whole congregation had divided into small groups. Lia craned her head. "Can you see the superintendent?"

With his height, Geoff had no trouble locating him. "He's over there, talking to Mr. Lovejoy. Looks like a fairly serious discussion. Why don't you take this opportunity to chat with his wife?"

"I don't think she wants to talk to me," Lia said gloomily. "Anyway, I know what she'd say."

"People can surprise you. She might listen."

"The superintendent listens to me. His wife does not. I do not understand how those two ever got married."

"The Lord works in mysterious ways," Geoff said.

Lia looked up at him, squinting against the sunlight. Speaking of mysteries... Last night, he had seemed so at ease sitting with her and Henri. His body language suggested that he might have come to care for her. But when he had said good night, his words had been formal and distant. "Did you ever think of getting married? Really married, I mean, not just a temporary engagement." Surprised at her own boldness, she felt as if she were testing the ice on a pond to see if it was strong enough to support her without breaking.

"The army is no life for a married man. It's a hard life."

Well. That didn't exactly answer her question. "Trapping's a hard life, but Maman never wanted to stay back at a trading post while Pa was out in the mountains. She wanted to be with him."

"In the army, usually a man's wife stays at home with the children. She can go years at a time without seeing her husband or even hearing from him. Or the couple goes off from post to post while raising a family, exposing their children to danger and disease. I've seen the strain it puts on the marriage. Many officers prefer to remain single until they resign their commission. It's not too horribly lonely. One develops a sense of camaraderie with one's fellow officers."

Was he trying to warn her off, keep her from getting too attached? She probed further. "What led you to join the army in the first place? Was it because you thought it would be exciting?"

Geoff shook his head, smiling ruefully. "I didn't really know what life in the army would be like. I knew it would involve seeing something other than Canterbury, and at that point in my life that was my whole ambition." He smiled, just a little curve of one corner of his mouth. "I remember the day I left home to go to school. My father said goodbye and went back to the obscure Greek text he was translating. Cook dabbed her eyes with a handkerchief and snuck me a packet of pastries for the trip. I climbed into the coach and went off to live with strangers. It never felt like home, when I went back for holiday visits. I didn't belong there any longer after my mother died."

He shut his mouth, looking as if he said more than he'd intended. She didn't like prying, but she was on fire with curiosity to know more about this man, to understand him. She was finally getting some answers, but instead of satisfying her curiosity, it made her want to know more. "Your father sounds like a hard man. Distant. I suppose you must have bonded with Bradford while in the army. He became like a brother to you."

"Bradford and I? We were thrown together by our superiors."

"But when you inherited your fortune, you chose to go off on an expedition with him. Why would you do that if you weren't friends?"

Geoff looked away, shifting his weight to his other foot. "Well, sometimes a man needs a change. Oh, look. The superintendent is talking to Mr. Pettygrove now. I wanted to speak to him about the new government they're forming up. For my book. Go talk to Mrs. Mason. This is neutral ground. She won't attack."

"I don't know if it would help. I don't think there's

anything I can do that will make that woman like me. If I could just be sure she would stop trying to replace me with her brother, that would be enough."

"If you can get her on your side, it might help smooth out your talk with the superintendent."

"I don't know how I let you talk me into these things," Lia muttered. But she found herself going over to where Mrs. Mason stood talking to Eugene. Eugene was looking embarrassed; he nodded politely at Lia but took her arrival as an excuse to slip away. Mrs. Mason greeted Lia with a tight-lipped stretching of her mouth into what might possibly be considered a smile, barely. She held herself erect, as if her spine were an iron rod, shoulders rigidly immobile. "Miss Griggs."

That was all she had to say, apparently. It was going to be Lia's responsibility to get the conversation going. She cast about in her mind for some common ground between them. Eugene. They both wanted him to succeed at school.

"As a teacher, I want to see all my students excel. I was wondering if it would help if I were to give Eugene a little extra help after school with his reading."

Mrs. Mason's shoulders became, if possible, more rigid. "Eugene is perfectly capable of learning his lessons without your kind assistance."

"Not from what I've seen." The superintendent had joined them. Geoff wandered over, as if idly, to stand by Lia's side. The superintendent nodded toward Geoff. "This gentleman tells me you're not planning on a wedding right away. Given that, I was hoping you might consider staying on until the end of the school year. My wife's brother has told us that he is going to return back east."

Maybe her words to Edgar had had an effect after all. It

was for the best. Edgar was not cut out for life on the frontier. He would do better to find a place where he could be happy. And she could keep Henri safely in school for the whole year. "Then yes, I could stay on as a teacher until spring."

Spring, when Pierre would come home to set up his trading store and she would have a position working with him there. She would have a home of her own, and people she loved to share it with.

Spring, when Geoff would leave.

"Then you could put on that exhibition," Geoff put in. He told Mr. Mason, "Miss Griggs used to hold an exhibition at the end of the school year when she taught at her old school. It gave the students a chance to show what they'd learned that year. I'm sure Eugene would be glad to join in."

Mrs. Mason froze, tense as an animal in a trap. Her eyes flickered to Eugene and back so quickly that Lia almost missed it. For a moment, the matron's guard was down. Fear, indecision, and fury. Clearly, the woman knew that Eugene was having trouble reading. The last thing she wanted was for the rest of the town to see his difficulties.

Lia felt an obscure impulse to help her out. "Perhaps Eugene could demonstrate his mathematical abilities? I was going to ask Henri to do a Bible reading." *That* would show them he was neither a heathen nor a savage.

Mr. Mason said, "Eugene should do a reading from the Bible too. He needs to spend more time reading it. It might help him stay out of trouble. You'll hardly credit it, Miss Griggs, but Eugene showed up for dinner yesterday with his clothes torn and his face all dirty. Been climbing trees, he said. Falling out of them too, by the look of it."

Obviously, the superintendent didn't know of Eugene's

difficulties. Lia said, "I can work with Eugene on his reading."

"That's kind of you, but I should warn you my boy's pretty lazy. Never wants to open a book. I wouldn't want him to make us look bad in front of the townsfolk. They'd expect my son to uphold my standards for literacy."

Mrs. Mason took her husband's arm. "Let's not monopolize these people, my dear." She all but hauled her husband away.

Henri came up to them. "I thought you'd never stop talking to her. Are you ready to go? Mrs. Whitlow was going to make ham sandwiches for lunch."

Behind him, Mrs. Whitlow said, "Leave them be, Henri." To Lia, she said, "This young man is going to accompany me while I visit with Mrs. Graham on the way home."

"Oh, I get it," Henri said sagely. "They want to be alone, 'cause they're courtin'."

Lia could feel how red her cheeks were turning. She dared not look at Geoff. His voice was gravely courteous, man to man, when he replied. "I'll make sure she gets home safely." He extended his arm to Lia. "Shall we?"

Lia kept the pace slow as Geoff escorted her back to Mrs. Whitlow's. Her plan to find out more about him was not an unqualified success. He would give information about his distant past readily enough, but any talk of what had led him here shut him up right away. Still, she felt she could get him to open up to her if she only knew the right way to go about it. He was as elusive as a fish trying to evade the net, but if this was a game they were playing, it was one she wanted to win. But perhaps she should try an indirect approach.

"Is your father still alive?"

"No. He died while I was posted to India. It was too far to return for the funeral. His man of business settled his affairs for me. I haven't been back to England since."

"Don't you ever want to go home?"

"I've been on the road for so long, I don't think of England as home."

"You never settled anywhere? Always on the road?" Almost like the life of a trapper, spending most of the time traveling.

He cast her a sidelong glance. "That's part of army life. You get used to it." He added quickly, "That was before I inherited my uncle's wealth and sold my commission, of course."

"Do you miss army life?"

"No," he said, sounding as if he were surprised by the admission. "Even though life outside the army is... complicated. Duty is simple. My father expected a dutiful son, the Army expects a dutiful officer. Actually, I think I stayed too long. I could've resigned my commission earlier. I stayed because... it was what I knew. It was safe." He paused, then said in a lighter tone, "Sometimes, I think I came out here so I could have a chance to prove myself. I grew up listening to my old nurse telling me of the Morte d'Arthur, don't you know, and hearing tales of the Knights of the Round Table doing great deeds. It's hard to prove yourself doing great deeds when you're stuck behind a desk reading an endless series of reports on the storage conditions of tinned beef."

He was going back into that Silly Englishman act that he'd put on for her when they first met at Tongue Point. There were some topics he had marked off with a tall picket fence, like the fence around Fort Vancouver that was supposed to keep off "savages" and prowling wildcats. Well, he had as much right to privacy as anyone else. All the same, it was frustrating. She would get so close to understanding him, forming a connection with him, and then he would veer off into something inconsequential. Didn't he trust her?

He opened the front door and stood aside while she entered. He made no move to follow her, so she turned around. She was tired of trying to pry answers out of the man, as if he were the enemy. It was time for a direct appeal. "You can come in for a moment. I'm sure Mrs. Whitlow wouldn't mind. After all, we are engaged."

He stepped over the threshold and shut the door behind him, but he looked uneasy. He was close beside her now, and looking up, she was struck again by the size of the man, his strength. He was a bulwark against the cold world. If only he would open the door and let her into his life.

"I should go. Bradford said something about working on the book today."

"Wait!" She stretched out her hand and he turned back to her. "Don't leave just yet. Give me something. A secret." She lowered her voice. "Something you wouldn't want to share with anyone else in the world."

He looked at her for a moment. Then he reached out his hand, lifting her chin with one finger. Slowly, giving her every opportunity to back away, he leaned down.

The touch of his lips against hers was so light it would have felt like a dream, except for the delicate tendrils of sensation that unfolded inside her, extending through every part of her body. His skin was warm, the callouses on his palm rough, and he cradled her face in his large hands as if she were as fragile as a soap bubble. All that power, all that strength, gentled into a tenderness that took her breath away. He straightened up, still without speaking, and turned away. The door shut behind him, a quiet *click*.

She went to the window. He was walking away from her, his step never faltering as he strode down the street. "Oh, you fool man," she said fondly to his retreating figure. "If you think that is going to stop me asking questions, you are in for a surprise."

CHAPTER 11

Lia's breath formed a white cloud in front of her as she walked to church with Henri and Mrs. Whitlow. Sullen gray December clouds hung low overhead, promising snow.

Henri tucked his gloved hands under his armpits. "You both walk too slow," he complained. "I'm going to run ahead and get warmed up."

He was off before Lia had time to respond.

Mrs. Whitlow sighed. "Wish I had half that much energy. Where's that young man of yours today?"

He's not my young man. She couldn't tell Mrs. Whitlow that their engagement was temporary. She had never even told Henri. She hadn't wanted him to feel it was his fault that she was going to such lengths. Instead, she told Mrs. Whitlow, "He's meeting us at church. He had to go somewhere with his friend this morning."

"There's something about your young man that doesn't seem right," Mrs. Whitlow told Lia.

"He's a fish out of water. He's a long way from home." It

was odd how she could find excuses for his behavior but still feel annoyed by it. Geoff had been spending more and more time with Bradford over the past few weeks. He still came to the Bible readings when he could, but invariably, as soon as Henri got up to go to bed, Geoff promptly said good night and left. She could not get a moment's conversation with him alone.

Whatever was going on in Geoff's head, he did care for her. Every instinct she possessed told her that. Their engagement could become real, if she could persuade him to reveal what he was hiding. At the moment, that didn't seem likely. It had begun as a game, but it had evolved into something more serious as the weeks passed.

Maybe she should let him go, once spring came. Let him disappear back east without knowing if she would ever see him again. But that felt wrong. The Lord had sent Geoff into her life for more than a convenient temporary engagement. When he wasn't around, it felt as if part of her were missing. Even if he was evasive and all kinds of stubborn, she missed him.

School was frustrating as well. Mrs. Mason refused to let Eugene stay late after school; she needed him at home for a variety of reasons, each excuse more flimsy than the last. The woman was evidently trying to help Eugene with his reading on her own. Lia could just imagine how well that would work, with the superintendent, skeptical and impatient, looking over Eugene's shoulder and commenting on his progress. Lia tried to speak to Mrs. Mason directly, but the woman avoided her.

On her way home from school one day, Lia glimpsed Mrs. Mason on the sidewalk, talking to Reverend Willett. She speeded up, hoping to finally catch the woman. Unfortunately, Mrs. Mason looked up and spotted her. She must have made some excuse to the reverend, because she turned away and disappeared around a corner with a flutter of skirts.

Reverend Willett's mild brown eyes twinkled. "You are clearly a fearsome woman, Miss Griggs, to have such an effect."

Lia frowned. She was not going to chase the woman down the street like a stray dog. "I don't know what I did to make that woman dislike me so. I took her brother's place as teacher, but it's not as if he even wanted the position."

Reverend Willett's expression grew serious. "People are out here thousands of miles from everything they're used to, trying to build a civilization where there's nothing but trees and mud. Put a weak person in a situation like that, and she's going to cling to what's safe and familiar, and she's going to cling to it with both hands."

"I wouldn't have called Mrs. Mason weak," Lia said.

"Her most of all," the reverend said. "She's afraid, you see. Every time a wolf howls off in the distance, she wants to go hide. And that makes her angry, so she fights back all the harder, clinging on to everything she has. And she's afraid of letting her son down, not doing the best for him."

"I offered to help her son to read. I suppose she saw that as some kind of slight."

"It's not your fault if she did. You cannot help someone who won't let you."

"I know." Lia sighed. She looked up to find the reverend watching her. "I was just thinking of Mr. Montgomery," she explained. "He's very secretive. If we're engaged, even newly engaged," *even temporarily*, she almost said, "shouldn't he confide in me?"

"Ah, Mr. Montgomery. A man with many secrets, I

suspect. I doubt he would have asked you to marry him if he didn't trust you. Give him time."

"We're running out of time," she said, and instantly wished she hadn't spoken.

The reverend looked at her with his innocent, round face and those shrewd eyes that always gave her the feeling he saw more than he would say. "If you share a secret with me, it will go no further."

She did not confide in strangers, but there was something about this little man that made her trust him instinctively. She found herself telling him about the whole engagement business, about Geoff and his attempt to make it right. "But it was my fault that we had to get engaged," she finished up. "*I* kissed *him*." Because she had felt sorry for him. Because she wanted to ease his pain. And—if she were being completely honest—because she had finally found a man that she wanted to kiss.

The reverend listened to her in silence until her words petered out. "My impression of your fiancé is that he's a man stuck carrying a heavy burden. I don't know what it is, but I can see how heavily it weighs on him."

"Yes," Lia said. "That's the feeling I get from him too." How could she understand him when he hugged his secrets so close? It irritated her, like an itch she could not scratch. Part of the jigsaw puzzle was missing, and she would not rest content until she knew. No matter how much she felt at home with him. How much she wondered what it would be like to kiss him again. If he couldn't trust her with his secrets, then she wasn't sure they could have any kind of future together. And she wanted one. She parted company with the reverend and continued on her way home in a pensive mood. At least things were going well with Henri.

Once he had overcome his fear of looking stupid, Henri

became interested in the nightly readings. He especially enjoyed the story of Daniel and the lions, as well as the psalms. Reading the Bible every evening was beginning to have an effect. Henri no longer had to follow along with one finger tracing the words as she read. He took his turn reading without hesitation. It warmed Lia's heart to hear him read from the scriptures each night, stumbling less and less as the weeks went by.

He was doing better in school, progressing through the lessons with ease. Occasionally, Lia would help him out with sounding out a difficult word. But once she had pointed him in the right direction, Henri could complete the work without further instruction.

Homework was becoming almost too easy. Henri had begun to grow restless. Lia remembered Geoff's suggestion that she give Henri something to focus on. She asked him to teach her the Kalapuyan dialect he had learned from his mother. It worked. Henri clearly liked being the one telling her what to do for once. It bolstered his self-confidence, which in turn fed his appetite to learn.

Lia wasn't the only one who noticed Henri's improvement. Eugene had made a few half-hearted jokes at first, but as the weeks went by he grew thoughtful. One afternoon, he lingered after class.

"Is there something I can help you with?" Lia had asked.

Eugene flung down his reader on her desk. "This book is too hard to read. It's old, and all faded. I can't make out the words."

"I think we have a spare in the cupboard." Lia fetched it. She watched the boy open the book and leaf through the pages. "If you like," she said, greatly daring, "I could ask your parents if you could stay late after school to work on the lessons." Not that she'd had much success with that before. But with the exhibition getting closer, perhaps Mrs. Mason might be more amenable to a little help.

"I don't think Ma would like it if I stayed late. She wants me to come straight home after school."

"Well, you could stay in for a few minutes at lunchtime every day."

Eugene was silent for a moment longer. "You're going to be asking everyone in class to stand up and show off at this exhibition of yours?"

"It's your exhibition as well. I'm going to ask all the students to demonstrate something they've learned. You have learned some things this year, Eugene. Your mathematical skills are quite impressive. It's just reading that is an extra challenge to you."

Eugene stuffed the new reader into his satchel. "I s'pose I could stay in at lunch. If Henri is going to stand up and read, I want to do it too."

"Of course." If competition was what it took to get Eugene to agree, she wouldn't argue. She was relieved that he was willing to work with her at all.

The lunchtime sessions were rocky at first. Eugene had had a late start, and he struggled, but at least he was making progress. He was clearly uncomfortable reading, but he was trying. Lia decided that she would assign a very short psalm for him to read. She wanted him to look as good as the others, and time was growing short.

EDGAR LEFT, sailing downriver to head back east by ship. In winter, there weren't many ships crossing the dangerous bar where the Columbia River met the Pacific Ocean, but there were some. It was the only way to head back east at this time of year. Storms blew in from the coast, one after another, with barely a day of blue sky in between the gray cloud cover. The near-constant rain they had in Oregon City was falling as snow in the mountain passes. Mount Hood was covered in snow.

Christmas came, and the biting cold settled in. The wind whistling down the Columbia River gorge brought a bite of cold from the high desert beyond the Cascade Mountains.

One frigid Saturday early in the New Year, snow began to fall, first gently, then more thickly. When Lia woke up the next morning, the entire town lay blanketed under six inches of pristine white, a rare heavy snowfall. Snow crunched under their boots as Geoff escorted Lia to church. After church, Lia was surprised and pleased to find several of her students' parents came up and spoke with her quite happily about their child's progress. Geoff stood by her side, hands clasped behind his back. Lia kept an eye on Henri as she chatted. He and Eugene had decided to use the snow to build forts. Once these were large enough to hide behind, the boys engaged in a brief but enthusiastic snowball fight.

That seemed to clear the air between them, in some mysterious male fashion. Lia watched them run off together in perfect amity, and shook her head. "They pelted each other with snowballs and somehow that made them friends? That makes no sense."

"Perfectly logical," Geoff replied. He offered her his arm. "Since your nephew has deserted you, let me escort you home."

Lia accepted gladly. Mrs. Whitlow had gone off to visit with the doctor's wife, who was expecting a baby. This was a chance to talk to Geoff alone. Once they'd moved out of earshot from the townsfolk, she asked straight out, "Why can't you ever answer a simple question about why you left the army? Or what you're going to do in Montreal that's so important?"

"You'll know all my secrets in time," he said equably. "Why rush? Let's enjoy the moment."

"I just want to understand you better." He said he was coming back, but he never would commit to anything beyond that. If the problem wasn't that he didn't care, then what was holding him back? That was the mystery she needed to solve, and she had the feeling that there wasn't much time left. Spring wasn't that far away, hard though it was to believe when there was snow underfoot and a cold wind blew down the street.

"There's not much to tell." He leaned over, drawing her shawl closer around her shoulders. He sniffed. "Lavender. I like it." His breath was warm on her cheek.

She jumped and took a step back. She could feel the hot rush of blood to her cheeks, but she wasn't sure if she was embarrassed or pleased. He was trying to distract her, she knew. But it was not exactly... unpleasant. She could not stop herself from smiling.

"You're full of tricks when you want to distract me. What are you trying to hide?"

"Speaking of trying to hide—are you going to tell Mr. Mason about your heritage?

The thought of Mr. Mason was like a bucket of cold water in her face. She sobered immediately. "If he asks me, I'll tell the truth."

"And if he doesn't ask? He keeps going on about the wonderful job you're doing. What if he wants to extend your contract for next year? How long will you keep hiding who you are?"

"There's something ironic about *you* giving *me* a lecture on hiding who you are."

"I am honest about the things that matter." He tucked a loose strand of hair behind her ear. His hand lingered on the side of her face for a moment, then he let it fall. "It changes you, pretending to be something you're not. The longer you try to pass as one of the townsfolk, the more effect it will have on you. I don't want to see you change. I rather like you the way you are."

She laid her hand on his sleeve. "I only want you to tell me more about yourself. Why all the secrecy?"

"Let's just enjoy the time we have together, shall we?" He tucked her hand into the crook of his elbow, his grip warm and firm. "I promise you, you will know everything about me in time."

"Is there something with Bradford, some scheme that he's involved with? You don't have to be tied at the hip forever, do you? Let him go his own way and we'll go ours."

"We can talk about the future when I come back. If you still want to."

"There it is again! Always qualifying things. Nothing is ever black and white with you."

"That's not how life works. There is always going to be a qualifier."

"Not with me."

For some reason, his smile looked almost sad. "Tell me that when I come back next year."

She stopped walking and glared up at him. He darted in and dropped a light kiss on her lips. She stepped back. "You can't get on my good side that way."

"It seemed like a good idea."

"It won't work."

"The superintendent obviously approves of you now. If you told him the truth, you'd feel better."

"I feel fine," Lia said repressively. "Or I would, if you could answer a simple question now and then."

She would have gone on, but just then Bradford came out of the saloon. He beamed at them both, his face flushed. "You two discussing that fancy show you're going to put on?"

"We could always use help," Geoff said.

"No, no, I would only get in the way. You've got it all sorted out. Excellent! Glad we could help before we leave. Montgomery, old chap, a word in your shell-like ear, old boy."

Lia watched Geoff walk off with Bradford and felt cold in a way that was not caused by the wind. She had come to depend on Geoff, not just his help with the exhibition but his presence. He was a bulwark she could lean against when the storms blew. The one man in all the world who made her feel as if she had found her place every time he walked in the door.

And he was going to leave her.

AFTER THAT LAST SNOWFALL, winter subsided. The days started to grow longer, and occasionally it stopped raining long enough for the sun to come out. Geoff and Bradford worked to gather all the information they could in the time they had left. Their efforts were hampered by the attitude of the townsfolk toward the British and their government's policies. Bradford complained that he could hardly walk down the street without men glaring at him. Geoff was in a better position, thanks to his relationship with Lia, but even he occasionally found himself on the receiving end of darkly suspicious looks. The near constant rain mirrored the town's mood, getting on everyone's nerves.

The chief factor at Fort Vancouver moved to Oregon City. The distance was a mere thirty miles, but the symbolic effect of the move was much more significant. Mr. McLoughlin had spent decades of his life working for British interests, and now he was throwing his lot in with the Americans. Bradford was indignant. "I can't believe the man would abandon his country."

"I gather he feels that his country has abandoned him."

Bradford eyed him. Geoff shook his head. "No, I am not thinking of following his lead. I'm going to complete this mission."

"You do seem rather... preoccupied with your little schoolteacher."

"That was my duty, you said."

"Yes, well, there are limits, you know."

"I know," Geoff said heavily. He wanted nothing more than to tell Lia everything. But he had sworn to do his duty. No matter the cost to him.

The unfriendliness toward the British wasn't helped when one of Her Majesty's ships sailed up the Columbia to Fort Vancouver. The *Modeste* was not the largest warship in the British Navy, but it was the largest one that the residents of Oregon Territory had ever seen. Many of the Americans seemed to take its appearance as the next thing to an open declaration of war. Geoff and Bradford were hard put to explain it away as a peaceful excursion. Matters were eased when the men of the *Modeste* put on a couple of plays and hosted a ball. The sight of grown men playing women's parts in the play was evidently amusing enough to lessen the threat from their guns.

For the ball, Geoff obtained some gauzy silk material from the stores at Fort Vancouver, enough for a gown, and some more hair ribbons for Lia. "That's going to make for an unusual entry in the accounts," Bradford observed when he brought it into their room one evening.

"It's important to keep up appearances," Geoff said stubbornly. Lia would look beautiful even if she came to the ball dressed in that funny dress she'd worn the first day in Oregon City, but he wasn't sure she knew that. He wanted her to *feel* beautiful. If that was all he could give her, he could at least make her feel as if she belonged. He just wished she didn't feel that she had to pretend half of her parentage did not exist.

"You're not... letting the woman get too attached, or anything of that sort, right?" Bradford seemed to be taking a great interest in polishing his boots. "Because, of course, there's no way to have that end happily."

"I know we cannot stay," Geoff said. "I have made it clear to Lia that I am going to leave. She knows that."

"So you've broken the engagement?"

"Not just yet," Geoff said. "The exhibition is coming up. She'll need my help." Bradford was frowning. Geoff added, a bit desperately, "It'll look odd if I end things too suddenly."

Bradford sighed. "Just so long as you've made your intentions clear, Lieutenant. You must end this relationship with the woman soon."

The trouble was that he did not want to end it. He wanted to give this woman the most fundamental truth he had, that he loved her and wanted to spend the rest of his life with her. But even that would be telling a lie, for the truth was that when spring came, he was going to have to leave her. He would have to go back to Montreal with Bradford and deliver his report. They would have to be on hand to answer any questions that their supervisors might have. There was the real possibility that this potential conflict, a bonfire already laid and waiting for a spark, would flare up into real war.

He needed to see her every day and talk to her. Hold her hand as he walked her home. Little things, but he depended on them. He had not realized how alone he had been before he met her. The thought of leaving her was unbearable.

Mrs. Whitlow had arranged for a seamstress in town to create a gown for Lia in the latest style. Geoff hired a boat to take him and Lia down the Willamette to Fort Vancouver for the ball. When they walked into the chief factor's home, Geoff noted with satisfaction that Lia was dressed as fashionably as any lady there. Not that she needed the dress to bolster her confidence; clearly, she had gotten used to voluminous skirts and wearing her hair up. There were far more gentlemen than ladies, and Lia was in great demand as a partner. Geoff watched her waltzing with the captain of the *Modeste*. Queen Victoria herself could not have exhibited more dignity and grace. Lia blended into the society of the men at the fort, traders and soldiers and sailors, with her head high and no sign of disquiet that Geoff could see. It still bothered him that she had to pretend to be someone she was not, but at least she could handle herself well now among strangers.

A couple weeks later, at the end of February, Geoff and Bradford rode up the Columbia gorge to check the snow level in the higher elevations. It was awkward moving through the deep powder, though manageable for a short-term effort. They would have to wait for better weather to try making it across the mountains.

Nevertheless, Bradford and Ogden began to plan their departure. Ogden spoke of caching stores. Early in March, he went up the gorge to gauge the amount of snow in the passes, returning half-frozen, the ends of his mustache white with frost. He rubbed his hands before the fire and shook his head. "Can't travel in the gorge for a week or more."

Bradford asked, "And there is no other pass across the mountains?"

"None you want to try this early in the season. You don't want to try to cross the Cascades in winter, boy. They're not forgiving of foolishness."

Geoff understood Bradford's impatience, but he did not share it. The weather would change soon enough. Spring was coming. The days were growing longer. Occasionally it even stopped raining long enough for the sun to come out.

He still made a point of walking Lia home from church whenever he could. He was going to leave her soon enough. Selfishly, he wanted to snatch a little more time to spend with her. He knew it was not only unwise, but dangerous. She was still determined to ask questions about his father and his family background. He gave her a few details of his childhood, but when it came to more recent history, he was stuck with the flimsy story that Bradford had tossed off so hastily. It was awkward.

"Why is it I never see you taking notes for your book?" she asked.

He tapped his head. "All the facts up here."

"Really?" She was looking at him suspiciously.

On impulse, he kissed her lightly. Her eyes widened. "Why did you do that?"

"It seemed like a good idea," he said with perfect honesty. He was running out of ways to distract her. He wanted so very much to tell her the truth. But he knew that might ruin everything. This woman made him feel as if she could see inside him to the things that really mattered. Would she feel the same when she knew the truth?

She grew more curious about him with each passing day. She was also growing more beautiful every day. No, strictly speaking, she was no prettier than she'd been the first day they'd met in the woods, when he had admired her freckles. *He* was the one who was changing. He was getting too attached. He had to leave now, while he still could. It would feel like ripping a bandage off an open wound, but it had to be done. The best way to do it was to rip the bandage off as quickly as possible.

THE WEEK BEFORE THE EXHIBITION, Lia gathered the students together to go through a rehearsal. The school was too small to hold all the parents and family members, so the pastor had suggested they hold the exhibition in the church instead. The children were all nervous, but the most nervous person of all was the school superintendent.

"This has to go well." He sat in the front row, drumming his fingers on the edge of the pew. "The people of the town expect great things. Are you sure your students are ready for this?"

"As ready as they can be. They've all worked very hard."

"And Eugene?" The relentless drumming of his fingers against the pew stilled. "Is he ready to get up on stage in front of other people?"

"Yes, sir. He's a bright boy. I think he will do very well." Probably.

The superintendent preened a little at the compliment to his son, but he watched the rehearsal with eagle-eyed alertness. When it was finished, he came up to Lia while the children were putting on their coats. "That was quite impressive, I must say. The townsfolk are going to approve. I have no doubt of it. It's just as well. At the rate the town is expanding, we'll need to build a bigger school, bring in another teacher to help. You could be head teacher." He peered at her as if to judge her reaction. Then he seemed to recollect. "If you're still here, of course." His eyes flicked to the back of the church, where Geoff was silhouetted in the doorway.

She made a noncommittal response, but his comment had crystallized her need for the truth from Geoff. She couldn't decide whether they had a future together or not. She needed to know where she stood with him before she could make any commitments elsewhere.

Geoff had never said tender words, never made her any sweet promises. Surely she had not imagined that he cared for her. It was in every touch of his hand, every glance he gave her. It was in the language his body spoke. But never in words. She'd had enough evasion. She was going to have to speak to him. Tonight.

The superintendent shepherded Eugene away, and other parents came to collect their children. Lia cleaned up the front of the church and swept away some chalk dust that had spilled from the blackboard. "Henri, could you take the globe back to the schoolhouse? I don't want to leave it here."

Henri left, and finally she was alone with Geoff. He came back up the aisle after having seen the last of the children out. He was smiling. "That was an excellent rehearsal. I'm glad the superintendent was able to attend. I heard what he was saying about your teaching next year. Head teacher! Your position here is secure."

"We could get married," she blurted. He froze, resembling nothing so much as an animal caught in a snare.

He said, carefully, "This is not perhaps the best time for this discussion."

More evasion. She was sick of it. "Do you care about me?" Geoff did not speak. She took a step closer. "Do you *not* care?"

"Lia..." His voice trailed off. He was looking everywhere but at her. It was excruciating.

She let her breath out in a huff. "Well, if you ever figure it out, be sure to let me know."

He bowed. "Ma'am." He started to leave, then turned back. "I cannot escort you to church tomorrow. Bradford requires my assistance on a small matter to do with our book."

"How kind of you to let me know." Lia did not bother to hide her frustration. He did not reply. He merely inclined his head and left.

She grabbed a broom and began to sweep the floor. It was perfectly clean, but she was going to sweep it anyway. She thwacked the broom against the planks as though the floor were a personal enemy.

Henri came in and stopped. "You okay?"

"I am *fine*." She swept harder, hitting the floor on each stroke. "That man is a confusing"—*thwack*—"mountain of"—*thwack*—"pure stubbornness."

Henri, wisely, said nothing. He found a chair on the side, well away from the broom.

Lia heard a sound in the entryway. For a moment, her heart leapt up in wild hope. Geoff had come back. She raised her head, half glad, half embarrassed. But the figure silhouetted in the doorway was thin, almost lanky, with dark hair that stuck out wildly in all directions as though he had combed it in a hurricane.

Lia dropped the broom. Henri stood up. Then he launched himself forward to fling his arms around the man. "Pa!"

Pierre had returned.

THE NEXT FEW moments were a confusion filled with words and hugs and laughter. Pierre stepped back, laughing, at Henri's torrent of questions. "Slowly! I didn't write because the letter wouldn't have gotten here any faster than we did. We caught a favorable wind that blew us here faster than I'd dared to hope." He raised his hand to the top of his head, measuring it against Henri's head. They were almost level. "When did you get so tall?"

"You're just in time for my exhibition." Henri grinned at his father.

"Your exhibition? What is that?" Pierre looked at Lia, brows furrowed in puzzlement. So Lia explained. Pierre seemed pleased. "It sounds like you've learned a whole lot while I've been gone."

"It's all thanks to Lia." Henri scuffed his shoes against the floor, suddenly bashful. "It was all her doing."

"I'm sure it was your doing as well." Pierre looked from Henri to Lia, beaming like a man with wonderful news. "In any case, once you're done with this exhibition, you'll need to start packing."

Lia picked up the broom and set it back in its place. "What do you mean? I thought women weren't allowed on trading missions. And anyway, you said this was going to be your last mission."

"It was my last trading mission—for the Hudson Bay Company. I'm setting up business on my own. I've come to take you both with me to Owyhee." He laid his hand on Henri's shoulder. "I've got a house right down by the beach. You'll love it."

Henri's eyes gleamed with excitement, but Lia felt more unsettled than ever. Everything was changing too quickly. "What do you mean, you've got a house?"

"Well, that's the other thing. I'm not just talking about going to Owyhee for a visit. I remarried a couple months ago. My wife is back in Lahaina, and I mean for us to make the islands our home. Settle there permanently."

CHAPTER 12

W hen she first arrived in Oregon City, Lia thought that her problems would be over once Pierre returned. Instead, they had multiplied. In the back of her mind, she had always counted on Pierre setting up a trading store here. Now, she had to choose between staying and keeping her family together.

Mrs. Whitlow offered to give Pierre a bed for the night, but he declined. "I'm used to sleeping in my hammock on the ship, thankee all the same, ma'am. But I've brought some packets of tea, fresh off a boat come from China, if you'd like to brew up some water."

Now it was Mrs. Whitlow's turn to decline. "I start drinking that stuff at this time of night, I'll be up 'til dawn. Bank down the coals when you're done using the front room." She went off to bed.

Lia busied herself with making tea, while Henri flung himself into a chair by the fire, peppering Pierre with questions about his travels, his new wife, and life in Owyhee. The novelty of having a stepmother intrigued him, and Pierre's description of the new things he would see made

Henri's eyes shine. They all talked for hours, catching up. Finally, Henri's questions got slower, and his yawns became more frequent. With difficulty, Lia finally persuaded him to go to sleep. "Your pa'll be here in the morning."

"I'll take you down to see the ship," Pierre promised. "Right after church."

With that, Henri went to bed, and Lia took the opportunity to ask questions. She sat down in the chair opposite Pierre. "I thought you said you were going to have a home here. No more going off for months at a time."

"Well…" He looked away, leaning forward to poke at the fire, though it was doing fine. "I do like coming back home between trading missions. I just don't like the idea of stopping altogether." As a child, Pierre had been constantly in motion, never mastering the art of sitting still for five minutes at a time. Even now, talking with her, he shifted in his seat as though eager to get up and do something, anything. "A merchant behind a counter? That's not the life for me."

Lia frowned. "Wait… you're not even going to set up a store in Owyhee? You said you were going to settle down."

"I have. Getting married is settling down." Lia's skepticism must have shown on her face. He said heartily, "You'll love Lahaina, Lia! It's beautiful. No snow, you could sleep outside if you want. It's paradise."

Lia refused to be deflected from the main point. "So you're still going to go off for months at a time?"

"I'll take Henri along with me when I go. It's time he started learning how to become a trader."

"And what should I do?"

Pierre wrinkled his forehead, puzzled. "Do?"

"Well, unless things have changed, traders don't take their sisters on their ships with them."

"Ah." His expression cleared. "Well, that's where Kail-iokalauokekoa comes in."

"Kalio—what?"

"My wife."

"All those syllables for just one person?"

"She's a good woman. She can show you the chores women do. You'll learn to fit in in no time."

"I don't want to 'fit in,'" Lia snapped. "I want a place where I can be accepted as myself, without having to change to make other people happy." She stopped, hearing Geoff's words in her voice. She didn't want to think about what this change would mean to Geoff. He had said he was going to come back next year, but that was a far cry from sailing halfway to China to see her. She might never see him again.

She had always known that Henri was going to go off on trading missions, but she'd thought Pierre would be settling down, so she'd still have a family and a home. She'd clung to that thought ever since Pa had died. Now, they were all going to leave. No matter what she did, she was going to be left on her own. She didn't count this strange new wife in Owyhee. She was no doubt a nice enough woman, but she wasn't anyone Lia knew and loved, like Pierre or Henri.

Like Geoff.

She didn't want to tell Pierre about Geoff. She would have to, eventually, but she wanted the chance to work through the confusion of her feelings. Somehow, the thought of staying in Oregon City without her family or Geoff just seemed so... lonely. As if she'd been abandoned.

She said, "This is like when Maman died. You stayed with Pa, 'cause you could help him with his work, and I got sent away to live with strangers because he didn't have any use for me."

"Oh." Pierre reached out, covered her hand with his. "It

wasn't like that. You were so young. I suppose he didn't tell you all the things he told me. He said I was like him: no good at book learning. You were so quick, Lia. You picked up reading like it was nothing. He told me he wanted you to go off and make something of yourself, and to do that you needed an education."

Some small, blackened scab of resentment, like coal dust sticking to her soul, slipped off. Her pa hadn't been trying to get rid of her. He had been trying to help her. "I wish I'd talked to him about this when I came back west." Some regrets could not be erased. "I was so set in my own way of thinking, I never stopped to consider it from his point of view."

"I know what it felt like to have a young boy to care for by myself. I was terrified," Pierre said frankly. "I think it would be worse dealing with a girl child growing into a woman with no woman around to show her how to get on."

He got to his feet. "It's getting late. I need to get some sleep. I'll be back tomorrow morning to go to church." He looked down at Lia. "I don't think I ever told you how much I appreciate all you've done for Henri. I thank the Lord every day that you were here when Pa died. Henri needed you."

He doesn't now. That thought twisted inside her like a knife as she said good night to Pierre. She stood in the doorway and watched him walk down the street. Henri didn't need her. But that was the role of any parent or guardian. Once the child was grown enough, you had to let him go free. And the truth was, Pierre didn't need her either. No one did.

What should she do now? She could teach in Hawaii, perhaps. But at the thought, loneliness rose up inside her until she felt as if she were drowning. It didn't matter where she went now. If Geoff wasn't there, a part of her would be missing.

Everyone was heading in different directions. Geoff was heading east and Pierre was sailing west, while the superintendent wanted her to stay here and teach.

What did she want for herself?

Reflexively, she reached into her pocket for the polished stone that Geoff had given her the first day they met. She rubbed her thumb against the stone. She could feel a thin line, an imperfection in the heart of the stone. A tiny crack, but it could split the stone open given enough force.

IT FELT STRANGE, the next morning, to stand next to Pierre in church rather than Geoff, to hear Pierre's light tenor beside her instead of Geoff's deeper tones. She loved Pierre, but everything felt just slightly wrong. She still hadn't told him about Geoff. She had wanted to introduce them. Maybe Geoff could find a way to describe their relationship. Every time she tried to work out how to explain it, her words sounded like complete nonsense. *We got engaged... except we didn't plan to get married really... only now I'm starting to think that I want to marry him after all...* no. She needed Geoff's help to get through this tangle of explanation.

"That superintendent sounded very enthusiastic about your work with the students," Pierre said as they walked back from church with Mrs. Whitlow and Henri. "Do you think maybe he'll want you to stay on and teach next year?"

"He said something about it, but I don't know if he is serious about wanting me to teach next year."

Pierre glanced at her. "Do you think you might want to stay here? On your own? That doesn't sound like you."

"Well, he hasn't made a formal offer."

"Besides, you're engaged now," Henri said.

Pierre stopped in his tracks. "What's this? You got yourself engaged, Lia? Who is the man? Where is he? And why didn't you think to mention this?"

Lia grimaced. She really wished she could have had a chance to talk to Geoff before trying to explain the situation to Pierre. "Let's go back to the house, shall we? I really don't want to discuss it here in the street. It's not exactly settled."

Now Henri was looking at her as if she'd gone mad. "What are you talking about? The whole town knows you're fixing to marry him."

Pierre shook his head. "I don't understand this at all. Are you engaged or aren't you?"

Only Mrs. Whitlow seemed unperturbed by Lia's comment. She merely nodded her head, as if confirming something she had already suspected.

"He has to go back to Montreal before we can think of getting married."

"Why?" Pierre crossed his arms. "Is he thinking maybe you're not good enough to go back to Montreal with him?"

"No. I mean, of course not." Lia tugged on his sleeve, trying to move him along. Pierre didn't budge. From the set of his jaw, he wasn't going anywhere until he got an explanation. "He's just—well, I was expecting to stay here with you and Henri while he was away."

"But if you don't need to stay here, then he'll marry you sooner? Maybe I should have a word with him, man to man."

If a hole had opened up in the sidewalk right now, she would have gladly disappeared into it. "Pierre—don't. I don't want to pressure him if he's not ready to get married yet."

"That don't make any sense," Henri said. "Any time you

walk in the room, he's got no attention to spare for anybody else. Why don't he want to marry you?"

"He says we need to wait to finalize things until he comes back from Montreal. If he needs more time, then I'm going to give it to him."

"Well, I'm not. No brother would. Even with the fast boats that the Hudson Bay Company uses he won't be back here until next summer at the earliest." Pierre frowned, puzzled. "Is he expecting you to wait here all that time? By yourself?"

Somewhat affronted, she said, "I can survive on my own."

"I don't like the idea of a woman living all by herself without any friends or family."

"I have friends." Lia could not believe she was arguing with Pierre over this. "Mrs. Whitlow will let me stay on." She glanced at Mrs. Whitlow, who nodded her support.

Pierre said obstinately, "Well, it all sounds rather funny to me. I don't understand this man. If he can't give you a good reason to wait, he's no one you want to marry."

She could not argue with his logic. Even so, instinct told her that Geoff cared for her. Unfortunately, that wasn't an argument that would hold much sway with Pierre.

"For all you know, he's got another wife back east. I've heard of men doing that, you know. Especially if their wife out here is native, and they married *au façon du pays*. They go back east and marry an American woman and forget all about their family out west."

"I can't believe Geoff would do that." Even as Lia spoke, doubts assailed her. Maybe Pierre was right; maybe Geoff didn't make her any promises because she wasn't the sort of woman he would want to marry. He had proposed before he knew her background, after all, and only because he had felt it was the honorable thing to do. "No," she repeated. "He wouldn't do that. He's too honorable." She wasn't sure if she was trying to convince Pierre or herself.

"Honorable but secretive." Pierre snorted. "If he's so honest, why doesn't he marry you now? You'd better come to Owyhee with us, Lia. I know you'll like Kailiokalauokekoa and I'm sure you'll find something to do there."

"You should have lunch before you do anything else." Mrs. Whitlow had been walking along so quietly, Lia had almost forgotten she was there. "I was going to make ham sandwiches, and I left an apple pie cooling on the shelf. Should be just 'bout ready to eat now."

"Well..." Pierre hesitated, but the mention of pie had Henri leaping up the front steps. Reluctantly, Pierre followed him. Mrs. Whitlow gave Lia a quick tilt of her head, indicating that she should take the opportunity. Lia smiled at the woman and escaped.

THERE WERE definite signs of spring out his window. Geoff frowned at the dramatic contrast of a spray of light pink blossoms against the dark green of the fir trees behind it, and then he went back to loading up the saddlebags with stores for their journey.

Bradford also looked out the window. "Pretty," he said, and went to get his pencil box. He sounded idly pleased at the prospect of something new to sketch. But to Geoff, the sight of the flowering tree was a sign of dread. He was coming to the end of his stay in Oregon. It was a matter of days, no more, before they could risk the passes. He could count on one hand the number of times he would see Lia again.

Bradford dragged his chair up to the window and began to sketch the blossoming tree. "We're almost ready to leave."

This was so obvious it did not require a response. Besides, Geoff knew that tone. Bradford was going somewhere with this conversation. Geoff waited. He had a feeling he knew what was going to come next.

"You've been seen in company a lot with Miss Griggs. I know—" He held up a hand to forestall Geoff's objections. "I know, I ordered you to pay attention to her. But you cannot continue to be in her company so constantly. It will look funny when we leave, if you're all lovey-dovey right up to the last minute. You'll want to break things off with her well before our departure, so no one asks questions. This exhibition should be the perfect opportunity. It will be a triumphant moment for her, securing her position in the eyes of the townspeople. There won't be any need for you to remain engaged to her after that."

This was reasonable. He knew it. But even so, he remained silent, driven by a stubborn impulse that he did not want to analyze closer. He put his hands in his pockets and scowled down at the ground. "I will break things off. When the time is right."

"You're not doing the girl any favors by putting it off any longer. You're just drawing things out."

Since this was exactly what Geoff *was* doing, he could not argue the point. But he wanted to. He wanted to spend every moment he could with Lia while she was still ignorant of his mission. While she still thought well of him.

"We're almost ready to leave. I don't know why you're even quibbling over this issue. End this engagement, Lieutenant. End it now."

Geoff slung the saddlebags over one shoulder. "I need to start saddling the horse. Ogden will be here shortly."

He escaped to the livery stables and saddled his horse. Ogden was going to use the horses to ferry supplies up the Columbia River to cache them there. Bradford did not want anyone to notice them preparing to leave. They were going to slip out quietly once all the preparations were made. Everything was in place for their departure. Except for that one last duty that he had to perform.

He heard a sound behind him and turned. Lia stood there. At the sight of her distraught face, instinct took over. He opened his arms and she walked straight into them.

She rested her head in the hollow below his shoulder, where she fit snugly, as if she'd been made to nestle against his body. He felt her take in a breath and let it out in a slow sigh. He pulled her in closer, leaning his head down until his breath ruffled her hair. He could stay like this forever. He wanted to. But he had to leave her now. By the time he came back, she would know the truth about him, and nothing would be the same. It took an effort to force himself to step back, lightly gripping her arms.

She tilted her head to look up at him. "My brother has returned." Not a flicker of emotion on her face as her eyes searched his.

"That..." He frowned. "I was expecting you to sound happier about it. I know you were looking forward to him coming back."

He listened without interruption as she told him about her brother's return and his plans for their future.

"Where is this Owyhee?"

"I think the English call them the Sandwich Islands."

Geoff had been expecting a village upriver, not a tiny cluster of islands over a thousand miles away. She would be even farther away than he'd thought. His hands tightened as though he could keep her close by physical force.

She was clearly expecting a response. He was not sure what to say. "So," he said slowly, carefully, "What happens now?"

"That's up to you, I think." Her voice was so soft he barely caught the words.

He stepped back, looking down at her. "Lia—"

"I know you *said* this was a temporary engagement. Maybe I would see you when you came back next year, maybe I wouldn't. But that was before I got to know you. You're saying one thing and doing another. I know you've got your secrets, but, well, this is good, what's between us. I think..." She took a breath. "I think we could get married." She looked up at his face, as though seeking a reaction from him. He could not tell her what he wanted to say, so he said nothing. She was hurt, and it was his fault. That thought burned him like a hot coal.

Lia went on doggedly, "I really want you to say something. Anything. You're still holding out on me. All I know is that now—right now—you're planning to leave me and I don't know why you have to go or when you'll come back. I don't know what kind of plans to make, whether to include you in them or not."

She looked so sad that he almost kissed her there and then, but fortunately there was a distraction.

Henri came into the stable, followed by a tall, dark-haired stranger. Geoff had never seen the man before, but he recognized him at once.

Lia's brother had the same dark hair and gray eyes as Lia. But there the resemblance ended. He was tall, with short, spiky hair that stood out in all directions. And Lia had never looked at him with such intense suspicion. The man was frowning at Geoff exactly the way Henri had, the day of that picnic above the river. And, it turned out, for much the same reason.

Pierre barely waited for Lia to introduce them before he spoke. "You cannot ask Lia to wait a year without giving her a serious commitment. It's not right. If you want her to wait for you, you need to promise—right now—to marry her when you come back."

The one thing he could not do. The words stuck in his throat. He could not bind himself to her, knowing she was going to feel betrayed once she learned the truth. He had to leave her free, for her own sake. He'd told Bradford that he was waiting for the right moment to break things off with Lia. But now that the moment had come, it was the last thing he wanted.

LIA WATCHED GEOFF, waiting for his response. He didn't look like an eager potential bridegroom. More like an animal caught in a trap. Had she misread his feelings? This made no sense. A few minutes ago, he had held her as if he never wanted to let her go. But now, he looked as if he wanted nothing more than to be a thousand miles away from here.

The door banged open as Bradford came in. "Montgomery, aren't you done yet with the— Oh. Good morning, Miss Griggs." A questioning glance toward Pierre. Lia introduced him, and Bradford brightened up at once. "So this is your long-lost brother, returned at last? Come back to take care of you? Splendid. Delighted to meet you."

Pierre looked a little bewildered by this flood of warmth from a stranger. He shook Bradford's hand, his expression wary. "I was just talking to your friend here about what he plans to do about my sister. Seems like he's planning to walk off and leave her after promising to marry her. That don't sound right to me."

It didn't sound right to Lia either, but that didn't mean she wanted to stand there and discuss the matter in front of them. It was too embarrassing. "Pierre, why don't you and Henri show Mr. Bradford your ship? I'm sure he would find it fascinating." She gave her brother a meaningful glance, but he didn't seem to pick it up.

"I wanted to talk to your Mr. Montgomery, find out what his plans are."

"I can do that for you," Lia said firmly. "For both of us." She put her hands on Pierre's chest and gave him a gentle push backward.

Pierre looked perplexed. He stepped aside as a groom came past, leading a lively bay mare. "Well, I guess maybe you two need to get things settled between yourselves. Why don't you go off some place quiet and talk it out?"

"Excellent idea," Bradford said, looking at Geoff.

She did not understand why they both felt the need to intrude into this whole business—it was between her and Geoff. But they were right. She and Geoff needed to talk.

She had been certain that Geoff would tell her the truth of his own accord if given enough time. But she had run out of time.

She led Geoff down to the school. On a Sunday afternoon, this was one place that she could guarantee they could talk in private. Dark gray clouds covered the sky. As they ducked inside the school, the rain began to patter on the roof above them. Geoff did not speak.

She turned finally to face him. "Henri and Pierre are leaving shortly."

He stood there, looking at her. It was hard to tell what he was thinking from his body language. He stood as rigid as a man facing a firing squad: shoulders rigid, face impassive, eyes fixed on her. When had she become the enemy? She would have sworn he trusted her.

He was a statue, standing there.

She took a step toward him and softened her tone. "I thought we got along well together. Well enough to make this a permanent arrangement." Her cheeks were burning. She felt like a fool. Had she misread him?

Her voice dropped to a whisper. "Or do you just want to get on your horse and ride off and never see me again?"

He moved then. His hands came up to grasp her arms, and he pulled her close to him. He leaned down until his breath ruffled her hair. "I have to go back to Montreal with Bradford, once the weather improves enough for us to get across the mountains. I gave my word." He said the words quickly, almost reflexively, as if they were a mantra he had repeated to himself so often that the words came out automatically.

"That doesn't mean we can't get married. I would travel with you—if you want me to. If you really do care about me, why wait?"

"I can't explain. Not yet."

"You keep saying that, and you never explain anything. I'm tired of your secrets."

"I'll come back from Montreal next year and then... we can talk. If you still want to talk to me."

Frustration boiled over into anger. They could not continue on like this. "Why? Can't you at least tell me that?"

"I can't." His voice was hoarse. "Please don't ask me."

He stood so still, he might as well have been turned to stone. It was a good comparison, she thought bitterly. His face was about as readable as granite. "Are you asking me to wait for you?"

His response was instant. "No. No commitment, no promises. Let's see how you feel when I come back. Your feelings... might change."

He said "might" but it was clear that he thought her feelings *would* change. Did he trust her so little? "I see. So you don't think I really care about you. Or you don't really understand what loving someone really means. Or you don't understand what honesty means."

The muscles around his mouth tightened. "You not telling the superintendent about your background because it *might* cost you your position. Is that honest?"

Even though she knew he was trying to change the subject, she felt too defensive not to respond. "I couldn't risk Henri getting thrown out of school. And I don't *know* that it would matter. Not for certain."

His silence held all the weight of an accusation. She plowed on, "If he asked me straight out, I would tell him. But if I stay, I can be the schoolmarm on a regular basis. Get junior teachers under me, more than likely. There are more people coming out to this area all the time. They're going to need a whole series of schools, and I could be there at the start, to guide things. Maybe I could make sure that natives are not excluded. That's something, isn't it?"

She was almost pleading, throwing out justification after justification in an attempt to get his expression to soften. "If I don't tell them who my mother was, who I am, then I can put myself in a position to help people. If he asked, I'd tell him the truth. And I don't *know* that telling him about my ancestry would lose me this position. It's just a guess."

"You don't understand," Geoff said. "It changes you, pretending to be someone you're not. Keeping secrets, telling half-truths. I don't want to see you suffer like that." He raised his hand, as if to reach out to her. Then he let his hand drop. He hunched his shoulders. "I don't want to see you get hurt."

"You hurt me," she said softly. "You won't let me share in your life."

He turned away. "I told you before that I would give you all the honesty I could. I can't give any more."

She felt emptied out, exhausted from an argument that went nowhere. "Then we should end this engagement already. It's not either of us any good, not any longer."

She hoped he would object. Instead, he said, stiffly, "That would probably be best."

"I won't promise to wait," she said, breath choked and rough.

The man was like a wall of granite, impossible to shift. He said, "When I come back... I promise you, nothing will be secret."

"Then when you come back, we'll talk." But she knew they wouldn't. This was an ending.

He stayed just out of reach. With a longing so intense it felt almost physical, she ached for the feel of his arms holding her close. She could draw her strength from him. But he did not kiss her. He did not hold her.

He reached out his hand and touched her face, very lightly running his fingertips down the curve of her cheek and across her lips, as if committing her features to memory.

Then he stepped back and bowed. Formally, like a stranger. Like a man she was never going to see again. He took another step back, hesitated. Opened his mouth as though he were going to say something. Then swiftly he turned away. The door closed behind him.

Lia stood in the center of the room, unmoving. She heard his footsteps retreating along the plank sidewalk until they faded into the distance and all that was left was the relentless dripping of raindrops from the eaves. She could still feel the touch of his fingertips running across her skin. The room was cold and empty, and she had never felt more alone in her life.

CHAPTER 13

That night, Pierre said, "So you've decided to come with us to Owyhee?"

"I suppose," Lia said listlessly. Like a boat cast adrift without a rudder, she was drifting with the current. She went to school the next day, going through the motions on the outside, lost on the inside. It was the last day of school. Children came up to her, offering shy thanks or little gifts, talking about the exhibition that night. She accepted their gifts, thanked them for their kind words or reassured them about the performance. She felt removed from everything, as if she were off at a distance, watching everything that was happening.

Her steps lagged on the way back at the end of the day. A man passed her, coming along the sidewalk in the opposite direction. She recognized him as the man she'd met on her first day in Oregon City, the one who'd told her about the schoolteacher position being available. He showed no sign that he recognized her in her fine clothes. He touched his hat respectfully and stood aside to let her go by, just as he would for any other woman in town. It was oddly unsettling that he didn't see her as different. She returned his nod and moved on.

She had carved a place for herself here, earned the respect of the people of the town and found a way to support herself without help from anyone. She could not picture herself living in Owyhee. It felt wrong to go live with some strange woman in her house, subservient, useless. She would not even have the company of anyone she knew. Pierre was already planning his next trading mission. He was aiming to head into the Russian Territory up north and take Henri with him. Henri was so excited, he could hardly sit still. Lia tried to be glad, for his sake. He was getting what he had always wanted.

She stopped in front of the mercantile. The storefront window displayed a selection of fabrics from one of the newly arrived ships from New York. A strange woman looked out the window: hair pinned up, wearing a dress and a bonnet like everyone other woman in town. It took a moment before Lia realized that she was looking at her own reflection. That shook her. Who had she become, if she did not even recognize herself? Was she still herself when she was pretending to be someone else?

Back in her room at Mrs. Whitlow's, she was relieved to find everyone else was out. She would not be good company in her present mood. Mrs. Whitlow was busy with the laundry. Henri had gone straight down to the ship after school. He had said he was going to come back and start packing after the exhibition. She decided to start packing now. If she could keep busy, it would help keep restless thoughts at bay. She was going to take life one step at a time, and trust the Lord to guide her on the journey.

GEOFF WRAPPED a piece of twine around the last bundle of notebooks and stored them in the bottom of his pack. Most of the reports they had prepared were hidden in the secret compartment in Bradford's pack. He had been much more conscientious about keeping them tucked away since that day at Tongue Point when they had met Lia and Henri. No, he was not going to think about Lia. Or Henri.

He looked around the now bare room. Bradford's belongings were all gone. Ogden had ferried everything else down to the cache he had arranged. Bradford had ridden off this morning, ostensibly on a sketching trip.

They had paid up until the end of the month. For the past couple weeks, they had been taking short expeditions around the area, gathering up the last bits of data about the population. Murphy would not be surprised if they were not seen for a few days. They would be missed eventually, but Bradford wanted to get started on their journey before anyone knew they were leaving to go back east. He wanted to avoid awkward questions.

His job today was to keep up the illusion that they were planning to stay here a while longer. Bradford was concerned about the mood of the town, and Geoff conceded that he might have a point. Even after they'd been staying in the town for months, he still got suspicious looks as he had wandered down to the river today.

All the same, things were going fairly well. Perhaps he might just make it through to the end of his visit without any problems.

He ambled around the corner of the livery stables, starting to feel optimistic—and ran straight into Henri.

He stopped dead. Henri stopped also. Geoff noticed with some surprise that the boy had grown during the past winter. His dark brown eyes were level with Geoff's. And they held a sense of accusation that verged on betrayal.

Geoff swallowed. "Hello."

Henri did not waste time in polite skirmishes. He said, point blank, "Are you coming to the exhibition tonight? Lia will want to see you there."

Geoff spread out his hands, as if he could pull a smooth, plausible explanation out of thin air. He sighed. "I can't." On sudden inspiration, "There's too much anti-British sentiment in town lately. I don't want to distract from the exhibition. This is going to be Lia's triumph. She's earned it. And you have too, of course," he added fairly.

Geoff hoped that sounded reasonable enough. All the same, the hurt look on Henri's face when he refused felt like a bayonet straight to the gut.

Henri scowled at Geoff. "Fine. I guess this is goodbye, then."

Geoff shook his hand, man to man. "Goodbye." Then he made his way around Henri and continued on down the sidewalk.

It was just as well he was leaving soon. He did not think he could have stood this situation much longer.

It really bothered him that he could not say goodbye to Lia in person. He had to fight the urge to wander by the school and see how she was doing. He was putting great effort into *not* thinking about that.

He could leave her a note. Ask her to wait. Ask her to trust him. No. There was no way he could even begin to convey everything he felt by scratching words onto a piece of paper. And he was bound by his oath not to tell her the things that she wanted to know. He was almost done with this confidential mission. Once he was east of the Rockies, he could go back to being a lieutenant in the British Army. He'd go back to army life, where he belonged.

Where he used to belong.

With surprise, he realized that he had already made the decision to leave the army once this mission was completed. Somehow, the prospect no longer intimidated him. It was time to resign his commission. See what it was like to live outside of the army. Go where he wanted, not where he was ordered to go. Maybe find a place where he could live without having to pretend to be someone else.

On top of all his other belongings, placed carefully between two stiff pieces of paper to protect it, lay the sketch that Bradford had given him of Lia on the ridge above Oregon City. "Something to remember her by, when we leave. I've already made a copy for the official report. I thought you might like to have this one." Geoff had accepted the sketch, though he knew he did not need it to aid his memory. He would never forget Lia. She was in his blood now. She was part of him.

There was no point in sitting here trying not to think about her. His thoughts kept spinning uselessly, like a clockwork automaton with stripped gears. He needed to get out in the air. He would wander about town, keeping up appearances, until it was time for him to leave.

He decided to head toward the mercantile. He wouldn't stay long—too many men liked to linger there and discuss politics—but he would stay long enough to make sure he'd been seen.

However, as he crossed the street toward the store, Reverend Willett came out of the livery stable, leading his horse. On seeing Geoff, he stopped, raising his hand. Geoff came over. "Are you going somewhere?" Willett's horse was saddled and laden with a bedroll and saddlebags.

"Yes, I'm off to visit the native villages. That's the best way to get to know a group of people, to come live with them in their homes. Something like what you've been doing here with us." The horse tossed its head up, the bridle jingling. "I think my horse needs to stretch his legs. Walk with me for a while. I was hoping that the Lord would provide me with a moment to talk with you."

Geoff followed, wondering. Despite the growing tension over the political situation, he had thought he had been successful in passing as a private traveler. Had the preacher seen through his pretense? Perhaps he had not been as successful as he'd thought.

The preacher walked beside Geoff on the rough track that led up to the ridge overlooking the town. He finally stopped on a point overlooking the river. He leaned against the fence separating the trail from a sheepfold, and looked out at the scene. "Quite a place, this Territory."

"Yes."

"Quite remarkable people in it, as well. We get all sorts here, rubbing elbows with each other. Works quite well, for the most part. Some people say they want to fight the British. Most just want to raise their families in peace."

"So I've noticed." Geoff leaned against the fence and relaxed. This talk sounded harmless.

"Y'know, a lot of people find themselves talking to a pastor when they don't think they can talk to the Lord directly about their problems. Maybe they just feel better talking to someone as fallible as they are. All I know is, I've had people with problems come talk to me about them. Sometimes they feel better afterward. But I never tell anyone's secrets. That's a promise. If you tell me something, it stays with me. Doesn't matter if you did something terrible, it stays with me." The man's tone was rang out with a firmness that Geoff had not expected from this round-faced man with his gentle ways.

"You're a good man, you follow the Lord, I can see that. But sometimes a man has orders to follow that come from other equally fallible men. One thing you learn in the army is that there's always going to be someone giving you orders that you don't like. You learn to accept it and deal with it. Until one day you're faced with the choice of whether to carry out an order at all."

Geoff stiffened. The other man's expression was as unassuming and mild as ever, but his eyes focused on Geoff intently. "All I'm saying is that if there's ever anything you'd like to get off your chest, I'm a good listener. And I don't share secrets."

Geoff smiled smoothly, like a man perfectly at his ease, while his mind raced to come up with a good response.

Reverend Willett smiled too, but with genuine humor. "On the other hand, some men prefer to carry their burdens on their own. If you don't want to tell another man your problems, I know someone else who is always willing to listen. And He's always there when you're ready to unburden yourself."

"Thank you," Geoff said. He wasn't sure what else to say. He had been braced for an inquisition; he had not been prepared for kindness.

His response felt inadequate, but the reverend didn't seem to find it lacking. He tightened his horse's girth and swung up into the saddle. "Goodbye, Mr. Montgomery."

Geoff watched as the other man rode up the trail until he went around a bend. Then he was gone, and Geoff was alone. He felt his loneliness as he hadn't felt it in years. He felt utterly bereft. "No," he muttered. "I know that You are with me sleeping or awake. I will not forsake you, when you have never forsaken me."

He turned back and headed down the trail toward town. He needed to see Lia. Just one more time. Even if he didn't speak with her, one last glimpse would be something to treasure on the journey he had to take.

ONE BENEFIT of Lia's depressed mood was that she didn't feel nervous about the exhibition. Not until she stood peering through the side door at the front of the church. Every pew was filled, and the chairs on the sides were all taken. People were even standing in the back. She scanned their faces.

"He's not here," Henri said quietly behind her.

Lia jumped, and let the door shut. She twisted around. She had to tilt her head up to see Henri's face. When had he gotten so tall?

He was looking at her with pity. "I saw him in town this afternoon. He told me he couldn't come tonight. Too many Americans all in one place; it would not be a good idea for an Englishman to show up."

"Oh." There was an ache inside her, as if part of her was missing. She would have to learn to live with that feeling. "Well, we don't need him to put on this exhibition." She raised her voice so that it would carry to the rest of her charges. "You children have done all the preparation work, and now you are going to go out there and show your parents how much you've learned this year. You can do it. I have faith in you."

She felt very alone as she walked out to stand at the front of the church. It was very quiet, only the rustling of clothing as people turned their heads to watch her. "Ladies and gentlemen. Thank you all for coming. Tonight we are going to show you how much the children of Oregon City have learned this year. We are going to start with the first class giving an exhibition of parsing sentences."

One by one, the classes of children trooped up to stand in front of the audience. They parsed sentences on the makeshift blackboard that Geoff had rigged up. She winced. She couldn't afford to think of Geoff now. She would concentrate on the children.

Math problems came next. The littlest children began by demonstrating simple arithmetic before the older children came up and tackled more complicated problems. Eugene wrote a long division problem up on the blackboard and solved it quickly, slashing through the numbers and writing the answer with a flourish. There was a smattering of applause from the audience. She saw the superintendent's face. His eyebrows were raised but he was smiling. Beside him, Mrs. Mason sat rigidly, her hands clasped in her lap.

The exhibition was a success. She could feel it. She was proud of them and all the hard work they had put into learning this year. She looked out over the crowd of people. They were all intent on watching their children, sitting forward and listening. Her gaze traveled to the back of the room. And stopped.

A tall figure stood silhouetted in the doorway. For a moment, she thought it was Pierre. But no, her brother was sitting in the front row, beaming as proudly as the other parents. Besides, she knew those broad shoulders and that proud carriage. She felt a warm rush of pleasure, tinged with bittersweet regret. Geoff had come after all. She could feel his strength and support like a lifeline extending all the way down the aisle to her. There was still a connection between them, even if he did not acknowledge it.

Henri got up and went to the podium. He was carrying his Bible, and her gut tightened with nerves. She was as bad as the superintendent, worrying about how well his child was going to do. Except that she was confident Henri could do this. He had worked hard on improving his reading. She knew, intellectually, that he would do well. But that did not stop the butterflies dancing in her stomach.

Henri himself did not seem nervous at all. He calmly placed the Bible on the stand and opened it before raising his head. "O give thanks unto the Lord; for he is good: for his mercy endureth forever." His voice had deepened at some point over the winter. The words rang out, sonorous. She could see the superintendent's eyebrows rise even higher. Mrs. Mason's lips were pressed tightly together.

Henri finished the psalm. He closed the Bible and started to walk away. There was a murmur of voices from the audience and then a man's voice rang out, harsh as a crow. "I don't believe it."

Henri stopped, and turned to face the man. "I beg your pardon?"

"I don't believe you were reading those words out of the good Book. Folk like you are too ignorant to read. You're just repeating back words you memorized. Even a parrot can do that." The murmuring around him increased, some people agreeing and others trying to hush the man.

Lia was on her feet now, moving toward where Henri stood. "This is a demonstration of the children's academic progress, sir. If you wish to discuss the merits of their learning, we can devote time to that after the demonstration is at an end." The last thing she needed was for Henri to lose his temper.

Henri, however, remained calm. He had grown in more ways than his height and his deep voice. Somewhere over the year, he had learned self-control. "I have no problem with reading something else, if that would set your mind at ease. Was there a favorite verse that you'd like me to read? Or I could ask Lia to pick something."

Lia could see Henri's accuser now, her eyes having adjusted to the dimness. The man was standing up, almost all the way at the back of the church. He had his hat in his hand and was twisting it around as he spoke. "How do we know she won't just pretend to pick something? Maybe she's the one who helped you memorize the verses in the first place."

Henri said, "Then I'll ask a member of the audience to pick a verse for me to read. Anyone you like."

Moved by an impulse she could not define, Lia took the Bible off the podium. She went down the steps to the first pew and handed the Bible to Mrs. Mason. "Could you pick something for Henri to read?"

Mrs. Mason's expression was unreadable. After a moment she reached out, hands jerky, and took the Bible. She leafed through it for a few moments, then held the book out to Lia. "There. Have him read that."

Henri took the Bible from Lia's hands. "Buy the truth and sell it not; also wisdom and instruction and understanding." He looked up and addressed the man in the back. "Is there anything else you'd like me to read?"

Red-faced, the man sat down without saying another word. The murmur of voices rose again, but Lia thought she could detect an approving edge to the tone now. It seemed almost anti-climactic when Eugene rose up after Henri to read the final passage. It was one of the shortest psalms that Lia could find, and Eugene had worked hard until he could read the words smoothly and not stumble. Lia saw Mrs. Mason's eyes fixed on Eugene, as if helping him along by sheer force of will. When Eugene finished and looked up, Mrs. Mason's shoulders relaxed for the first time that evening. Lia beamed at him as he walked off. She was proud of him. She was proud of all of them.

At the conclusion of the program, Lia directed all the children up to the front. The applause was thunderous. Lia stood on the sidelines, applauding them as well, until Henri dragged her into the center of the line so she could share in the attention. Lia looked out over the audience. Her eyes went again to the doorway at the back of the church, but she could no longer see Geoff. She could still feel that intangible sense of him supporting her, even though he was no longer there.

The superintendent bustled up to her, rubbing his hands together. "Oh, this was an excellent evening, Miss Griggs! The townsfolk are all pleased. I must say, this has really helped convince them of the excellence of our school. The school board has agreed to add an additional school and hire a couple additional teachers." He looked around. "I don't see Mr. Montgomery anywhere in the crowd. I wasn't sure if you were going to put off your wedding until the fall, but if you were—"

"We are no longer engaged." She had to get the words out quickly. It took an effort to force herself to say it, but that was the truth.

"Ah." Mr. Mason had the decency to pause, to try not to look too pleased with the information. "Well, that's unfortunate on one level, of course, but on the other hand it does open up additional possibilities. In that case, we'd like you to stay on. You'd be the head schoolteacher, of course, with additional teachers reporting to you, but I don't expect that you'll have any difficulty with that."

She wasn't conscious of a decision being reached, but

there it was right in front of her. After all her soul-searching, it wasn't a difficult decision. There was no other option. "That's very kind of you. Actually, it occurred to me that perhaps I should take a trip back to the Red River settlement, visit my mother's relatives in the Métis community there. It's been a long time since I contacted them."

"Ah." A longer pause. The superintendent was no longer smiling. He said carefully, "Of course, I have not actually spoken to the school board about extending your contract. It might be premature for me to ask you to take on that responsibility."

"Of course. I understand perfectly. You have to think of what the townsfolk might think." He didn't even hear the irony. He went off to join his wife, who was talking to Eugene. Eugene was gesturing toward Lia. The superintendent took his wife's arm as though to escort her out. There was a brief conversation, then Mrs. Mason shook off her husband's arm and marched over to Lia. She held her head high, a determined glint in her eye. Lia waited, a bit weary. She was done with this fight.

The matron looked her straight in the eye. "I didn't agree with my husband hiring you, but I pay my debts, and I owe one to you." Her fingers tightened their grip on her reticule. "Edgar got sent to school, and I stayed home and learned how to be a lady. Mama taught me well, but I wonder, sometimes, what I missed. I might not have been any good at it, but I might have liked to find out." She took a breath. "That doesn't matter now. What I wanted to say was this. Eugene would never have been able to get through that exhibition without your help. Thank you." She gave one decisive nod before she turned away and went back to where her husband waited by the door. He tipped his hat to Lia, cool and distant, but not impolite. And they were gone.

GEOFF LEFT town without anyone noticing him go. He led the rangy chestnut gelding with one hand on the bridle to prevent it from jingling. It was the perfect time to leave. Everyone in town was packed into the church, watching the exhibition. The sun was starting to sink behind the western hills, but there was still light enough to see the route he had to take.

His last sight of Lia had been seeing her surrounded by a crowd of beaming parents congratulating her. As Geoff turned away, the school superintendent was shaking her hand. Her future was secured. It was time to look to his own future. Finish this mission at last.

He went up the track he'd taken with Reverend Willett. The plan was to turn off on a shortcut that zigzagged up a narrow trail over the ridge to where Bradford and Ogden had set up camp. His feet felt like lead, and the muscles of his chest tightened. The worst was that he had not been able to say goodbye to Lia. Even if he never saw her again, he could have let her know that his feelings for her were genuine.

He put one foot after another, plodding up the hill, leading the horse. Every step felt like he was taking another step away from where he was meant to be. But he had to fulfill this one last mission. *Lord, I am wandering in the dark. Show me the path I should follow.*

He really, really wanted to leave her a note. A piece of paper with words chosen by him, written down by his own hand. Something of his that she could touch and hold on to while he was far away. It seemed terribly important, though he wasn't quite sure *why* it mattered so very much.

Ah. He remembered the night his mother had died. That

was when everything had changed. Life had become about duty. His duty as a son, trying to meet his father's expectations. Then his duty as a soldier, putting the mission above everything else. Including walking away from the one woman who made him feel whole again.

That night, he had stood in the hallway outside his mother's bedroom, clutching his old blankie and being pushed out of the way by doctors and important adults who bustled in and out of the bedroom, talking to each other in important tones. They had completely ignored Geoff. His father had been at his mother's bedside, refusing to leave to sleep or eat, holding her hand and talking to her in gentle tones. Then something had changed. The room went completely silent, apart from his mother's rasping breath. "Death rattle," he heard someone murmur. "Won't be long now."

Geoff's nurse tried to bring him into the room then, to "say goodbye" as she put it. Geoff did not budge. He did not want to say goodbye to his mother. So long as he didn't face her, she would still be alive in there. He knew, even at that young age, that he was being irrational. But driven by fear or superstition, he clung to this notion until his father, harried by his own grief, dragged him into the room. He gripped Geoff's shoulder so hard that his fingers felt like pincers. Geoff wiggled, but he could not get away.

All the bustling had stopped. Inside the bedroom, silence reigned. The adults stood solemnly around the bedside. His father towed him over to his mother's bedside. "Say goodbye," he instructed, in a harsh, choked voice. "It's too late now for her to hear you, but say it anyway. Do your duty."

Geoff mumbled some words; he couldn't remember now what he'd said. All he could remember was what he'd felt. His mother was lying in the bed, eyes closed as if she were asleep, but in some indescribable way she was gone, and he could not escape the feeling that he had been responsible.

After the funeral, his father had buried his grief in his books, turning away from his son. All he had wanted from Geoff was for him to be a dutiful son. Perhaps he hadn't known any other way to cope.

Geoff had learned that lesson well. Duty was safe. Deep down, he was still the little boy hiding in the dark hallway, afraid to go into the room and face the truth.

He paused at the top of the ridge and looked down at the church, the lanterns in the windows sending out a warm glow in the gathering dark.

He had lost the opportunity with his mother to feel her hand grip his one last time, to have the chance for one last loving look, one last hug, the last whispered "I love you." He had lost those moments due to fear and hesitation. Now it was duty that barred him from speaking the words he felt in his heart. And there was no more time. The sun had dropped below the ridge across the river. He would have to hurry to make camp while he could still see the path in front of him.

He turned his back on the town, with its light and warmth, and plunged down the trail into the encroaching darkness.

LIA WENT BACK to Mrs. Whitlow's with Pierre and Henri for the last time. The evening meal was both festive and sad. After dinner, Lia packed up the last of her belongings. She worked methodically, mindlessly, keeping busy to keep from thinking. She had tried to return Mrs. Whitlow's fancy dresses, but the woman refused.

Mrs. Whitlow came into her room. "Mrs. Graham's getting close to her time. Her husband thought it would ease her mind if someone stayed with her until the baby came. I'm leaving first thing tomorrow morning, going upriver to stay with her at Champoeg. I'll be away a few days."

"We'll be gone by the time you get back." Lia straightened from her packing, placing a hand on the small of her back and stretching. "This is goodbye, then. Thank you for all your help. I don't know what I would have done if you hadn't been there when I first came to town."

"Pshaw. You'd've landed on your feet, girl." Mrs. Whitlow's eyes were a bit damp, but her voice was matter-of-fact. "You and that young man of yours." She picked up Lia's old dress, the one that she had worn her first day in Oregon City. "I'll find someone who can use this. You'll want to look nice when you get to Owyhee, or wherever you're going. That old dress doesn't fit you any longer."

"Yes," Lia said. *It's time to let go of things that don't fit.* "Why do you say 'wherever I'm going'?"

Mrs. Whitlow's eyes were too knowing. "I just thought your young man might have come to his senses by now and patched things up with you."

"He's not *my* young man." Lia kept her head down, blinking back tears.

She could hear the pity in the older woman's voice, softened by kindness. "My poor child. Of course he is."

As if a dam had broken, tears started to slip down her face. Mrs. Whitlow's arms came around her and hugged her tight. Lia leaned her head against the older woman's shoulder, absorbing the comfort of a loving touch. Then she straightened up, wiping her eyes. The situation had not changed, but she felt better. "Thank you, for everything. I am glad we came to stay here this winter."

"I'll miss you, that's for sure." Mrs. Whitlow looked a little misty-eyed, but her voice was as firm and no-nonsense as ever. "But you have to find your own road through life. I'll say goodbye now. Take care, Lia."

Alone in the room, Lia looked around the bare room one last time. Everything was accounted for. She laced up the pack. The rest of her belongings would be loaded on the boat, but she was still too much the trapper's daughter. She needed to carry a pack with food, water, and supplies. She lifted the pack, testing its weight.

Then she put it down again. "No," she said to the empty air. "I won't."

CHAPTER 14

Lia emerged from the livery stable, blinking as her eyes adjusted to the unfamiliar sunshine. Behind her, the horse nudged her gently, and she turned. She had never owned a horse before, and this one was darling, a little bay mare with a white streak down her face and white socks. Petting the horse's soft muzzle, Lia realized this was the first time she'd bought something—anything—on her own. Not something for Henri, for Pierre, for Pa. Just for her. Being all on her own was still a scary notion, but there was a certain amount of pride in the notion that she was independent for the first time, making decisions for her own life. The purchase had taken a sizable dent out of her savings, but it was worth it. She took a firm grip on the bridle and led the horse out into the street.

Pierre followed her out. "Are you certain about this, Lia?"

"Yes, absolutely." *Well, almost.* It *felt* right, but after the debacle with Geoff, she was not as sure about her instincts as she had been.

He smiled faintly. "You're a rotten liar. You know that."

"I know. I plan to keep it that way. Narcissa said that I would be welcome back at the mission in Waiilatpu. Without Henri to support, I can earn enough to support myself. It might even be a benefit, my being part-native." She smiled, but then her smile faded. "I will miss you both."

"We'll still be coming back here every year, don't you worry." His arms came around her in a final, warm hug. They walked down to the river's edge, where Pierre's ship was docked. The hands were on deck, preparing to make sail. It was almost time for them to leave.

Henri caught sight of them and trotted down the plank, his old pack slung over his shoulder. He held it out to Lia. "Pa bought me a new pack, so I packed all the stuff that I wanted to take with me in it. I was thinking maybe you could give the old pack to the folk at the mission, if they want it."

"Well, that's one way to get you to clean out your pack," Lia teased.

"Um..." To do him credit, Henri did look a little embarrassed. "I just took out the things that I wanted to keep. There are some school papers down in the bottom of the pack that I never got a chance to go through."

Lia shook her head, but she had to smile all the same. "All right. I will clean out your pack for you."

"Thanks, Lia." Henri's grin flashed.

Something about that grin wrenched at her heart. She blinked back tears. It would be a year, maybe more, before she saw him smile again. "Goodbye, Henri. I love you."

He hugged her again. Low in her ear, he muttered, "Love you too."

Lia watched Henri walk onto the boat, and she had to bite her lip to keep from calling out, asking him to stay. It felt as if part of her were being torn away. But at the same time, the sense of pride that she'd felt at the exhibition returned. Tears blurred her eyes, but she smiled and raised her hand in farewell. He was ready to move on, as prepared as she could make him. It was time for him to stretch his wings.

Pierre gave Lia one last hug, then he followed Henri up the plank to the ship. Lia stood on the shore, blinked against the bright sunshine, waving as the ship rowed out into the current and the sails were raised. Pierre stood at the tiller, with Henri tall and proud by his side.

Lia refused to cry. Henri's last sight of her would not be a face bathed in tears. She blinked the tears away and watched the boat as it made its way downstream. Henri waved a hand one last time as the boat went around the bend. And then they were gone. She let the tears fall then, running hot down her cheeks. She ached for Geoff's reassuring presence, for the feel of his arms around her, for just his physical presence, warm and reassuring beside her. She missed him all the more intensely because he was so close. Up Main Street, above the newspaper office, seventeen steps up to his door. She could knock. Invent some excuse. Just to talk to him one last time.

No. She had closed that door herself when she had ended their engagement.

She snuck a glance all the same, as she passed by on her way back to Mrs. Whitlow's. The curtains were drawn back now; the room inside was dark. He was out.

Everyone was leaving her. Reverend Willett had ridden off to Celilo Falls. Mrs. Whitlow had gone upriver to visit with her friend at Champoeg. Pierre was gone. Henri was gone.

She was not going to drop in on Geoff one last time. Like all the other people in her life she cared about, he was going one direction in life, she was going in another, and she was just going to have to accept that. *Lord, be with him. Guide his steps in the wilderness and if it be Your will, bring him back to me.* If he came back next year, she'd be here. Well, she'd be up in Waiilatpu, but she'd given her directions to Mrs. Whitlow. Anybody who wanted to find her could look her up. And next year, when Henri and Pierre came back to visit, well, she would have had a year standing on her own two feet. She would prove something to herself and to them.

Lia wanted to cling to the hope that Geoff loved her enough to come back. But she had to make her own way in life now. She would make the best of it.

Back at Mrs. Whitlow's, she packed up all the supplies she needed to travel up to Waiilatpu. There was no need to linger now. She was only putting off leaving because it felt so final. But it was time to bring things to a close.

Speaking of which, she needed to clean out Henri's backpack so she could pass it on to someone who needed it. She began to take out all the little bits and bobs that Henri had stuffed into his pack and never cleaned out.

She smiled wistfully as she went through the papers. Old notes from spelling lessons, some math problems, a grammar lesson. She set these aside. There was one last paper down at the bottom of the pack. It had been crumpled up half-under the seam, and she had to tug on the paper to free it.

She smoothed it out. It was a piece of ruled paper, torn from a notebook. But the handwriting on it was not Henri's. It was Geoff's.

Of course. She remembered their first meeting at Tongue Point, with Bradford's pack and Henri's pack and papers scattered in all directions. This must have been part of Geoff's book, gathered up by Henri by mistake. His mysterious book. So he had written down some notes about it after all. She unfolded the paper and began to read.

The paper was covered in penciled notes. Phrases leapt out at her. *A battery of cannon on Chinook Point will control the north channel. Will investigate Tongue Point for evaluation next.*

The pieces of the puzzle began to fall into place. She could see the whole picture now.

Cannon. Controlling the shipping channels, the life's blood of trade between the Oregon Territory and the rest of the world. Geoff, who'd had a career in the army as an engineer, deciding where to build forts. A career he *said* he'd given up.

Lies. He had been lying to her from the moment they'd first met. Her hand clenched into a fist, crumpling the paper.

LIA LED her horse up the trail, her boots sinking into the icy mud. She could think again. She could feel. She did not know which was worse.

Geoff had been lying since the moment they met. A private traveler, indeed. Everything he'd ever said to her was a lie. Every kiss, every caress. The relationship she'd thought they were building on a solid foundation had been a house built on shifting sand.

She had gone to their room above the newspaper office. It had been swept clean, beds stripped. Not a scrap of paper or any indication that they had been there. Discreet questioning of the boy at the livery stables had led to the information that Geoff had taken his chestnut gelding out late yesterday afternoon. Bradford's gray hadn't been in the stables in a couple days, and no one could recall seeing him.

They had left, and she felt sure they had left for good. But the stable boy had given her the direction Geoff had gone, at least. It hadn't rained for a few days, and few horses in town had a stride as long as Geoff's rangy gelding. Once she'd picked up his trail, it had been easy enough to track.

She had stayed long enough to put on the comfortable old men's hunting clothes that she used to wear when trapping. Then she saddled up the bay mare, with her pack secured behind her bedroll, and set out.

She had not told anyone that she was going after him. There was no one in town she could confide in. Reverend Willett was away. Mrs. Whitlow was upriver. No one else would listen to her. The superintendent had most likely shared the information about her ancestry by now. She had been a good teacher, but what mattered to some people was who her parents were, not who she was. Not what she did. She had not spent the winter lying and scheming and plotting to overthrow the government.

She had the vague idea that she needed to stop him, confront him. Take him hostage until the authorities could be notified. But really, she just needed to see him. See his face when she knew him, who he really was. He had swept away the ground from under her feet; she was certain of nothing any longer.

A light mist beaded raindrops along the brim of her hat; when she turned her head, drops splattered onto her jacket. She followed the tracks up over the flanks of Mount Hood. As the trail led higher, the light misting rain turned to a dusting of snow, but the white covering wasn't thick enough to blur the hoof prints. She found the place where he'd camped the night before. They, rather. Two men had stayed there, judging by the tracks. They had only been gone for a few hours; the embers in the camp fire were not completely cold. Going forward, the horse's tracks were joined by another horse's tracks. No doubt Bradford's.

She urged the mare on, feeling encouraged. They were only a few hours ahead of her; she stood a chance of catching up with them. That night, she wrapped herself in a blanket covered with furs, not troubled about being alone in the forest. Up on the side of a mountain, surrounded by nature, she felt like a child safe in her father's arms. The next day, she saddled the horse before the sun had cleared the looming bulk of Mount Hood and rode on, following the faint tracks downhill to the banks of the Columbia River.

The rain grew heavier, dissolving the trail in mud. It did not matter now. There was only one way he could go from here: up the gorge that the river had carved through the mountains to the high desert beyond. The way east.

A rising wind lashed her face with the rain. It was growing colder. Farther on, the ground was sure to turn icy. That could pose a problem. An ice storm could shut down the gorge for up to a week, making the ground underfoot too slick for man or beast. If she got caught in the gorge when it iced over, while Geoff and Bradford had already gotten through, they could get so far ahead that she would never catch up.

She could not think about what she'd do once she caught up to him. That was too far ahead. Her mind was fixed on one thing. Catching him.

SHE SLEPT UNEASILY THAT NIGHT, sheltering under trees that stood close to the river. Memories of Geoff kept coming to her mind's eye. She remembered all the times he'd rescued her, when it gained him nothing. Offering her the polished

stone to cheer her up when they first met on the bank of the
Columbia, this same river that was rushing by, an endlessly
restless current in the dark. Helping her up after she'd
fallen in the street. Buying her a parasol and using his horse
to create a distraction when she needed to get away from
Mrs. Mason and her husband. When it would benefit him
nothing, he had seen her distress and been moved to try to
comfort her. This was not the act of a man who was doing
nothing but using her.

Where did the lies end and the truth begin? She needed
to know. She had to stand before him and see his body
language when she told him she knew the truth.

She wrapped the furs tighter around herself. The
warmth of her anger was fading now, and she was aware of
the darkness and the silence and the rain falling out of the
black sky. She felt completely alone, even though she knew
she was not. *Lord, you know his heart. Help me to understand
him.*

The next morning, she continued. She was starting to
wonder if she would catch him after all. The trees were thin-
ning out as she proceeded up the gorge. There were some
open stretches where she should have seen men on the trail
ahead of her.

The rain hadn't let up all morning. Perhaps they were
holed up in some shelter, waiting for the storm to pass. She
could not have missed them; the trail wound along a narrow
strip of land between the river and the cliffs. All she could
do was ride on. She turned up the collar of her jacket and
kept her head down against the rain.

Toward the middle of the afternoon, she stopped at a
creek to give her mare a chance to drink. She slipped off the
horse and stretched, looking around. On the other side of
the ford, a thick stand of trees blocked her view of the trail

ahead. The mud on the far bank of the creek looked to have been churned up recently. Hoof prints were sunk deep into the mud, as if a horse had slipped. And was that the impression left by a man's boot next to the hoof print? She rather thought it was.

She led her horse across the stream, bending low so as not to miss any signs. The trail led into the trees. The sound of the creek behind her grew softer. She could see the Columbia River through the trees on her left, but the current was a distant murmur. The farther on she went, the quieter the woods around her became. The ominous stillness set her nerves on edge. Her horse seemed to catch her nervousness, tossing its head up so that the bit jingled. The noise sounded overloud, and she soothed the mare until it quieted. She hadn't heard anything untoward, or seen anything either, but instinct overruled her senses. Quietly, she began to load her rifle. There was a creaking of breaking twigs, the sound too heavy to be a bird. She whirled and raised the rifle. And stopped where she stood.

Geoff stood before her, his expression unreadable.

Bradford broke the silence. "Not a bear after all."

"No," Geoff agreed, still looking at Lia. "A dilemma."

CHAPTER 15

Geoff was fairly certain that Lia had not had time to finish loading the gun, but as she was pointing the rifle straight at his stomach, it didn't seem like a good moment to find out he was wrong. "Do you suppose you could put the gun down? We could talk."

Instead, she raised the rifle until it pointed directly at his heart. "What good would talking do? So far as I can see, every word you've said to me has been a lie."

"Not every word," Geoff said softly. *And you know that, deep down, my love.* He was still reeling from the reality of her presence right in front of him. He wanted to reach out, run his fingers along the curve of her cheek, to *prove* that she was standing right in front of him. But when he had ended their engagement, he lost the privilege of touching her. No matter how much he wanted to.

Perhaps something of his inner conflict showed in his eyes. She hesitated. Then she went on raggedly, "You're a spy. A professional liar. You've been lying to everyone in town so that you could find out things about us. And you're going to take that information back to the British government."

There was little point in denial. "What gave me away?"

"I saw a note from that 'book' you've been writing." She did not bother to keep the bitterness out of her voice. "Your pages got mixed up with Henri's belongings back at Tongue Point."

Bradford winced. "Well, how it happened doesn't matter now. That's all in the past. Leaving aside the question of how you learned about us, the question is: what should we do now?"

"We finish the mission," Geoff said firmly.

"No," Lia said. "I'm going to take you back to the authorities. They'll know what to do with you."

Well, at least you don't want to shoot me outright. That's something. "We can't return to Oregon City. We have to go on."

Bradford nodded. "You shouldn't try to stop us. It's the best thing you can do for your country—and ours. We have to go back to Montreal and tell them what we've seen."

"Tell them the best way to control the river traffic and all the access points to town."

"Tell them that there is no way to win," Geoff said. "That is why I have to go back to Montreal and report in person. On paper, our report *could* be read as encouragement to send the army in. We have the superior military force. Britain could control the river traffic on the Columbia, could occupy Oregon City and control it. But we couldn't hold the Territory. The Americans aren't coming over the mountains in a trickle. It's a flood, and there's no way we can stop it. The numbers are overwhelmingly in favor of the settlers."

"He's telling you the truth," Bradford said seriously. Lia's attention was diverted momentarily, and Geoff eased a step forward. Gently, gently. She was tense as a spring, but if she truly wanted to shoot him she would have done so already. She needed to be convinced not to. Perhaps she *wanted* to be convinced.

"Well, of course you'd agree with him." Her finger curled around the trigger. "You're both in this together."

"It's a matter of numbers," Geoff said. "There might be a battle or two, but for the most part it would be a war of attrition. The British would win the battles. But we cannot win the war. I am going to go back and tell the authorities that we should not even try."

"We both are," Bradford said. Geoff took another step forward and to the side. Lia's eyes flicked to him and he froze.

"You're trying to creep up on me."

"Lia, you don't want to shoot me."

The rifle was still pointing directly at him. "Are you so sure?"

"Yes," Geoff said firmly. Lia caught her breath in what might have been a sob. The rifle wavered, then dropped. Geoff stepped forward and took the rifle away from her. "You don't need a gun to hurt me," he said under his breath.

She looked up at him and he saw the shine of tears in her eyes. The sight twisted something inside him like a knife to the gut. He had done that to her. "I'm sorry. I know it's not an adequate apology, but... I *am* sorry I hurt you. I could not tell you the truth about my mission. I swore an oath to follow orders and serve my country. I keep my promises."

Bradford said, "Well, if she's not going to shoot you, and presumably you're not going to shoot her, what are you going to do with her?"

"Nothing," Geoff said. "We go on. If she heads back to Oregon City, the townsfolk won't be able to catch up to us. If she tries to ride ahead and tell the natives in Celilo Falls, well, they're staying out of the argument between the British and the Americans. It's not their concern." It didn't matter who she told, not by this point. And honestly, he no longer cared. That wasn't what mattered right now. She knew the truth now—the truth about him—and she was still talking to him. Spitting mad, but talking. It was insane, but he felt almost hopeful. He was a condemned man who'd gotten a reprieve just as the hangman was tightening the noose around his neck. "We could talk as we walk along. I've got nothing more to hide from you now."

Bradford grumbled, "I agree. I'm not getting any drier standing here getting rained on. If we keep walking, we'll stay warm."

"Walk?" Lia looked at their horses.

"I can't ride," Geoff explained. "My horse got a stone in its hoof. I removed it, but the poor beast is still lame." He rested his hand on the gelding's neck. "That's probably what enabled you to catch up with us." That or Divine Providence. *Lord, give me the right words to say. Help her understand.*

Lia gathered her mare's reins. "I will walk with you," she said coldly. "And you will give me answers. There is a lot that I want to know."

As she started to brush past him, he said, low, "I'm glad you're here, Lia." She did not respond, merely clucked to her horse to start it moving.

The path was broad enough for all three to walk side by side, leading their horses. Geoff walked between Lia and Bradford. His mind raced, sorting out various approaches, trying to find the right words to persuade her to give him a chance. If there was even the slightest possibility that he could get her to think about waiting for him to come back next year, he would take it.

Finally, she turned her head to address him. "Where are you going?"

"We're heading to Celilo Falls for the night," Bradford said. "Then up the river until we can cross the mountains."

Lia said, "I was not asking you."

"Well, I'm the one in charge, so maybe you should be. I am the commanding officer of this mission."

"It was my mission as well," Geoff said. "I take full responsibility for my actions over the past six months. If you want to blame someone, blame me."

"It's really irritating when you start being noble and self-sacrificing," Bradford said, exasperated. "It was my idea to use her as an excuse to stay in Oregon City. Why not have her hate me rather than you?"

"No," Geoff said. "I'm not hiding anything from her any longer. Everything's out in the open now."

"Oh, is it? Then you won't mind answering a few questions. I take it you didn't have a rich uncle who left you a legacy."

"No."

"You are still in the army."

There seemed little point in denying it. "Yes."

"You've been lying to me since the moment we met." Her eyes met his, a brief, intense glance that raked him like grapeshot.

"Not about everything." It was a weak response. He was going to lose her if he couldn't do better than that. "I told the truth wherever I could. I wanted to tell you everything—but I couldn't."

"You lied when it was necessary for your duty," she said flatly.

He sighed. This discussion was going nowhere. Perhaps she needed more time, a chance to vent her anger, before he could ask for forgiveness. "We will find a place for you to stay in the village before you go back in the morning."

"Don't change the subject."

"Lia, I have to make sure you've got somewhere safe to stay. I can't stop caring for you." *Not everything I said to you was a lie.*

She stopped, halting her horse as she turned her whole body to face him. Geoff stopped as well. Bradford glanced at him but kept on walking. He was several paces ahead by the time Lia spoke again.

Her voice was raw with emotion, and her eyes seared Geoff with their intensity. "I don't even know if that's true. I don't know what is true about you and what is false. I thought I was good at reading people. I thought I was good at reading *you*. But I guess I was wrong. You could have asked me to wait for you. If you cared. Once you came back, your secret would no longer matter. But you didn't even ask."

Geoff clenched his fists to control the urge to reach out and take her in his arms. "How could I? How could I ask you to promise when you did not know what—to whom—you were making the promise? It wasn't fair to you."

"You should have trusted me."

"Lia, it isn't a question of trust."

"It is to me," she said, very softly, and tugged on her horse's reins to encourage it to walk on. Geoff shook his head, as if that would clear the chaotic jumble of thoughts inside him.

Bradford had halted a little way down the trail, and they soon caught up with him. The trees were beginning to thin out. The rain still fell steadily, but the wind had changed direction, blowing warmer air up the river from the ocean. If this warming trend continued, the snow would melt and they would have no trouble getting through the gorge.

The sun had sunk low in the west. It would be getting dark soon. The river curved around a bluff, hiding the trail ahead. If the map Ogden had given him was accurate, the village should be just around the bend. Geoff darted a side-long glance at Lia. She was looking straight ahead. Still frowning, but not at him. At least, not for the moment.

This might be his last chance to talk to Lia in private. "Bradford? Why don't you ride ahead and scout out the trail? We should be close to the village. And... I think Lia and I need to talk. Alone."

For once, Bradford didn't make any comment about being the superior officer and the one who should be giving commands. He just looked from one of them to the other. Then he nodded.

Geoff waited. The sound of Bradford's horse faded into silence. The rain dripped down from the branches above them.

Finally, Lia spoke. "I understand why you had to do what you did. I'm not saying that I like it, but I understand. Doesn't mean I'm not still mad at you."

It was a start. Maybe... maybe he had a chance. *Lord, if it be Your will, soften her heart and help her forgive me for all the hurt I've caused.*

THIS WHOLE SITUATION would be so much simpler if Geoff would only have the decency to behave as the villain was supposed to. He just stood there looking at her with those eyes that had always made her feel warmed through with love and understanding. Only now those feelings were so mixed up with anger and pain and uncertainty that she could not begin to sort out what she felt or what she should feel.

He did not move, curse him. He was willing to stand there and wait if that was what it took for her to make up her mind on her own. A tear slid down her cheek, then another. She blinked away the rest of the tears that threatened. This was no time for weakness. She could cry later.

She could not stop caring about him, no matter her anger. They were connected, a bond she could not sever no matter how much he'd hurt her. Nor did she want to, she discovered. But at the same time, she did not know how to go forward.

The silence stretched between them, underscored by the raindrops dripping from the tree branches onto the leaf litter below. His silence held all the regret he was honor bound not to put into words. What had it done to this man to be forced to lie, day in and day out, to everyone he met?

He took a deep breath, still watching her closely. "You said I should have asked you to wait. Do you think... do you think you could wait for me to come back? Once I make my report, I'm going to resign my commission. I'll be free then, to do what *I* want for once. Will you wait for me to come back next year?"

She did not even have to consider that. *Anything can happen in a year. You could be hurt on the trail. You could die, and I would wait never knowing what had happened. I could not bear that.* "No. I am done with waiting for someone I love to come back to me."

"I suppose I shouldn't have expected any other answer." The pain in his voice melted her anger the way the rain was softening the snow on the hillside. The raindrops splashed down into the snow, creating a puddle of melted water, widening it, joining it with other puddles. Soon patches of the spring grass growing underneath would emerge.

Something inside of her was melting as well. That hardened lump of anger in her throat eased. She could look at him again without pain. He stood there watching her, his face hidden by shadows, his broad shoulders silhouetted against the dying light in the west. He did not move.

She took a step toward him. "You didn't trust my love for you enough to ask me to wait."

"It wouldn't have been right," he said miserably. "You didn't know the full truth."

Another step. "I know I love you," she said. "And I thought you knew that too. God's love for you is unconditional. That's the way love is supposed to be. I'm not your father, laying duties on you and judging you. I love you, Geoffrey Montgomery."

"Then... why won't you wait for me?" For once, he was not standing stiff and erect. The soldier was gone, and in his place was just a man, standing there with his shoulders hunched as he looked down at her. He wore no hat. Rain fell into his hair, running down his face like tears.

He looked wretched and she longed to put her arms around him, comfort him, to be the one to rescue him for once. She resisted the impulse. He had to want her as much as she wanted him, or this would never work. "You don't trust me."

"It's not about trust."

"It is to me," she said softly.

Hoofbeats sounded, coming down the trail fast. Bradford rounded the bend, riding hard. He pulled up in front of them. "Settlers," he panted. "Coming this way, down the path to Oregon City."

Geoff straightened. "They could tell anyone in town we were here," he told Lia. "They can't see you."

"Why not?" she said sourly. "*I've* got nothing to hide."

Geoff grabbed Lia around her waist and swung her around to the back of the nearest tree, a broad oak. He put her up against the trunk of the tree, covering her mouth with his hand.

CHAPTER 16

"We don't have time for an argument," Geoff hissed, close to her ear. "Just keep still, please." His hand covered her mouth in a firm, gentle grip and his body pressed against her, holding her still. She heard the thud of slow, steady hoofbeats and the jingle of harness as the settlers came closer. Geoff's body was like an iron bar, holding her immobile. She glared at him, and he looked back at her, apologetic but unmoving. After a few moments, the hoofbeats stopped and she heard Bradford call out, "How do you do?"

She could hear the men talking: Bradford's easygoing, genial tone and the low murmur of the others. She couldn't make out the words. Then the sound of horses moving on. One of the men laughed.

The rhythm of hoofbeats started up again, receding now. Bradford came back into the trees. "It's all right," he said. "They weren't men that we'd met before. I told them I was holding the horses while my friends were off hunting. I think they bought my story."

Geoff released his grip from Lia's mouth and he stepped

back, but did not let her go. "I couldn't risk you crying out. Are you all right?"

"You didn't break anything," she retorted. She straightened her jacket. "I've had enough of secrets and lies. Why did you hide me and stop me from speaking?"

"I didn't want them to hear you. You were too angry to think about what it would do to your reputation in town if you were found alone with us."

"You're a spy on the run, trying to escape before you get arrested or worse—and you're worried about my reputation?" She couldn't decide whether to laugh or cry. "It doesn't matter, anyway. My reputation is beyond repair. I told the superintendent about my mother. The whole town will know by now."

Bradford looked confused. "Your mother? I don't understand."

Lia looked at Geoff. "You didn't tell him." The knowledge warmed her. Out of all the lies and uncertainties, this was something tangible. This was something she could hold on to. Softly, she said, "You kept your promise."

"I have *never* made a promise and not kept it," Geoff said doggedly. "That's why I didn't want to commit to marrying you next year. I knew you'd be angry when you found out why I had come to the Oregon Territory." He took a deep breath, running his hand through his hair, slicking it back. "But that's not an issue any longer. If you care for me, can we try to make this work out between us? Wait for me to come back."

Bradford sighed, loudly. "As your superior officer, might I remind you of your current situation? You're a spy in enemy territory trying to escape back to safety. You probably won't see each other in months, if not years. This isn't the best time to make a commitment."

Geoff said evenly, "Bradford, old chap. You may be my superior officer, but if you interrupt this very private conversation one more time, I will make it my mission to make your life a misery for the next two thousand miles."

"Ah." Bradford paused. "I feel a sudden inclination to scout behind us, see if anyone is on our trail."

"Wise decision, sir." Geoff didn't wait until Bradford had ridden out of earshot. "I promise you that if you wait for me, I will come back and ask you to marry me."

She whispered, "After all the lies you've told me, you're asking me to trust your word on this?"

"Yes," he said simply.

He did not move closer to her. The gap between them was a couple of feet, but it felt like a chasm.

"And why should I do that?"

"Because I love you," he said.

Four simple words. Odd, how they could make her feel as if the earth had shaken beneath her feet. It was the way he said them, the expression in his eyes. There was no longer any discrepancy between his body language and the words he was saying. Everything aligned, and it was as if the last puzzle piece had been put into place and she could see the whole picture that comprised Geoffrey Montgomery. The congruence gave his words a force that resonated deep inside of her. This, at last, was the truth of the man.

Geoff stretched out his hand to her. "I want to live with you and make a life together somewhere we can both be happy. I don't care if that's in America or England or anywhere else on the globe. Once I finish this mission, I intend to spend the rest of my life making you believe I love you. If you'll let me."

She blinked rain out of her eyes. Slowly, she reached out and grasped his hand. A small gesture, but it felt like finally stepping across the threshold of her own house after years of wandering in the wilderness. She knew what she needed to do.

~

GEOFF CLOSED his hands around hers and held on tight. "No more lies. I swear it."

All he could do now was give her the truth. And pray that it was enough. "Lia, I know it's a lot to ask of you, but do you think you could—" He stopped, his attention caught by the sound of hoofbeats coming fast up the trail behind him. Bradford came into sight, riding at a gallop. He pulled up in a jingle of harness and a scattering of mud. The horse snorted, but Bradford slipped out of the saddle and grabbed its reins to keep the animal from stepping away. "Natives coming up the trail behind us. They'll be here any minute. Do we hide the girl or do we try to brazen it out? They're heading for the village. If you're not serious about bringing the girl to Celilo with us tonight, you'd better hide her."

"You can try." Lia told Bradford. "I'm done with hiding. Don't imagine you can get me off the trail without making a great deal of noise and trouble. Which they'll no doubt hear."

"Are you going to tell them about us, what you know?" Bradford demanded. "Or are you going to let us go on and complete our mission?"

"She won't betray us," Geoff said.

"Are you sure?" Bradford said nervously. "You're willing to bet the success of this mission on this girl keeping quiet?"

"Yes." Geoff looked at Lia. "I would trust her with my life."

Bradford opened his mouth, clearly ready to argue, but

then he stopped. The natives came around the corner, walking single file and carrying packs.

Lia moved forward, not looking at Geoff or Bradford, and addressed the natives. A tall man in front answered her. Geoff knew enough about the native ways to understand that the man's flattened forehead indicated he was a man of high rank, but he could not understand what he said.

After a few minutes of conversation, Lia turned back to Geoff. "They do not speak English. These men are from the Ahantchuyuk tribe near Pudding River. They speak a different dialect of Kalapuyan from the one Henri taught me, but it's close enough for me to understand them. They're bringing baked camas root from the Willamette valley to trade for beads, furs, dried fish."

Bradford said nervously, "And are they going to tell any Americans that they've seen us? Are they curious what we're doing here or where we're going?"

Lia spoke to the man again. Whatever she said caused the man to grin broadly. He nodded at Geoff and Bradford, and then the native men shouldered their packs and went past them up the trail.

Geoff said, "Whatever you said, it left them in a good mood."

"Yes," Bradford put in. "What did you tell them about us?"

"I told them we're going to see Reverend Willett. He's up at Celilo for a while. It's all right," she added, seeing Bradford's alarm. "He's not going to tell anyone that he's seen you. Seen us. And Geoff, you don't need to worry about my reputation any longer. I told the men that we were going to see the reverend to see about getting married."

Geoff jerked his reins suddenly. His horse threw its head up and snorted indignantly. Geoff patted its neck absently, but he still stared at Lia. He couldn't take it in. "But... you said you wouldn't wait for me. Did you change your mind?"

"Never mind that right now," Bradford said impatiently. "Can we trust this reverend not to report back to the Americans? What if he thinks that we're his enemy?"

Lia shook her head. "Reverend Willett will understand. You can trust him not to share anything he's told in confidence."

"And you'll wait for me?" Geoff had to force the words past the thick lump in his throat. He was so afraid to hope. "We can have Reverend Willett marry us when I get back?"

"Oh, no." Lia smiled. "I figure that this is my opportunity to make an honest man of you. You'll have to make up your mind what to do about me right now. Either marry me or let me go. Celilo's only a few minutes away. You've got until then to decide what to do about me."

"I believe I need to go check on the—on the— Oh, it doesn't matter what I need to check on. I'll meet you at the village." Bradford suited his deeds to his words. Geoff barely noticed him go. His mind was in a whirl.

In the rapidly fading light he could just make out Lia's determined expression. She said, "I am not going to stand here and watch you walk away from me. The only thing I am sure of is that the Lord has given us this moment together. I'm not willing to throw it away."

This must be how a man on the gallows would feel when he received a last-minute reprieve. He wanted to hope, but he was almost afraid to believe. "But how can we get married tonight? What about Henri? Your brother?"

"I'm free," she said simply. "You told me once that there was always a price to pay, and I've paid it. I let Henri go to become what he wants, and I've told the superintendent who my mother's people were. I paid with honesty, and it cost me my position—and a few tears, when I saw Henri leave—but it bought me my freedom. I can go anywhere I want."

He reached out a hand to touch her, but then he stopped, hesitating. "Are you sure? Please. I need to hear you say the words." It didn't seem real, that she was free to marry him tonight. That they were both free to start a life together built on honesty and trust.

"Yes, I am sure. I want to marry you right away." She stepped closer, reaching up to cradle his face in her hands. She traced the outline of his lips with one thumb. "I've never been more sure of anything in my life."

Disbelief melted away at her touch, swept away in the flood of joy that surged through him. He didn't care that he was getting rained on, or that the ground was fast turning into mud, or that his feet were freezing. None of that mattered. He slid his arms around her and pulled her body against him, reveling in the sheer, unbelievable fact that she was with him and he was able to hold her without guilt or deception. She was warm in his arms, solid and real.

Slowly, he brushed his lips down the curve of her cheek. "Once the question of war has been settled, we can come back to this Territory. I imagine there's work for a husband and wife guiding wagons on the Oregon Trail. With all this new land to explore, I'm sure we can find a place that we can call home."

"I am already home," Lia said. "I'm with you." And she kissed him.

AUTHOR'S NOTE

In 1845, the British Colonial Office in Montreal sent two army lieutenants, an engineer and an artist, on a confidential mission to the Oregon Territory. Their orders were to pose as private travelers while they mapped out potential fortifications, drew up a plan to occupy Oregon City, and determined how much effort it would take for Britain to defend the Territory against the American expansion westward.

This was not their story.

I kept to actual events as far as I could find documentation for them. The newspaper quote that Geoff read was from an essay published by John L. O'Sullivan in the *United States Magazine and Democratic Review*, Volume 17 (New York:1845). The lieutenant who was an army engineer did purchase hair ribbons, yards of silk, and a pair of ladies' shoes at Fort Vancouver and charged it to his account as part of the mission. Peter Skene Ogden did call the lieutenant who was an artist a "disagreeable puppy." And the city of Portland, Oregon, did receive its name as the result of a coin toss at a dinner party one night in Oregon City. But the personalities and actions of Geoff and Bradford do not, to the best of my knowledge, resemble the actual Lieutenants Vavasour and Warre.

Lia was inspired by Amelia Douglas, wife of a factor at Fort Vancouver. Lady Douglas, however, never tried to pass as anything but a woman whose father was of French-Irish descent and whose mother was Cree.

I hope you have enjoyed Geoff and Lia's story. If you liked it, could you leave a review on Amazon or Goodreads? (Or even if you didn't like it. Either way, you'll help other readers.)

If you want to know more about my next stories, please visit me at EvelynHillAuthor.com. Sign up for my newsletter and I'll update you on new releases and sales.

Keep reading for an excerpt from my debut Harlequin Love Inspired Historical book, *His Forgotten Fiancée.*

ACKNOWLEDGMENTS

Biblical quotes are from the King James Version. My thanks to Lynne Tagawa for editing, Emily Nemchick for proofreading, and Cover Shot Creations for the cover.

I also want to thank the kind docents of Newell Pioneer Village in Champoeg, Oregon for their endless patience in answering my questions and the Confederated Tribes of Grand Ronde for sharing their Chinook Jargon language resources.

HIS FORGOTTEN FIANCÉE

Chapter 1

Oregon City,
Oregon Territory, 1851

"Who am I?"

Liza Fitzpatrick dropped the cleaning rag onto the counter of the dry goods store and spun around. A man stood in the doorway, his rough, working-class clothes soaked to the skin. He stared at her as if she were the first woman he'd ever seen.

Ten steps to the back room, half a minute to grab Pa's rifle. She might be able to make it. Sober, the long-legged man could easily outpace her. But not the way he was swaying from side to side. It was getting dark outside, and she found it difficult to guess his age in the light from the single lantern, but beneath the beard and the bedraggled brown hair that fell to his shoulders, he looked under thirty.

"Well?" Impatience edged his tone like a well-honed knife.

She cleared her throat. "Um… good evening. Mr. Vandehey, three doors down, serves liquor—"

"That's the last thing I need." He sagged against the doorframe, his head drooping.

She took a couple of cautious steps closer, to get a better look at the man. Red streaks trailed down his forehead. "You're hurt!"

His head came up. "Obviously." Those thick eyebrows could have been designed to scowl at her. His dark eyes woke the memory of a pain that she had thought buried safely away. Recognition twisted inside her like a knife plunged straight into her heart. He repeated, "But who am I?"

"You don't know?" She stared at him. This encounter was starting to take on the unreal qualities of a nightmare. That was ironic, considering she had been dreaming of this moment for months. She had imagined all the different ways the scene would play out — or she thought she had.

"I am trying to be patient, madam." The man spoke with a cultured accent at odds with his wild, mountain man appearance. "I would appreciate the courtesy of an answer to my one—simple—question. Do you know who I am?"

"Yes," she said. "You are the man I am going to marry."

He swayed further, and his eyes closed. Then he leaned against the doorframe, sliding slowly down to the ground in a faint.

Liza had thought she would never see him again.

She looked down at the man sprawled on the floor. His eyes were shut, dark lashes long against his pale skin. Liza had a thousand questions that needed answers, but now was not the time, not when Matthew Dean lay passed out at her feet.

Her emotions were in a whirl. She had been waiting for this day for over a year, hoping for it, praying for it, sometimes almost dreading it. And now that he had finally come back to her, it didn't seem real. His skin was cold, but his pulse beat strong against her hand. For a moment, he responded to her touch, his fingers curving to grasp her hand. He murmured something under his breath, and then his hand drooped.

She didn't know whether she should laugh or cry. He had been gone for so long, without a word. Why had he come back now?

Her mother had always told her that the Lord never sent you anything unless he had faith in your ability to withstand it. Sometimes, she wished the Lord didn't have quite so much faith in her.

She fetched Jim Barnes, from the livery stable on the corner, to help her get the unconscious man into the bed in the back room. Jim cleaned him up while Liza routed out some dry clothes. Mr. McKay, the owner of the dry goods store, was shorter and much wider, but his homespun trousers and red checked shirt would have to do. Matthew's clothes weren't merely damp; they were soaked through. She rubbed the rough, sodden fabric between her fingers, then spread the clothes out by the fireplace in the front room. They hadn't had rain in weeks. He must have fallen into the river to get this wet.

Jim came out of the back room, shutting the door quietly behind him. "Restless man, won't hardly lie still," he said. "Like there's something burning a hole in him."

"How badly is he hurt? Memory loss sounds pretty serious. I should probably send for the doctor." She frowned, torn between worry and frustration.

"Doc Graham won't be back until tomorrow, but I don't think he's in bad shape." Jim reassured her. "Just that cut on his head, which has already stopped bleeding. Looks like he got roughed up some, is all."

"I appreciate your help." Liza hesitated, unsure of whether to ask for an additional favor. Jim, placid and unflappable, had accepted her explanation that the man was her fiancé without any questions. But other people would be more curious, asking questions she did not know the answers to. *I need to know why he came, after all this time.* "I'd appreciate it if you did not mention this incident to anyone."

He gave her a look that was unexpectedly shrewd. "Anyone like Mr. Brown, you mean? I won't say a word to him about it, but I'll send Granny Whitlow over to keep you company. Wouldn't be proper, otherwise."

Matthew was hardly in a position to pose a threat to any woman at the moment, but Liza nodded. "Thank you, Jim." After he left, she began to tidy up, sweeping the floor and straightening the goods on the shelves. The dry goods store was the front room of the McKay's home. It still had the original puncheon floor and the cat-and-clay fireplace that was used for cooking and to heat the house, but the walls were filled with shelves of nails, rope, and harnesses, as well as the latest bolts of fabric off ships from Boston and New York. The back room was the family's private area, and the children slept up in the loft. Liza had agreed to mind the store for the McKays when they went upriver to Champooeg to celebrate their eldest son's wedding.

It was getting late. She could not close up the store yet, there was one more visitor coming to see her tonight. She was already dreading it. Meeting with Mr. Brown was never pleasant, but if he knew her fiancé had come, he might decide to change his mind and go back on their agreement. She had to get Pa's IOU back from Mr. Brown before he found out about Matthew. With any luck, she could do it.

Hopefully, Matthew's arrival tonight had gone unnoticed. It was possible. In the year since Liza had come, the town of Oregon City had doubled in size. More people were coming in from the Trail each week, making their way around Mount Hood on the Barlow road or risking the passage down the Columbia river past The Dalles, all eager to find a place of their own.

She recognized that longing for home; it was what had brought her out here on the Oregon Trail herself. It was all she had ever wanted, since she was a child, a place she could call her own. No one to look down on her for being the daughter of an Irish immigrant. Here, they were all immigrants together. This was a place where she could put down roots. She could have a family—she winced away from the thought. It led back to the man lying unconscious in the bed in the back room.

Perhaps he had an explanation for what he'd done. Perhaps he had come to apologize. It had been almost a year since she'd last seen him.

The front door opened. Old Granny Whitlow stomped in, bringing a rush of cool evening air with her. "What's this I hear? Some man barged in here?" She looked around. "Where's he now, then? Don't just stand there, girl!"

"He's resting. I don't want to disturb him." Liza shut the door behind Granny. She only wished she could close the door on this conversation as well. She had wanted a chance to talk to Matthew privately first.

"Hmph." Granny did not look impressed. As one of the

founding members of the Ladies Social Club, she seemed to feel it was her duty to collect and spread the latest news among the townspeople. "I was hoping to get a look at the fella."

"He's been injured," Liza said. "There's really no need for you to stay. He's not going to hurt me."

The dry goods store served as the social center for the women of the town, so Mrs. McKay had placed a couple of rocking chairs by the fire, for visitors, and a table with Mr. McKay's prize chess set on it. Granny settled herself in one of the rocking chairs, and then looked up at Liza. "You sound pretty certain about a total stranger."

"He's not a stranger." This was harder than Liza had expected. She had to force the words out. "He's the man I got engaged to on the Trail."

The silence was so profound that she could hear the tinny piano being played all the way down in Vandehey's saloon.

"Well, if that don't beat all. You've been refusing offers left and right on account of your being promised to some man none of us have ever seen, and here he pops up all out of nowhere." Granny nodded her head.

Liza felt her cheeks growing warm. "When he went off down the California Trail instead of coming on to Oregon with me, he promised me he'd come up once he'd gotten a stake, and then we'd get married. It just took longer than I thought, that's all."

"Months and months. California's full of them pretty Spanish girls, I do hear."

"He loves me." Was she trying to convince the other woman or herself? She shoved that thought aside. "He asked me to marry him, and he's an honorable man."

"Hmph. Men change their minds just as much as

women do. If he was coming up here to marry you and all, why was he down there all that time and never sent you a letter?" Granny spoke triumphantly, hammering the final nail in the coffin.

Every word she said was true, but Liza didn't want to hear it all the same. "He asked me to marry him. He promised he'd come back to me. Now he has."

Granny said skeptically, 'And he just happened to wander straight to your door? Just you go and fetch those quilts from up in the loft. I can't manage that ladder, but no matter. I'll be comfy as anything right here in this chair for the night."

Liza got a couple of quilts for herself as well, spreading one across the other rocking chair. "Anyone in town knows I've been minding the dry goods store while the McKays are upriver. He could have been given directions before he got attacked." Granny still looked skeptical. "Likely, he came here because it was the only place open this late, apart from the saloon."

"You really shouldn't keep the store open this late. I'll help you put up the shutters."

"No." Liza put out a hand to stop her. "I can't close up the store yet. I'm waiting for someone."

Granny narrowed her eyes. "At this hour? Who?"

As Liza started to answer, the door was pushed open again. The man in the doorway was of medium height, slim, with brown hair and a neatly trimmed mustache. There was nothing remarkable about his appearance, but dread curled into a knot in Liza's stomach. "Good evening, Mr. Brown."

"Good evening." He nodded to Granny. "Mrs. Whitlow." He paused. "Might I speak with you privately, Miss Fitzpatrick? Perhaps we could use the back room. There is a matter I would like to discuss with you."

"No," Liza said quickly. "We can talk here. It is all right if Granny stays."

"Don't mind me," Granny said brightly. "I'll be quiet as a mouse." She folded her hands, eyes bright with curiosity.

Liza went behind the counter, where she had her reticule waiting. "I have the money here." She handed him the coins. It was almost all the money she had in the world, but giving it to him was worth the sacrifice if that meant keeping the claim. "There. That is the last payment. Now Pa does not owe you anything, and neither do I."

Mr. Brown put his wallet away inside his jacket. He withdrew a piece of paper. "And here is the IOU. It was unfortunate that your Pa needed to borrow money, but I'm glad at least that I was able to be the one to help you in your time of need."

"Thank you." She had to force the words out. "I am sure Pa thought he was doing the best he knew how, but I would prefer if he did not borrow money from anyone in the future. I can take care of him until he gets on his feet again." *And next time, he can* tell *me when he borrows money to keep the claim going.*

"Can you?" The question was mild, but those pale green eyes were intent upon her. "Apparently, you have not heard. Your hired hands quit this afternoon." His thin lips curved up into a faint smile. "They should be halfway to Astoria by now."

The words settled into her like lead weights. "I expect we'll manage." She only wished she knew how. There was no way she could get the harvest in by herself.

"It looks like you've gotten some new supplies." Mr. Brown scanned the bolts of fabric on the shelf behind her. "I'd like a few yards of that braided trim if you would be so kind."

Liza measured out the yards of the fabric and wrapped it up for him. He was playing with her, wasting her time. What use did a man have for trimming? None.

He never shifted his gaze from her. "You could sell the claim to the Baron, you know." Mr. Brown's boss, Barclay Hughes, had come out to the Oregon Territory a few years back. He had quickly made a fortune, becoming a lumber baron by cutting down trees and shipping the lumber down to San Francisco. To his face, everyone called him Mr. Hughes. Behind his back, he was known as The Baron. "He wants the land. He'll be pleased if I can get it for him. I can make sure that he doesn't cheat you on the deal, you know. He listens to me. He will give you a good price for your claim, and you could find permanent work in town."

"Sell the claim? And give up our independence? Thank you all the same, but no. My father is going to prove up his claim, and I am going to help him. No one is going to take it from us." She finished wrapping up the fabric and pushed it across the counter to him.

Mr. Brown leaned forward, and she had to repress the urge to step back. "Frankly, Miss Fitzpatrick, you can't do it. Not just you and your father."

He thought she would give in. Thought she had no choice.

Since that tree had fallen on Pa's legs, breaking them both, getting the crops in had become a major worry in her life. Without the harvest, she and Pa would not be able to afford to stay on the claim over the winter, which meant they would lose it. The law specified a man had to live on his claim if he wanted to prove it.

She didn't have time to go hunt for new men to do the work. Anyone around here was too intimidated by the Baron to go against Mr. Brown, and she didn't have time to get outsiders to come help. The wheat was ripe now. If she put off the harvest, the rains would come and the crops would rot in the fields.

Her thoughts flitted to the man in the back room. She went to the front door and held it open. "Please don't let me keep you."

"I'll talk to you tomorrow, when you've had more time to consider. I know you're a stubborn little lady, but I'm sure by morning you'll understand that I only want what is best for you."

From her place by the fire, Granny called out. "You'll be wanting to go back to the hotel before you lose your chance of supper. I don't know why you don't just board with some respectable family instead of paying all that money to stay at that fancy new place, but that's young men for you. Always have to present a good image to the world."

Mr. Brown opened his mouth to speak, then he shut it again, pressing his lips together. Anger stained his cheeks with bright red patches. Abruptly, he turned and left.

Liza shut the door behind him and bolted it. She leaned against it, closing her eyes for a moment, and a sigh escaped her.

"There's a man who dearly likes to get his own way." Granny's dry voice came from behind her. "Mr. Brown won't be happy until he's gotten your claim for the Baron."

"That's what I am afraid of." Liza sat down in the other rocking chair and wrapped the quilt tightly around herself. "I don't know what to do about the harvest." There. She had said it out loud.

"Why is that man so obsessed with your claim? He's bought up most of the claims around. You'd think he'd be satisfied."

She shook her head. "He wants to please the Baron. He thinks if he goes through me, Pa will agree to sell the claim."

"That's true enough. Whole town knows your Pa would do anything for you."

"*For* me, yes." It never occurred to him to let her share the burden. That was part of the problem. Granny was looking at her, eyebrows raised, so Liza explained further. "After my mother's death, Pa left me with my aunt while he came out here and threw all his energy into building a new home for us on the claim. I think it helped him deal with his grief, as well as giving him a way to provide for me. It was his legacy, he always said." She did not want to think of what losing the claim would do to him. He would feel a failure, not just as a farmer but as a father.

"Come sit by me and say your prayers, child." Granny spoke gently, instead of her usual, acerbic tone. "Let the Lord carry your troubles for the rest of the night."

It was good advice, but Liza found that she was not able to stop worrying. The fire was getting low in the fireplace. A log sank down into a bed of glowing embers. She settled into the other rocking chair, and wrapped a thick quilt around her and stared into the embers.

Why had Matthew taken so long to come to her as he promised? She had waited, first hopefully, preparing the loft in the cabin for two people. Then anxiously, wondering if something had happened to him. She had no way of knowing where he had gone, exactly. Just a hastily scribbled note saying he was going to find gold and that he would come to her in the spring. Six months without a word, just wondering.

She was familiar with the feeling of being left. After Pa had left, she had waited back in Iowa for three years before he had sent for her. Even though his concern had been to make sure there was a proper home for her, he had left her. That awkwardness still lay between them. They never spoke of it, but she could tell sometimes, when he was in one of his moods, that the guilt weighed on him. She still struggled with her anger at being left behind.

She had travelled the Oregon Trail with strangers, a respectable family that her pastor had introduced her to. They had been kind enough, though preoccupied with their own affairs. She hadn't realized how lonely she had felt, until she met Matthew. He had been traveling without family too, and somehow that had formed a bond that had quickly strengthened into something stronger. Or she thought it had. He asked her to marry him. He said he loved her. Had he changed?

The memory of those dark eyes, looking straight at her with no sign of recognition at all... she shivered, despite the quilts. One thought chased another through her mind until finally she fell back to reciting her favorite psalms to calm herself. Finally, she slept.

The next thing she noticed was sunlight falling warm on her face.

Granny bent over a kettle hanging by the fire. "Good morning. I just checked on your man. He's still sleeping, but his color looks good. I'm thinking he's not hurt that badly. Looks like he's not been eating regularly, worn himself down." She patted Liza on the shoulder. "The tea is almost ready. I'll be back later, see how you're getting on." She must have read the apprehension on Liza's face, because she added, "You'll be fine. The Lord knows what he's doing."

It was quiet after Granny had left. Liza stood in the middle of the room. She could hear early morning noises outside: birds singing, the occasional rattle of wheels as a wagon rolled by. From the back room, nothing but silence. She had to face him. Butterflies danced in her stomach at the thought. To put off the inevitable, she whipped up a batch of biscuits. While they were baking, she combed out her hair, braided it and pinned it up into a crown around her head. Her mother had always told her that her light-blond hair was pretty, but Liza found it annoying. It was too fine. Wisps slipped out of the braid despite her best efforts. She wrestled with it, finally settling for pinning the plait into a crown around her head.

Dallying over her hair was only putting off the need to go in and talk to him. She straightened up and put her shoulders back. She had walked the length of the Oregon Trail. She was not going to fail at the end.

Despite her resolution, it took an effort to knock on the door to the back room. When there was no response, she opened the door tentatively. No sound came from the blanket-covered mound on the bed. She pushed the door open wider.

She laid down his folded clothes at the foot of the bed, putting on top of the pile the comb and the new-fangled harmonica that she'd found in his pockets. That was all he had had on him, no money or identification.

He didn't move, so she took a couple steps closer. She studied him as if seeing him for the first time. He'd always been thin, but now he was downright skinny. His cheekbones stood out prominently, and there were dark circles under his eyes.

Under the quilt, his legs twitched as if he were about to run. He looked so like a boy, with that strand of dark hair tumbled down over his forehead. A troubled boy. Whatever he'd been doing, he'd not had an easy time of it.

Unexpectedly, tenderness welled up inside her. She

smoothed the hair away from his face. Very lightly, she trailed her fingertips across his warm skin. She smiled.

His eyes flew open. Dark eyes, fierce as a hawk, stared straight into hers. Then he moved swiftly.

She found herself flat on her back on the floor, with those fierce eyes intent upon her and his hand at her throat.